To Author Susan May Warren,
with gratitude for investing yourself in future novelists.

Cruise
TO DEATH

SARA L. JAMESON

Scrivenings
PRESS
Quench your thirst for story.
www.ScriveningsPress.com

ACKNOWLEDGMENTS

My deepest thanks to my sister, Susan Pearcy, for her hours of brainstorming and suggestions; and to my prayer partners who have upheld every part of the writing and publication process: Peggy Bell, Amy Jablonka Nelson, GG Gould, Elgonda Brunkhorst, and Amy A-Zotter. To Heidi Van der Wal for providing a place to stay while editing the book. Many thanks to Robert C. Goodwin for his invaluable assistance with technical matters in this story.

And deep gratitude to Linda Nixon Fulkerson and Shannon Taylor Vannatter for believing in this book and giving it a publication home. Linda, as always, your cover designs are superb. Thank you so much for your line edits on the book. Shannon, thank you so much for investing your editing expertise on this book. It has been a privilege to work with both of you.

1

Brussels, Belgium
June 1st

Despite the cool night air, sweat plastered Agent Jacob Coulter's shirt to his skin. He'd never have raced over to Schaerbeek in a business suit—not even for his best bud—but panic had riddled Noel's voice on the phone like a machine gun gone rogue.

Jacob inched a few feet along the brick wall between the brothels. The beams of red light around the windows still caught his six-foot-one frame in their crosshairs. Five years of analyzing terrorist intel at an Interpol desk had left his field skills rusty.

A parade of vehicles snaked past him, filling the air with diesel fumes and raging male hormones. The odor of beer and cigarettes spilled from the bars, clogging his lungs. He yanked at his necktie, clawed its noose-like knot. Surely Noel could have picked a less seedy rendezvous. No Brussels newspaper encouraged loitering in the red-light district after dark. All too often it turned deadly.

Especially on Rue d'Aerschot.

Across the street, two teenagers cloaked in hoodies and

sweatpants shuffled outside the North Train Station's rear exit, another no-go zone for tourists after five. If they valued their lives. The two guys eyed Jacob then ducked into the shadows.

He patted his chest where his shoulder holster should've been. And would have been if office staff were allowed to carry weapons. And handcuffs.

One guy slithered his hand inside the kangaroo pouch of his hoodie then piled plastic packets in the other's cupped hands. Within seconds, the buyer stashed them in a shoulder bag and slipped the first man a white envelope. The seller pocketed it and swaggered inside the train station.

Jacob slammed his fist into his palm. He couldn't even arrest a couple of drug dealers. So far his sole contribution to mankind was pinpointing possible *jihadists* on paper. As an undercover policeman with Interpol, Noel, his buddy since boarding school, worked the streets, ferreting out terrorist cells. Sacrificing time with Christine and cuddling their three-month-old son.

Brakes squealed, and a black Peugeot stopped. In the backseat, three men elbowed each other, clamoring for the window, their shrill catcalls piercing his eardrums. The oglers' eyes ravished the scantily clad women, perched on their stools in the windows like prize parrots.

Heat surged through him. One of the girls seemed no older than his pubescent sister. Jacob resisted the urge to race inside the shop, snatch her from her stool, and take her to a Christian halfway house. No woman should have to sell her body to make a living.

He glanced toward the back door of St. Jean et Nicolas church up the block. A door that looked as if it hadn't been opened in fifty years. A door that should lead to the salvation of these girls. And the neighborhood. Instead, Belgium had declared the building a historic monument.

The Peugeot's driver leaned out the window. Tufts of greying chest hair poked between his gold chain necklace. "Hey man, what's keeping you?" He thumbed a finger at Jacob. "Go in and have some fun."

Restraining himself from hauling the heckler out of the car by his necklace, Jacob clicked the light dial on his watch. Nine p.m. Acid coated his tongue. Three hours late. Something must have gone wrong. His bud wouldn't blow two months infiltrating a terrorist cell unless the situation was urgent. Life and death urgent. International-consequences urgent.

But why had Noel broken protocol and phoned him instead of his case manager?

Gears ground on the Peugeot and the car shot forward. Jacob walked past the red-lit windows, the corner café, and turned up Brabant Street behind the brothels. Within twenty feet, he'd left a human flesh market and entered little Mecca.

Shop signs in Arabic hawked everything from *hijabs* and sumptuous wedding gowns to housewares and electronics. As a kid, he'd never considered blond hair and blue eyes a deterrent to protecting the world. Here, his American haircut and suit might as well be draped with the stars and stripes. This was Schaerbeek, home to disenfranchised Muslims and a terrorist bomb-making factory.

The tantalizing smell of kebab shops hit him, but he headed for the electronics store. If Noel worked in the area, he might not have been able to get off work to meet him. Terrorist-cell infiltration meant he would be watched day and night. Even making the phone call could've unmasked his cover. And after two months, he might be unrecognizable if he'd grown a straggly beard and donned traditional Muslim garb.

Inside the store, dimly lit glass cases housed an array of Mac and PC computers and neat rows of cellphones. Two computers lay on the counter. One of them, tuned to AraBel FM, blared an Arab song in French.

Shoulders gyrating in time to the music, the salesclerk drummed his fingers on the counter while a young man in jeans and a T-shirt toyed with the other computer. The clerk glanced up. He muttered something and flicked his head toward the rear of the store. The young man grabbed the computer and fled through the black curtains behind the counter.

Jacob rammed his fists in his pockets. Another missed op. First thing in the morning he'd make certain HQ put this place on its radar. He stepped outside the shop. *Focus. Focus.* He was here to find Noel.

As he sidestepped the clothing racks blocking the narrow sidewalk and strolled toward a group of women shrouded from head to toe in black *hijabs*, they averted their gaze. Whisked their baby strollers between the clothing stands, mother hens shielding their chicks from the big, bad American trespassing in Muslim territory.

Without missing a beat, the bearded keeper of the dress shop planted himself in the doorway. He folded his arms, his glower razoring Jacob like *jambiya* daggers.

Jacob hesitated. Some Muslim neighborhoods banned the entrance of any non-Muslim. Everyone knew Brussels' police officers often refused to enter certain districts without a vanload of backup assistance. Vans that might not show up.

Next door, the grocer laid down the apples and oranges he'd been arranging in his sidewalk bin and snatched a handful of broccoli rabe from the crates stacked beside him. Giving Jacob an I-dare-you stare, he wrung the stalks until their necks went limp. He spat on the ground and tossed the ruined vegetables into a bucket at his feet.

The stench of rotting greens and overripe fruit filled Jacob's nostrils. He'd never be able to convince these people he had peace-loving Muslim friends. Friends who were as horrified as he was at the rise of *jihadists*. He risked a smile. "*Bon soir*, good evening."

The shopkeepers glared at him, mute.

At the moment, his choices were minimal. Either head for St. Jean et Nicolas up the block, or the slalom-sloped Dupont Street to his right. If he returned to his post outside the brothel, he might not find Noel.

Behind him, footsteps pounded on the pavement. Jacob whirled as a dark-haired man staggered up Brabant Street, his breaths heaving as if he'd run six back-to-back marathons. Crimson lakes splotched the midsection of his T-shirt and jeans. His white-rimmed eyes glazed like a man fleeing a half-crazed mob.

Jacob's stomach knee-jerked his heart. *Noel.* He sprinted after his friend. "Hey, man."

Oblivious to him, Noel plodded up the hill of Dupont Street.

Seconds later, two skinny men in T-shirts and jeans rushed past Jacob. The one in a stocking cap gripped a dagger in his left hand. The shorter one aimed his gun at Noel.

"Stop! Halt!" Jacob sprinted after them, his pulse pounding in his ears. His only hope was to tackle one of them. "Halt!"

The shorter man stopped, spun toward him and bull's-eyed his pistol at Jacob's chest.

He feinted to the right, but the bullet pierced the sleeve of his jacket. Hot coals seared his arm. Lurching back into the chase, Jacob pulled out his phone, dialed emergency, and requested an ambulance. "Hey, guys. You missed." Blood trickled down his wrist. If he could draw their attack, maybe Noel could make it to safety. "Hey bud, I'm coming."

Halfway up the hill, his friend tottered and sank to his knees. He flung out his arms like a marathoner too weak to cross the finish line. Then his arms fell to his side, his head flopped onto his chest.

"Don't give up, man. Run, run." Jacob's yell shrieked off the buildings. He forced his legs to pump harder, faster.

As if fueled by a bloodlust, the stocking-capped man picked up speed. Streetlights glinted on the silver blade in his grip. Six more yards and he'd reach Noel.

"No!" Jacob shot his hand toward his friend. His best friend. His only friend.

As Jacob sprinted toward them, the knife-wielding assailant hurtled toward Noel and tackled him.

Noel's fingers scrabbled for the man's stocking cap and managed to pull it off. Long hair tumbled over the attacker's shoulders. *A woman.* Crouching behind him, she locked his neck in a chokehold and drove the blade into the front of his body. He crumpled to the asphalt.

Without a backward glance, the assassins fled up a side street.

"No, God no, please." What was taking the ambulance so long?

"Hang on. I'm right here." Jacob whipped off his jacket, knelt beside Noel and rolled him over. "I'm getting you to the hospital." He wadded the fabric against the abdominal wound, but the blood surged over his hand. "Noel, can you hear me?"

Noel's eyes fluttered open. "Nymph." His lips quivered, his words garbled.

"What?" Jacob bent toward Noel's mouth.

"Boat."

Dear God, don't let him die. "Hey man, you're gonna make it." Jacob stroked the sodden hair from his friend's forehead. "Don't you dare give up."

"Ant—"

"What was that?" Jacob leaned closer to Noel's mouth.

"River." His stale breath rasped against Jacob's ear. "Soon. Agent ..."

"You're gonna make it." Jacob squeezed Noel's hand. Already his fingers were chilled.

"Tell Chri—" Noel's chest rose and fell with three short shudders then stilled.

"No. No." Jacob cradled Noel and rocked his lifeless body, weeping for all the things he'd never said to his friend. Things it was too late to say.

Antwerp, Belgium
June 3rd

RILEY WILLIAMS EXITED the Antwerp Cruise Terminal and headed up the walking street that led to the medieval town square, her phone pressed to her ear. Overhead, a breeze whipped thickening black clouds. "Quit worrying, Frénie. Of course, I can do your job." How hard could singing Broadway ditties be?

"But Rileeeee ..."

She grinned. Seven years after meeting Vielle Fréneau, she still found Frénie's French accent charming. "Relax, you can count on me. I never break a promise."

"But *chérie*, you're an opera singer, not a cruise-ship performer."

"No problem. I love musical-theater repertoire. With my piano skills, I can accompany myself." Then she wouldn't have to memorize the songs.

"But you need three twenty-minute sets with different songs every night."

Riley's heel caught on a cobblestone. *Wow.* Her longest opera role was only forty-five minutes of singing. "How long did you say the cruise lasts?"

"Twelve days."

She did the mental math. Good grief, she couldn't even name fifty Broadway tunes. "Sure. Sure. Nothing to it." Maybe it was a blessing she had no summer gigs—no opera roles to learn, no recitals, no oratorio appearances—ergo, no income.

"And do not forget, you must dance with the guests." The way Frénie hissed the word 'dance' you'd think they were discussing an outbreak of bubonic plague.

"And we both know dance was not your best subject." Vomiting sounded in the background on the phone.

A gulp lodged in Riley's throat. Surely Frénie hadn't seen the Düsseldorf review of *The Land of Smiles:* 'American Soprano flatfoots Mi into slapstick role'. What did audiences expect from a five-foot-ten redhead playing a petite Chinese girl? Not even her black China-chop wig had saved her performance. She eased back into the pedestrian traffic and walked toward the cathedral.

"All those hours I coached you, so you wouldn't fail the course."

Riley cringed. Their Bucharest Conservatory classes. If only payback time didn't include moving her feet on a dance floor. She really ought to split Frénie's salary with her. Even her two-step was a guaranteed fiasco.

"*Chérie*, I worked so hard to get this job. Oh, ugh."

"How long does food poisoning last?" Riley zipped past an old man leaning on a cane. "Once you recover, maybe you can join the cruise in a few days." Before she ran out of songs, before the men who danced with her had to have their feet amputated. "Aren't you feeling any better?"

"*Non*. I am so seeeek."

"That's why you need to relax. Get well first."

"In a hospital? *Chérie*, you are not a realist."

"I'll try to stop by the hospital this evening."

"*Bon*. Good. Please bring my bath towel and washcloth. And a nightgown and my toiletries. They don't supply these in Belgian hospitals."

"You're kidding."

"*Non*. And *absolument* do not be late for the staff meeting at three. Today."

"I promise." Maybe she could sneak in a Belgian waffle for lunch. "Cross my heart." She blew a kiss into the phone and disconnected. Holding up her hand, she ticked off her Broadway repertoire on her fingers—eight songs. This afternoon she'd look through Frénie's songbooks and learn a few numbers. A few? Who was she kidding? She needed two-hundred-forty-two more songs.

Every café surrounding the medieval guild buildings of the town square, Groete Markt, had succumbed to hordes of red-hatted, red-shirted tourists. She paused in front of the statue of Brabo, Antwerp's mythical rescuer. With his massive foot planted on the slain giant's body, Brabo tossed the ogre's severed hand into the Schelde River. According to legend, his courageous act saved the citizens of Antwerp from an evil tyrant.

Her shoulders sagged. Everyone needed a rescuer.

A petite, tuxedoed violinist stood beside her, a Bach gigue rippling from his nimble fingers and bow. Except for his grizzled grey hair, the man was a ringer for Joel Grey in his Cabaret role, complete with false eyelashes and red pointy lips. She dug in her purse for a five-euro bill and laid it in the open violin case at his feet.

Pursing his lips, he blew her a pouty kiss.

If her opera auditions failed, she might end up like him, warbling the Queen of the Night's arias on the back streets of Europe.

The scent of waffles and dark chocolate made her stomach rumble. While she ate, she'd feast her eyes on the guilds' step-gabled roofs, gold signs, and leaded windows. At the end of the first row of tables, a silver-haired gentleman nursed a coffee. He stroked his goatee and nodded at her.

The cruise would probably bring her even more unwanted attention. She flicked him her don't-get-any-ideas smile, then threaded her way between the tightly packed patrons and a stroller with a squalling infant whose parents seemed too frazzled to care. Her table was sandwiched between a polyester-clad couple arguing about the menu in New Jersey-speak and two dark-haired men huddling over glasses of Stella Artois.

Her feet froze to the cobblestones. The man's black leather coat, poorly fitted suit, and razor-sharp eyes unleashed a flood of memories. Memories of ten hours of interrogation in a Bucharest prison cell. Interrogation by a Romanian security police officer dressed like him.

Muscles bulged beneath the navy-striped jersey of his

9

stubble-jawed companion. His faucet-shaped nose seemed to have been hammered by multiple fists.

As she stood there, riveted to the pavement, portly Eagle Eyes raked her from her head to her white canvas shoes. Then Hawk Nose's rodent-like eyes fastened on her.

Sweat prickled her skin. She looked for another table. Nothing. Sitting with her back to Eagle Eyes, she gave the waiter her order in Flemish. Fortunately, her German skills bridged the language gap for her in Antwerp.

The waiter brought her hot chocolate and a Belgian waffle then slid Mr. and Mrs. New Jersey's plates of black-skinned eel, floating in a moss-green sauce, onto their table. Their chitchat died mid-sentence. Forking a bite of the crusty waffle and strawberries, Riley let the whipped cream spill across her tongue and settled back in her chair. Belgian chocolate. Waffles. Life was good.

"*Da, ştiu*. Yes, I know," Eagle Eyes' voice sounded awfully close.

Romanian. The waffle soured in her stomach. Somehow, she had to bury the past.

"He has the vials?" A nasal twang mottled Hawk Nose's voice.

"Tudor will see to everything. The bidding, the sale."

Riley sipped her hot chocolate. She really shouldn't eavesdrop.

"Who's bidding, Al-Qaeda, ISIS?"

She choked. The hot liquid sloshed through her eyelet top and scalded her skin. Terrorists. The Romanians must think no one in Antwerp spoke the language.

"What difference does it make? As long as we get our money."

Keeping her back to the men, she scanned the square for a policeman or woman. Not a blue uniform or cap in sight. She dug her phone from her purse and tapped the recorder button.

"But where are—"

The baby in the stroller wailed, drowning out Hawk Nose's words.

She tilted the phone at her ear toward Eagle Eyes. Every muscle in her legs tautened, urging her to run, sound an alarm. But if she left, they'd probably vanish. The police would have no leads. Unless she could snap the Romanians' photos.

"Tudor will give us the vials the day of the transaction."

"Think of what you can do with your cut." Hawk Nose snickered.

"And what the highest bidder can do with the vials."

"*Da.* Agent *X* will bring governments to their knees."

A chill shot through her. New York City or Washington D.C. could be targets.

"In two weeks, we'll be wealthy."

"Make sure you're not in the same country or you won't be around to spend the money."

Behind her, a phone rang. "*Da.* Yes," Eagle Eyes said. Seconds later, the sound of coins clinked on the table, chairs scraped the cobblestones.

Summoning an innocent tourist's smile, she shut down the voice recorder app. Hawk Nose cut between the tables at the other side of the café and loped across the square like a just-docked sailor. Eagle Eyes trailed behind him. Despite the summer heat, he'd put on the black leather coat and flipped up the collar.

Imagine that—she drops by a café for a waffle and overhears a terrorist plot. Frénie would never believe her. Riley slid ten euros beside her plate and strolled toward the men. The police would need every bit of information she could give them. Descriptions. Decent photographs.

Waving her red pennant, the tour guide motioned her red-hatted flock to follow her to the statue of Brabo. As the tourists surged toward her, the street violinist grinned and swung into "She'll be Coming 'Round the Mountain."

Hawk Nose disappeared around the opposite side of the statue, but Eagle Eyes paused in front of it and lit a cigarette.

Ten more feet and she could snuff out his match. Riley dug her cell from her purse and faked a phone conversation in German. "*Ja, ja. Wunderbar.*" With her heart climbing into her throat, she activated the camera app on her phone.

Red-shirted tourists swarmed in front of the two men.

No, no, not yet. Riley aimed the lens at Eagle Eyes and snapped a photo. She glanced at her picture. Red hats blocked the Romanian's face.

Overhead, black clouds released the first raindrops.

Hawk Nose headed toward the Meir, the main shopping street. Eagle Eyes strolled toward the cathedral.

Which one should she follow? If Eagle Eyes had worked for the Romanian secret police, he'd never let her escape with her camera. Like a salmon swimming upstream, she shouldered past the last of the red-hatted tourists and followed Hawk Nose. Raindrops pelted her hair, dripped down her neck. Thirty feet ahead of her, Hawk Nose kept his head down and wove between the crowds scurrying for shelter inside specialty shops and department stores.

The stoplight changed, and he crossed the ring avenue that bordered the medieval city center. She zigzagged around the pedestrians huddled in front of shop windows. Central Train Station was only two more blocks. With three levels of incoming trains, the building had more hidey-holes than a rabbit warren.

Maybe the men were staying in Brussels. The city had attracted a large Romanian community and had a history of home-grown terrorist attacks. She dared not let Hawk Nose disappear.

Yellow warning tape blocked a construction site. As she skirted it, she skidded on a patch of mud. Wind-milling her arms, she two-stepped on the slippery cobblestones. Murky water squished between her toes and splattered her white slacks.

Mud dripped from her hair and stained her top. She squinted at the crowded sidewalks leading to the train station.

A tram bell clanged a warning, and the streetcar to Mortsel glided past. Seated beside the fifth window, a man turned and stared at her. Hawk Nose.

Ice slid down her spine. The men may have realized she'd understood their conversation. She did a slow three-sixty, looking for a police officer, a police car, a police station.

Riley checked her watch. Yikes—ten minutes until the staff meeting. Her mind whirled. *You can trust me, Frénie. I always keep my promises.*

But if she waited to report the men, millions of people could die.

2

Day 1: Aboard the *River Nymph*, June 3rd

Five hours he'd wasted, waiting to see the captain. Jacob dug his heels into the plush carpet in front of Captain Thor Lundstrom's desk, bare except for a computer and a two-tiered wooden in-and-out box. By now he could've searched the staff's quarters and bugged the cabins of suspected terrorists. If he'd had a passenger manifest and information on the staff. A steward's uniform and a passkey. If Interpol hadn't insisted he play by the captain's rules.

Gale-force winds whipped across the Schelde River, slamming the *River Nymph* against her moorings. The picture windows shuddered in their frames. Like Interpol's plan, the storm had blown up out of nowhere.

In the forty-two hours since Noel's death, Interpol had scrambled to decipher his information, placed agents on any boat docking in Antwerp, put Jacob through refresher hand-to-hand combat courses, temporarily assigned him to Interpol's police division, and cobbled a plan for intercepting the terrorists. A plan that had more holes in it than a kitchen sieve.

He steeled himself for another tirade. He'd feel a lot more powerful in a business suit. Instead, he was dressed in the staff's white slacks and light-blue polo shirt.

The sleeves of the captain's black uniform were decked out with more rows of gold braid than a Rear Admiral's. He even looked like a white-haired Admiral, the gold buttons on his jacket concealing a few too many five-course meals. "Passenger safety and a pleasant cruise are my priorities." A purple vein bulged and pulsated at Lundstrom's temple.

Jacob's supervisor had reacted the same way when he demanded to be assigned to the *River Nymph* as the onboard Interpol agent.

"Understood?" The captain's voice thundered like an Antediluvian rockslide.

"Yes, sir." The knots in Jacob's shoulders ratcheted ten degrees. If the terrorists' plans played out the way Interpol feared, honoring the captain's request might be impossible. He owed it to Christine and Noel's son to help capture Noel's murderers. "Sir, I'm not sure you understand what's at stake."

"Of course, I do. You *think* your information *might* be accurate." Lundstrom pulled a bottle of antacids from his drawer. "A pity we're fully booked." He shook out two tablets, tossed them in his mouth, ground them between his teeth. "Traveling as a tourist would've been best."

Not really. The security checks at boarding would've uncovered the ordnance and equipment Jacob had snuck onboard with his land partner's help. "Sir, I'd like to have a steward's uniform and a passkey."

"That's highly irregular." His right eye twitched like a semaphore. "And the legalities ..."

"Sir, Interpol is hoping you'll cooperate."

The captain held up his hand. "I'll be watching you. A number of our passengers are repeat cruisers with us. The Ackelroyds, Mrs. Cochran, Mr. Molnár. Any slip-ups in your crew position, or any complaints about your work from passengers or your cruise supervisor, you'll be terminated. Immediately."

Jacob flexed the knots in his shoulder blades. The captain read his intentions as easily as a Nesbø thriller. The man realized Interpol's predicament. If Interpol forced the cancellation of the river-boat cruises and the ships in port, HQ could lose their only lead to the capture of the terrorists. And if the captain wouldn't authorize a passkey and steward's uniform, using a lockpicking kit could attract attention.

"Sir, I'll need a list of any changes in the crew and passengers who made last-minute bookings."

"The last passenger booking was three weeks ago. Suite 408." Captain Lundstrom turned the monitor on his desktop computer toward Jacob. "Mr. Khalid Hosseni and his wife, Sora, are joining us at Cologne."

A current jolted through Jacob. The Hossenis—known Iranian assassins—could be the people Noel had tried to warn him about. Somehow he had to get into their cabin. Maybe this time Interpol would have sufficient evidence to make a conviction stick. He texted Helmut Schwarz, his supervisor, about the Hossenis.

Unless suspects surface on other boats, the *River Nymph* may be the terrorists' target.

"We've had several last-minute crew changes." Lundstrom made a few clicks on the keyboard and another spreadsheet opened on the computer. "Our singer-dancer, Miss Vielle Fréneau, was hospitalized two days ago with food poisoning. The doctor said she's fortunate to be alive."

"Oh?" He'd let Brick, his land partner, know. A terrorist might have tried to kill her to insert one of their people in the job.

"She recommended a colleague, Miss Riley Williams, an American opera singer, age twenty-eight. She and Miss Williams were classmates at the Bucharest Conservatory."

Warning bells clanged in Jacob's mind. Romanian dictator Ceauşescu had allowed Arab terrorist-training camps to operate on Romanian soil. Even more recently, authorities had arrested several Romanians plotting terrorist activities. For the right price, Riley might have poisoned her friend.

Years ago, the CIA had financed struggling musicians in Europe, provided they agreed to vacate the apartment periodically for CIA purposes. Terrorist cells found the practice equally useful. "Do you have a copy of her résumé?"

"Yes." Lundstrom switched to her online bio. "Her engagements include a smattering of opera roles, concerts, and operetta in Europe. Normally we'd hire a performer with musical theater or nightclub experience."

"Did anyone else apply for the job?"

"No one." Lundstrom took a manila folder from his inbox and pulled out an eight-by-ten glossy photo. "And since we depart tomorrow ..." He handed him the picture.

The camera had captured her generous smile that seemed to laugh at the lens. A mesmerizing energy radiated from her luminous eyes, enveloping him with its seductive power. He caught himself wanting to run his fingers through the irrepressible waves of her shoulder-length hair. If he didn't know better, she could be a modern-day Lorelei, luring men to their deaths.

Using his encrypted phone, Jacob snapped her photo and forwarded the picture to Interpol Headquarters in Brussels. "Will Miss Williams have a roommate?"

"No. Miss Fréneau's contract includes a private cabin." Lundstrom shoved Riley's photo in the envelope. "You know singers. Divas. Every one of them." He stamped the brads flat then passed Jacob a passport photo. "A new steward, Manuel Rodriguez, was hired two weeks ago. He's a Mexican national."

The grainy snapshot suggested an emergency stop in a train station photo booth. Nevertheless, the camera had exposed a glint of cruelty in his shrewd eyes. Jacob copied the picture and forwarded it to headquarters. "An unexpected replacement?"

"We ask crew to give a month's notice, but considering our former steward Carson's shoddy work, he probably expected to be dismissed."

"I see." Jacob tossed Manuel's picture on the desk. He'd have Brick check Carson's whereabouts and any suspicious deposits to his bank account. "Sir, about that passkey and steward's uniform."

"I gave you the *maître d's* room." Lundstrom flicked his gold-braided sleeve over the cuff of his shirt. "A decision that guarantees both of us enemies."

"I appreciate your decision." No way could he carry out his undercover work with a roommate. His orders were to avoid using his electronic lock-picking equipment and to blend in with the crew. On a boat carrying 132 passengers, keeping a low profile might be tricky. "Sir, about that key." Having a key card amounted to cruise-line permission to enter cabins.

The captain snatched another manila folder from his inbox and flipped through Jacob's job application papers. "I see you've waited tables in France. Tour guide in Indonesia." He stuffed the application in the folder. "But no experience as a steward."

The one job critical to his undercover work on the boat. "I'm sure I can do the job. As for waiting tables, I'll need permission to go ashore with the passengers every day. And I'd like to be assigned to the Hossenis' table."

"Tell Dieter, the *maître d*.'" Lundstrom shook two more antacids into his hand. "I'll authorize permission to go ashore." Morosely, he eyed the tablets on his palm. "That guarantees more friction among the staff." Then his eyes lit. "However, going ashore makes working as a steward impossible." He poured the tablets back in the bottle and shut it in the drawer.

"Sir, I must insist on a steward's uniform and passkey."

"Sorry. Time for the staff meeting."

"Then I'll have to report your decision to Interpol."

Lundstrom slapped his palms on his desk. "I'm certain you'd do more than make the beds. If you're seen using a passkey, I could lose my job, my career."

Jacob thrust his face inches from Lundstrom's, his tone every bit as fierce. "If we don't stop these bioterrorists, millions of people could die."

"If a passenger or a staff member finds one of your devices and accuses Explorer Cruises of illegal surveillance—" The vein on Lundstrom's temple throbbed a frantic SOS. "The company's reputation would be ruined."

"When the public hears terrorists were known passengers or staff on this boat and you refused to take steps to prevent them—"

Beet-red flushed Lundstrom's neck, his cheeks. He pulled a key card from his pocket and slapped it on Jacob's outstretched palm.

"Thank you, sir. I'll do my best to keep you out of any fallout." If he were caught.

As a subliminal suggestion of Delft pottery, the designer had staged the boat's library, bar, and dining room with blue-and-white décor and Dutch ginger jars. Jacob did a quick head count in the lounge. Thirty-plus people dressed like him, all in white slacks and light-blue polos, relaxing on the blue couches and armchairs. Except for Manuel and Riley.

Lounging against a wall in the back corner, the steward picked at his fingernails. Every few seconds, he eyed Riley, who hunkered on a couch beneath a bank of windows.

She was easily recognizable from her photograph, and taller than Jacob had envisioned. A froth of auburn curls framed her mud-streaked face. The brown splatters on her top and slacks looked as if she'd been trapped in a paintball fight. Odd, a performer showing up poorly groomed. Maybe she'd raced to the boat from a meeting with the terrorists.

Jacob walked over to her. "Mind if I join you?"

"No." But her tone carried an I-wish-you-wouldn't.

Ignoring it, he took the vacant spot beside her and she scooted away from him. "Excuse me." He pulled a tissue from his pocket. "Looks like you found quite a mud puddle." With a smile, he offered her the tissue and pointed at her nose.

"Thanks. I barely made it back to the boat." Her smile quivered. "I didn't have time to change clothes." She moistened the tissue on her tongue and rubbed her nose. "Did I get all the dirt?"

"Almost." He rubbed a spot above the bridge of his nose. "One more speck." If he didn't watch out, she could cloud his judgment. "Looks like you've had quite an adventure." Great job, secret agent. Use a gruff voice and get an uncooperative suspect.

"You have no idea." She crossed her legs and drummed her fist on her thigh, faster than a panicked telegrapher. "I can't afford to jeopardize this job."

He tried to peel his gaze from her thick lashes, those hazel eyes, the tasteful gold earrings, the mud in her silky hair. Where had she been? "Are you new, too?"

"I'm filling in for a friend who took sick." She covered the side of her mouth. "Don't tell anyone, but it was food poisoning, onboard."

Jacob faked a grimace. "You're kidding." Sidling toward her, he slid his arm along the back of the couch. The odor of dried sweat mingled with her Chanel No. 5. His last girlfriend had liked that perfume. "How come you were free to fill in?"

"I was between gigs." She moved to the end cushion and gave his outstretched arm a would-you-mind stare. "I'm a freelance coloratura."

So much for his fatal charm. He lowered his arm to his lap. "Colora-what?"

"Soprano. The one who sings the stratospheric high notes in opera. You know, like a trapeze artist who performs without a net."

"Wow." He hated to admit it, but she fit the prototype of a terrorist dupe. A struggling artist short on income. But dupes had been known to become pawns. "Sounds like you enjoy a bit of risk. Or danger."

Every inch of Riley's shudder screamed diva. "Nope. Strictly a small-town Texan who's gonna have a career in opera. No matter what." She glanced out the windows. Tapped the face of her watch, the rhythm almost frenzied.

Jacob wanted to reach over and still the incessant tapping, the foot gone wild. What would she be willing to sacrifice to promote her career—her friend? Her country?

As Captain Lundstrom walked to the podium in the center of the dance floor, the murmured conversations died. Most of the staff sat to attention in their seats. Not Manuel. If anything, his slouch worsened. The captain picked up the mic and tapped it. Riley shrank on the couch. But Lundstrom's frosty gaze nailed her.

Her cheeks pinked and Jacob almost felt sorry for her. She fingered the brown stain on her top. With those long legs, she'd never be able to hide the mud on her pants.

If only he could shield her from Lundstrom's merciless scrutiny. *Whoa, Coulter. Get a grip. She's a person of interest to Interpol.*

The captain launched into his welcome remarks, and the mic squealed.

But Riley stared out the windows facing the cathedral and gnawed off the last of her pink lipstick.

Tuning out the captain, Jacob angled toward her. Noel's killer had been a woman. Maybe she was watching for her terrorist contact.

She shifted away from him, her chest heaving beneath her blouse.

If her breaths grew any shallower, she'd hyperventilate. Riley, my girl, you're promoting yourself from a person of interest to a prime suspect. Jacob's phone vibrated against his hip. He slid his cell from his pocket, but hid the screen and text message below his left side.

Ask RW about her Romanian-Arab boyfriend.

3

I f this staff meeting didn't end soon, she'd launch into one of Verdi's *Andiamo* choruses—let's go already—and march out of the room. By now the terrorists could be miles from Antwerp. Or Belgium.

"Most importantly, I wish you a pleasant cruise with happy passengers." The captain zeroed in on Riley, then the Hunk beside her. "Satisfied. Passengers. Who will be eager to re-book with Explorer Cruises."

Happy passengers. She squirmed on the cushion. Had Frénie warned him her sub couldn't dance? Riley shifted her knees away from the blue-eyed hunk. Too bad her appearance hadn't dimmed his interest. No way was she letting some gorgeous man come between her and her career.

"Dismissed." Firing her a final salvo in his glare, the captain laid down the mic and left the lounge.

Maybe now the new whatever-he-was employee would settle his blue eyes on someone else. Riley leapt from the couch and headed for the stairwell. She'd been so upset about the bio-terrorists, she hadn't asked his name or about his job onboard. Not that she was interested, but her mother had raised a polite Southern girl.

She let herself into her cabin, shucked off her dirty clothes and stepped into the minuscule shower. Needles of hot water pelted the knots in her shoulder muscles. After alerting the police she had to practice ballroom dancing and come up with twelve songs—fifteen to be safe—for tomorrow night's performance. She wrapped the bath towel around her torso.

How luxury-loving Frénie endured these postage-stamp quarters was unfathomable. Only a scuffed-up dresser, a closet that barely held both their evening gowns, and a desk with a molded plastic chair so uncomfortable her bottom would ache in no time.

Riley unzipped her suitcase on the lower bunkbed and slipped into a navy-blue pantsuit and heels. Looking professional couldn't hurt. She stuffed Frénie's toiletries, nightgown, and towels in a tote bag and dashed up the steps to the sundeck.

Beyond the boat, the Gothic spires of Onze Lieve Vrouw Cathedral towered over the cityscape. Narrow gable-roofed buildings cowered below the church, like helpless souls. Riley crushed the strap of her shoulder bag in her fingers. If she couldn't convince the police to believe her story, somewhere in the world there would soon be even more lost souls.

Two crew members worked at the bow, splashing buckets of water and slapping mops on the deck. The Hunk had parked himself beside the gangplank, his arms bracing his back against the shellacked railing like an actor in a Hollywood movie scene. A pair of reflective sunglasses hid his eyes. He shifted from the direction of the swabbies to face her.

Who did he think he was—a self-appointed sentry? She turned her back to him and web-searched directions to local police stations on her phone. The Oudaanstraat station was the closest. She strode across the deck toward the gangplank.

The Hunk cupped her elbow in his hand. "Hey, where's the fire drill?"

Riley bit back a groan. The guy was turning into a pest. "No fire. Just an urgent errand."

"Maybe I could help you." He pulled off his sunglasses, fixed his blue-eyed gaze on her.

If she weren't careful, his razzle-dazzle smile could fell her faster than Paul Bunyan. A glint of alertness flickered in his eyes and catapulted her to her career-girl senses. She jerked her elbow free. "I don't think so." Catching her lip between her teeth, she tilted her chin to her shoulder and gave him her best Shy Di glance. "Uh, girl things. You know."

"Oh." He moved back from the gangplank. "Sorry."

Stifling a chuckle, Riley hurried down the gangplank, her heels clattering on the metal ramp. She headed south on Ernest van Dijckkaai, along the Schelde River. Although the storm had abated, a fishy smell rose from the water.

A few buildings farther, she stopped in front of a shop window, checking for anyone following her. No sign of Hawk Nose or Eagle Eyes or the Hunk. Now she could focus on convincing the Belgian police she'd overheard a bioterrorist plot.

An innovative architect had designed the multi-story Oudaanstraat police station to resemble an enormous cement waffle. In front of the nearly empty parking lot, bicycles leaned between the black-railed fence. Inside the gleamingly modern lobby, she handed her passport to the female officer manning the desk. "I'd like to report a terrorist plot."

The young woman's eyebrows shot up. "*Ja?*" She dialed a number on the desk phone. "Inspector Vlincke, there is an American woman to see you." She scanned Riley's passport under a code reader, returned the document to her, then pointed toward the bench beneath the windows. "Have a seat over there."

Fifteen minutes later, the elevator doors opened and a business-suited man with ruddy cheeks and an unruly thatch of grey hair walked over to her. "Miss Williams?" The scent of beer hung on his breath.

"Yes. Are you with the Counter—"

"Please." He gestured her toward the elevator.

The elevator hummed and buzzed as it rose to the ninth floor. Trying not to flinch under his piercing gaze, she studied the mud-stained floor, the walls, the control panel.

With a ding, the elevator doors parted. He motioned her inside his office, to a chair in front of his desk. A desk that, apart from a computer monitor and a desk phone, was as sparkling clean as the windows behind it.

Ticking off in her mind the best way to start her story, she set her tote bag beside the chair.

"Now." Inspector Vlincke planted his elbows on his desk and laced his fingers as if he were the department psychiatrist. "Tell me all about it."

The words flew from her mouth as she told him about the Romanians' conversation.

His left eyebrow hiked. "These men were speaking English."

"No. Romanian. I studied in Bucharest for five years." *Idiot.* If Vlincke checked with Romanian authorities, they'd give him police reports on her. Reports serious enough to discredit anything she told him.

Narrowing his gaze somewhere on the ceiling, Vlincke leaned back in his chair, its joints squeaking.

"Aren't you going to take notes or something? We're talking Al-Qaeda, ISIS."

"So, these men were speaking loud enough in a noisy café to hear their conversation at another table."

"Not always. But they mentioned a man named Tudor who will give them the vials of Agent X to deliver to the highest bidder." She set her phone on the desk and played back the recording she'd captured at the café. *Buzzbee, buzzbee.* Silverware clinking. Voices too faint and garbled to identify. She punched off the app. "I can describe the men."

"And you are just now coming to tell the police."

"I came as soon as I could. I tried to follow the men but I lost them." She tore a page from her notepad, scribbled her name and phone number on it, and slapped the paper on his desk. "I'm subbing as the singer on the *River Nymph* cruise boat."

Vlincke picked up the paper. "Who else knows about this?"

"No one."

"Good. Say nothing about this to anyone."

"Then you believe me, you want me to look at photos, right?"

His expression went stony.

How could he be so obtuse? "Don't you understand—they could use this Agent X on Antwerp. Or Brussels. Or America." She snatched her tote bag and marched to the door. "After all the terrorist activities in this country, I can't believe you people would ignore this information."

The pink in his cheeks reddened.

"When Agent X is released, I'll make certain every newspaper in Europe learns of your stupidity."

INSPECTOR VLINCKE WAS WRONG, wrong, wrong. How could a law enforcement officer be so dimwitted? Maybe she ought to do a Facebook post. Send out the alarm herself. Riley grabbed her streetcar ticket from her purse. But she'd given him her word she'd keep mum.

Tram No. 4 slid to a stop before her. Boarding the car, she shoved her ticket in the reader then plopped into a seat near the exit. In less than twenty-four hours she'd be cruising on the Rhine River, unable to do anything to stop these madmen.

The train click-clacked past narrow three-story buildings that looked like dollhouses compressed like an accordion. Red brick. White brick. Yellow brick. All of them dingy with gleaming windowpanes. The architecture differed so from her European base—Vienna, Austria, and her parents' home in Cuero, Texas. If she'd overheard the Romanians' conversation in Texas, she'd bet the police wouldn't have disregarded her warnings.

The tram rolled past a café and her stomach growled. Her

few bites of the waffle at lunch were long since gone. At Sint-Vincentiusstraat, she disembarked and walked toward the hospital. The balls of her feet screamed for relief from her high heels. What wouldn't she give for a pair of sweats and flip flops and a tall glass of iced tea.

Ahead of her, dusk shrouded the hundred-plus-year-old hospital, Sint-Vincentius Ziekenhuis. Despite architectural updates, the foreboding red-brick façade looked like a boarding school straight from Charles Dickens' pen. Her stomach cramped, her appetite fled. Hospitals. How she hated them.

Inside the gift shop, she purchased a get-well card and a set of sparkly bangle bracelets, then forced down a ham-and-cheese sandwich in the cafeteria. At the sleek front desk, she asked for directions to the women's ward. If American visiting hours had been limited from two in the afternoon until eight in the evening, she'd never have survived.

The elevator doors caged her in. Her gut twisted into a dozen knots, just as it had during the hundreds of visits she'd made to see Lacy. The faked smiles, the false cheer. Always upbeat despite the urge to weep. But twins read each other's thoughts. Felt each other's pain. Riley stepped into the hall. It had been twelve years, but the corridor's familiar smells—floor wax, antiseptic cleansers, and urine—overwhelmed her with memories she'd worked hard to bury.

Drawing a breath, she crossed the eight-patient ward to Frénie's bed at the end of the room. Riley tried for a smile, but her lips froze tight as a sealed coffin. The effects of the food poisoning had carved new hollows beneath Frénie's high cheekbones. Today, her pixie haircut was matted around her heart-shaped face.

Riley's heart nosedived. Lacy had looked wan and thin, too. "*Bon soir.*" Skipping the traditional cheek kisses, she set the towel and washcloth and toiletries on the nightstand. "At least they supply the sheets around here." She gave Frénie the card and bracelets. "For you, my friend."

"*Merci, ma chérie.*" Eyes dancing, she slipped the bracelets on her arm and let the overhead light sparkle on them. "Now I am *chic* again."

The curtain rings screeched as Riley drew them around the bed then helped her friend into her nightgown. She arranged the covers, pulled up a chair, and grasped Frénie's cold hand. "Feeling any better?"

"*Oh, la.*" Frénie clutched the pink plastic tub in her lap and hefted her shoulders in a Gallic shrug. "I will never eat again."

"You'll be out of here in no time." The words caught in Riley's throat. She must've told Lacy the same thing a thousand times. "Once you regain your strength, you can join the cruise in a few days." The words tumbled from her mouth, the panic-ridden pitch sounding like the lies she'd told Lacy. Lies she knew neither she nor her sister had believed.

Frénie beaded Riley with a caught-your-hand-in the cookie-jar gaze. "You're in trouble."

"Trouble, me?" She had to get a grip on herself. "Everything's fine."

"Oh, *chérie*, I know you too well. Besides, this afternoon a handsome man came to visit me." Frénie's eyes twinkled with the mischief that had gotten both of them into far too many scrapes in Bucharest. "He wanted to know everything about you."

Heat burned Riley's cheeks. They'd barely met on the boat. How dare that wannabe Romeo pry into her personal life. She shifted on the wooden seat. Even more disconcerting, how had he known where to find Frénie? "Let me guess. Blue eyes, a tall blond hunk."

"*Non.* Medium height, hair black as midnight, eyes green as the Emerald Isle."

Riley's fingers iced. She hadn't noticed this man watching her. On the boat or onshore.

"And *oui*, a hunk, as you say." Frénie brought her thumb and two fingers to her lips and kissed the air. "Where did you find him? Does he have a brother?"

Definitely not Hawk Nose or Eagle Eyes. Maybe there was a third Romanian. "Wh-what did he want to know?"

"Everything, down to your measurements."

"How much did you tell him?"

"Everything. Except your hip measurement."

"Tell me you're joking. Did he say how he knew me?"

"He said he worked for the Antwerp Opera."

"I assure you no green-eyed general manager attended my audition or the one in Ghent."

"Oh *chérie*." Frénie flicked her hand, jingling her bracelets. "Knowing you, you'd block him out of your mind. I doubt you remember any of the men you saw a week ago."

"True." But she'd not forget Hawk Nose. Riley gripped the edge of her chair. Someone besides Inspector Vlincke knew she was subbing on the *River Nymph*, knew where she'd be every day for the next two weeks. Her mind sped through her chase of Hawk Nose. If only Vlincke hadn't ignored her warning.

"You are ready for tomorrow night, *oui*?"

"Huh, tomorrow?"

Frénie paled. "The cruise. Your songs. Dancing with the guests."

Riley's jaw slacked. She steered her gaze toward the linoleum. Away from the tell-me-you've-mastered-ballroom dancing plea in her friend's eyes. "Oh yes, yes. Ready."

Ready, she'd never be.

4

What he wouldn't give to make himself invisible and follow Riley into Antwerp. If she checked any more often over her shoulder, she'd crash into a wall. With his phone to his ear, Jacob strolled along the sundeck railing. She'd ferreted out tails like a pro. Maybe she'd learned the shop-window trick from her Romanian-Arab boyfriend. On the fifth ring, his land partner answered.

"Yo, dude."

American slang sounded ridiculous with Brickley's British accent. "I need you to tail Riley Williams."

"Sorry, chum. At the moment I'm following a bloke from a cargo ship. Orders from Headquarters."

Jacob jammed his fist in his pocket. "Doesn't Schwarz get it? The *River Nymph* has a boatload of suspects."

"Peace, chum, peace. Ours is not to reason why HQ sends us on a myriad of wild-goose chases."

"Yeah. Get back to me as soon as possible."

"Right-O."

He disconnected the call and went downstairs to the dining room. With the precision of a Prussian eagle, Dieter circled the tables, checking the place settings. The pot lights gleamed on his bald head. Jacob slipped from the room and trawled the A-deck corridor that housed passenger suites. Carrying a stack of white towels, Manuel entered the room across from suite 408, the Hossenis' cabin.

If he hurried, he might get Dieter and Manuel's rooms searched. Jacob fetched his passkey and surveil kit from his room then checked the dimly lit hallway. All the cabin doors were closed. Inside one of the rooms, a German sportscaster's voice shrilled over the madly cheering crowd as he described a soccer match. Outside Manuel and Dieter's cabin, Jacob did a one-eighty then knocked once and let himself inside.

A set of water-filled travel weights were piled in the corner beneath the porthole window. At the head of the lower bunkbed hung a poster of a bare-chested Dieter, flexing his over-developed pecs and biceps. The skinhead had a tiny swastika tattooed around each nipple. Jacob slapped a listening device beneath Dieter's mattress. Expecting a *Sieg Heil* in the dining room hadn't been off the mark.

Beneath the blanket on the top bunk, a mounded sheet bulged at the foot of the bed. A bath towel lay wadded beside the scrunched pillow. Jacob touched the towel. Damp. Manuel ought to make steward of the month in no time.

Jacob knelt beside the closet safe, held his electronic decoder next to the lock. Either one of these gents might return any minute. Five beeps and the code flashed on the screen.

Hotel-style safes were so insecure, he could've lifted the safe a few inches and dropped it on the shelf to dislodge the lock or keyed in the usual administration override codes. He turned the knob and the safe door clicked open. Starting with the lower shelf, he counted the cash and removed a small box. A Nazi tie clip and lapel pin were nestled on a square of cotton.

Shifting over to Manuel's closet, Jacob opened the safe and unzipped a leather case on the top shelf. He flipped through an Egyptian passport with Manuel's picture but registered to Apophis Bayek. Jacob photographed the passport pages on his phone and forwarded them to Interpol Headquarters. Nothing like rooming a skinhead with a possible terrorist. The opportunities for blackmail were endless.

Maybe Captain Lundstrom was mistaken. These two guys might decide they were a match made in *jihadist* heaven. The longstanding relationship between WWII Nazis and Egypt's Muslim Brotherhood hadn't ended with the war. Even today they had far more in common than anti-Semitism and world domination. He attached listening devices under the desk, the chair, and in the closets. Dieter and Manuel could be working with Khalid and Sora Hosseni.

Seconds later, Jacob tapped on Riley's door then let himself in with the master key. He picked up the small dual-framed family photos on the dresser. The first picture looked about twenty-years old. Seated on their parents' laps, two little girls with unruly curls wore matching frilly dresses with ruffled socks and shiny patent-leather shoes. Sporting an impish grin, a boy of about seven, stood next to the man's chair.

The second photo seemed to have been taken a decade later. One girl, her head bound in a scarf, sat between her shell-shocked parents. Despite the cadaverous shadows beneath her cheeks and eyes, her steady gaze radiated a peace that could only come from God. The other girl stood behind the chair, her hands resting on her sister's shoulders, eyes flashing like an avenging angel. The boy hovered next to his sister's chair, wet spots visible on his cheeks and shirt.

Jacob set the picture on the dresser. What would it have been like to live with his sister, to watch her play with dolls and do her girlie stuff, to protect her from teenaged boys on the make? Thanks to his parents, he'd never know what it felt like, any more than Noel's son would.

In her closet, he opened the two boxes inside her suitcase. Wigs. He closed the boxes carefully, making sure the hair fibers were as he'd found them, then moved to her dresser. Searching for evidence connecting her to the terrorists was one thing. But handling her undergarments made him feel like a pervert. Drawing a breath, he opened her drawers, careful not to disturb her neatly stacked pajamas and underwear.

A cluster of evening gowns too small to fit her were crammed at the end of the closet. He thumbed through a few pairs of slacks, tops, skirts, and ten evening gowns, each more beautiful than the last one. White, black, red, several shades of blue and green. Lace and lots of sparkles. He tried to clear his mind of how stunning she'd look in any one of them. If she asked him to choose his favorite, he'd be speechless. And if she knew he'd searched her room, she'd kill him.

In the bathroom, he checked the contents of her makeup bag. The usual toiletries and face paint. Three black-lidded, glass vials filled with clear liquid sat on the counter. He unscrewed the lids and sniffed the contents. A minty liquid. Some kind of oil. Chanel No. 5.

Working swiftly, he wanded the room for bugging devices then stuck a mini mic in the wall joint between the dresser and the desk. Nothing here suggested she was anything other than a female singer on a cruise. No pictures of a boyfriend, Romanian-Arab or otherwise. Maybe they'd broken up. Maybe she'd seen the error of her choices. Or maybe she was too savvy to pack his picture.

After locking her cabin, he picked up two ham-and-cheese sandwiches and bottled water from the staff dining room. He settled on the starboard side of the stern and snarfed down one of the sandwiches. What was keeping Riley? If she'd gone to a pharmacy for feminine products, she ought to be done by now. He wiped the breadcrumbs from his lips. She didn't seem the type to miss supper.

His phone vibrated against his thigh and he checked the caller ID. HQ's encrypted ID, his boss, Helmut Schwarz. Jacob pressed the cell to his ear. "Yes, sir."

"Just had a call from an Inspector Vlincke of the Antwerp Police." Schwarz cleared the smoker's rasp from his throat. "Miss

Williams paid him a visit this afternoon." He filled Jacob in on Riley's information.

With everything in him, he didn't want her to be involved with the terrorists. But considering how little information Noel had been able to give them, this lead seemed too fortuitous. "Then you're not concerned about the Romanian Security Police reports on her work for her boyfriend."

"Yes, I am, but we can't afford to ignore her story." A cigarette lighter clicked in the background. "It may tally with the information you've sent us regarding the *River Nymph* crew and the passengers."

"The whole thing could be a setup. The terrorists could be using her as a decoy, deflecting our attention from the real operatives."

"Yes, that's possible." Schwarz's exhale blew into the phone. Cigarette smoke, no doubt. "In the meantime, ply Miss Williams with your irresistible charm."

That was one assignment he'd enjoy. Jacob grinned. "So, we keep her in the dark as much as possible."

"Something like that. I've pulled Brickley off duty from the cargo ship. He's been brought up to date." A phlegmy cough rasped into the phone. "He's all yours." Schwarz ended the call.

Jacob gulped down his other sandwich and the bottled water, stashed the garbage in the can, and went upstairs to the A-deck. With Riley demoted on the suspect list, he could focus on bugging the Hossenis' room.

The door to Room 408 stood open. Manuel stood at the foot of the king-sized bed, contorting a bath towel into an unrecognizable shape.

Jacob tapped on the door. "Need a hand?"

"No."

"What's it supposed to be, a life preserver?"

Manuel's jaw worked like a flexing fist. "A swan."

"*El cisne*, huh?"

The guy gave him a blank stare.

Obviously 'swan' wasn't part of Manuel's Spanish vocabulary. "Watch closely." Jacob unfurled the towel and laid it landscape style on the reasonably well-made bed. "The first lesson's free." Holding a finger to the top center of the towel, he folded the corners downward and inward into a cone shape. "Guess you're new at this."

Manuel's Adam's apple shimmied like a California earthquake.

"Maybe I can help you out. Until you get the hang of things."

The Egyptian's face went sphynx-like.

After knotting the end of the cone, he tucked the loose ends into a ball. He flipped the towel over, shaped the body upward into a Z, then folded back the bird's head. Amazing what one could learn on YouTube. "*Comprende*, got it?"

Manuel nodded.

"I'll need a hand towel for the wings." Jacob's fingers closed around one of the microphones in his pocket.

As soon as Manuel left for the bathroom, Jacob crouched beside the bed, the mic in hand.

"Hey. What are you doing?" The steward swatted him in the face with a hand towel and the mic fell to the carpet.

"Watch it, don't disturb the artist." Jacob tilted his head, squinted at the swan, and grabbed the mic. With a magician's sleight of hand, he repositioned the bird and jabbed the mic into the bottom of the mattress. "Been working on ships a long time?"

"Yes." Manuel squatted beside him, his face close enough to smell the garlic on his breath. "What about you?"

"I'm a bit of an odd-jobber." Jacob stood and creased the hand towel into accordion-like rows, then centered the towel over the back of the swan and splayed the folds. "Like I said, if you need any help—"

"You go." Manuel jabbed Jacob in the chest. "Now."

"Hey, man." Jacob held up his hands and backed toward the

hall. "No *gracias?*" Tomorrow morning, passengers would board the boat. And the killers' stateroom was barely bugged.

———

THE MAN WAS STILL TAILING her, leaving only three buildings between them. Riley clutched her purse, the empty tote bag to her side. Staying so late at the hospital had been a mistake. This time of night, Europe's streets weren't any safer than America's. She should've paid more attention to her surroundings, the people around her.

Instead, she'd spent the tram ride fuming over Inspector Vlincke's lack of interest in the Romanians and worrying about the man who'd quizzed Frénie.

Leather shoes tap-tapped on the pavement and her stalker crossed to the opposite side of the Meir, drew level with her.

If only the tram from the hospital hadn't been delayed for an hour. She risked another look at the man, quickened her pace. Dark hair, medium height. He could be the third Romanian.

The street was almost deserted except for types of people she wouldn't want to meet in the daytime, let alone ask for help at nine-thirty at night.

She approached the lanes near the cathedral. Darkening, deserted lanes. Best stick to the main walking street to the Schelde River.

Murky shadows bled from the cathedral. A wizened man lurched from the side of the church and thrust his arm toward her. His Flemish was garbled, but the leer on his face and the beers on his breath were translation enough.

She veered away and peeked over her shoulder.

In mere seconds her stalker had closed the distance between them. Fifty more yards and he could nab her.

If only she'd learned karate, jujitsu. But she could scream.

As she race-walked toward the Schelde River, her ankles skewed left and right in her high heels.

She was close now, oh so close.

The soft lights on the *River Nymph* beckoned like a sanctuary. She hurried through the cruise boat terminal and up the metal gangplank, the *takka takka* of her heels spitting like gunfire. Gasping for breath, she stepped on deck and turned toward the cathedral. Beyond the rooftops, the spot-lit spire glowed yellow against the dismal grey sky. At the street corner, the man who'd been following her stood by a brick building, a phone at his ear.

Fumbling for her room key in her purse, she fled downstairs to her cabin. What an idiot she'd been. She'd led him straight to the boat. Ten minutes of checking online, and he'd know where she'd be for the next two weeks. Her heart hammered her sternum.

She double-locked her cabin door, kicked off her shoes and hobbled over to her bed. Nailing Zerbinetta's high notes was more than enough excitement.

No way was she cut out to be a secret agent.

5

Day 2: The *River Nymph* departs Antwerp

An opera singer who rose before noon and skipped five a.m. breakfast? Jacob pressed his ear to Riley's doorjamb and knocked again. He should've interrupted her last night while she was singing songs so faintly they'd barely carried through his earbuds. Half an hour later, she was doing some kind of cardio workout, counting 'left, two, three.' When he'd knocked at eleven, she hadn't come to the door. Probably a diva who slept with earplugs.

He pulled his passkey from his pocket. Waiting to tell her he was her onboard Interpol contact was one thing. But their need for her to identify the two Romanians was a ticking stopwatch.

A door opened down the hall and one of the staff stepped into the corridor. "Morning." Jacob waved a greeting.

The man acknowledged him with a cold nod, then rammed his shoulder. Jacob memorized the man's face, his gait. Another disgruntled crew member or someone else of interest to Interpol?

Jacob let himself into Riley's room. The bed was beautifully made, her damp bath towels folded with precision on the bathroom rack. He went upstairs to the sun deck and phoned Brick. "Bad news, the songbird's left the boat."

"Not good. That cuts into photo-viewing time, if we find her. What if Chatty Cathy tells her friend in the hospital or calls home with the news? You know, one of those, don't tell anybody, but ..."

"Better pray she doesn't talk. If she starts a press-generated panic, the terrorists might scrap the sale for now. We'd lose the only leads we have. I'll come ashore and help you look for her."

"Leave her to me."

"Yeah, you'd like that, wouldn't you?" Jacob chuckled. His partner would lose no time wooing Riley: Interpol Agent saves the day, wins the girl.

"Thought you were supposed to be figuring out how many bioterrorists are on the boat and checking out the crew."

"Passengers board later this morning, and I need to take care of a cabin." Suite 408, the Hossenis'. Manuel might have found and disabled the bug.

"Our fill-in diva may be planning to play Ms. Tourist and not return to the boat until you depart."

A sick feeling wormed through Jacob. He should've knocked on her door last night and not been so considerate of her time. If he were going to make the grade as a field agent, he'd have to get a grip on his emotions, his Mr. Nice-Guy instincts.

OUTSIDE THE OUDAANSTRAAT POLICE STATION, Riley checked her beige turtleneck and slacks for dust then surveyed the square. If she weren't paranoid about being followed by Romanians, she could enjoy a few hours of sightseeing before they sailed. Ruben's house, a lace shop, Burie's chocolate shop. Instead, she'd notify the police about the man who'd followed her last night then return to the boat.

She ignored the protests in her stomach for skipping

breakfast. If yesterday were any indication, the Hunk probably would've sat with her, and the less she saw of him, the better for both of them. He didn't seem the type to take no for an answer.

"Well, a good morning to you."

Riley whirled toward the British-accented voice. A dark-haired man, wearing a blue blazer, a white turtleneck, and grey slacks, tossed a cell phone from hand to hand, a self-satisfied grin plastered across his face. She edged toward the police station. "Who are you?"

"Brickley Landon, at your service. But you may call me Brick."

"I'll call you, Gone. As in, get out of here before I scream."

"Wouldn't want to damage those vocal cords, would you?" He gave her what he probably considered a zap-the-girls-gaga smile. "And ruin poor Frénie's job?"

A shiver sliced through Riley. He could be the third Romanian. Europeans who studied English with Brits often picked up their accent. She took two more steps toward the police station. "You'd better leave now. I'm on close terms with the Antwerp police."

"So am I." He checked his watch. "Inspector Vlincke told me about your visit."

"Wh-who are you?"

"I'm an undercover agent for Interpol." He showed her his ID.

"How do I know it isn't fake?"

"You don't."

A teenaged boy in sweats and a hoodie clattered away on a bicycle. Two blocks away, an old woman lugging a shopping bag hobbled down a side street. Not a blue uniform in sight.

"I know you must be terrified."

"Were you following me last night?"

"Yes." He shot his palms upward in a stop gesture. "For your safety. And yes, I pumped Ms. Frénau for information about you and to find out if her food poisoning was of natural causes or arranged."

"Arranged? By whom?"

"We thought perhaps you might have done the job."

"Me—she's my best friend."

"Ever since Bucharest, your Conservatory days. Yes, we know."

She nibbled at her lipstick. He knew way too much about her. "Who's 'we'?"

"Interpol."

The top of her turtleneck squeezed her throat. Had she really been on Interpol's radar ever since she dated Radu? "I don't think you're being totally honest with me."

"We'd like you to look at Interpol's photographs of known or suspected terrorists." He rechecked his watch. "And ID those two men before your boat sails."

The air whooshed from her lungs. So Vlincke had believed her. "Fine."

"Atta girl." Brick made a phone call. "Found her. We're on our way inside the police station." He pocketed his cell, grasped her elbow and walked her inside the building.

She lengthened her stride to match his. *Dear God, let Hawk Nose and Eagle Eyes be on record. Bring them to justice before they can carry out their plans.*

At the front desk, Brick flashed his ID.

The same woman who'd been on duty yesterday nodded at them, her face grim.

Riley returned the nod. Word about her story must have spread through the station.

Seconds later, the elevator doors whished shut, enclosing her in the odor of stale cigarette smoke, beer, and Brick's cologne. As the elevator flew past each floor, a bell dinged. Dinged like a portent of doom. "How likely are these men to be in Interpol's database?"

The lines around Brick's eyes and mouth brittled beneath the fluorescent light. "How many needles have you found in a haystack?"

"None. But when I was a little girl, I stepped on one barefoot."

"Ouch. Hopefully locating these chaps won't be as painful." The elevator doors glided open. Brick rested his hand on the small of her back and nudged her inside Vlincke's office.

Smoothing his unruly thatch of hair, Vlincke rose from his chair. Today, a tray with two cups and saucers, a carafe, and a plate of spice cookies had been placed near the computer monitor. "*Dag*, Good day Miss Williams." His eyes held a warmth they'd lacked yesterday afternoon.

"Morning, Inspector." She tried to forget his grilling only fifteen hours ago.

"I will leave you two to your business." Vlincke motioned her to his desk chair. "There's coffee in the carafe. Call if you need me." He left and pulled the door closed.

Wasting no time, Riley sat in the inspector's padded leather chair.

"If you'll face the window, I'll get us into the site." Brick leaned over her shoulder, his citrusy aftershave tickling her nose.

"Of course." She swiveled the chair toward the spotless windowpanes, checked her watch. Less than six hours to ID the Romanians.

Clicks flew from the keyboard. Brick's arm brushed hers. "All right. The site's up." He perched one hip on the edge of the desk.

Riley swung back to the computer. Mugshots filled the screen. Men of all ages and sizes. Some swarthy, others bearded or clean-cut, some dressed in white garments and skullcaps. But their eyes had one thing in common. A spirit of murder. She gripped the mouse, moved to the next page. Thirty photos out of six thousand. "I had no idea Interpol was tracking so many potential terrorists."

Closing her eyes, she refreshed her memory of Hawk Nose and Eagle Eyes. No. She'd never forget those two men.

The scent of freshly brewed coffee wafted toward her as Brick filled two cups. "Cream and sugar?"

"Yes, please." Today she'd need every ounce of brain energy she could summon. With her forefinger poised over the mouse, she planted her elbow on the desk and propped her chin in her palm.

He leaned over her shoulder and stared at the computer screen. "Now you see what law enforcement is up against."

THE COMPUTER SCREEN WENT BLACK. The coffee she'd consumed hourly churned in her stomach. Riley shifted in the seat, trying to release the knotted muscles in her back. "It's two o'clock and not one of the photos resembled the Romanians."

"That's the way it goes, kid."

She'd been utterly useless. Useless to Interpol. To America. And anywhere else these terrorists planned to release Agent *X*. "What happens now?"

"Leave that to Interpol." Brick reached over and closed the website, brought up CCTV film.

"Good. There's more." She scrolled through the grainy clips. Clips of her disembarking the ship. Passing the cathedral. Crossing the town square. Then an almost imperceptible shot of Hawk Nose from behind, burrowing inside a group of pedestrians on the Meir. She jabbed the image on the screen. "That's him, right there."

Brick peered at the photo. "We're going to need a frontal shot." He tapped commands on the keyboard and video from trams rose onscreen. "Here you go, madame."

One by one, she clicked through the shots. An hour later, she reached the last video. "He ought to be somewhere in those films."

"Looks like your guy picked the right tram. A couple of cameras were out of service that day." He sighed. "Time to get you back to the boat."

Tears welled in her eyes. She stood and blinked them away. "Agent *X* sounded awful."

Brick thumbed her chin upward until she met his gaze. "You're extremely valuable to us and a threat to the terrorists. You can identify two of them." He gripped her arms. "You can't tell anyone what you know."

"I understand."

"Based on your information, Interpol thinks the vials will be sold at one of the stops on the *River Nymph's* itinerary. It's likely the Romanians will be there. With your help, Interpol will be waiting to nab them."

The past twenty-four hours had become an unending nightmare. "How do I get in touch with you if I spot them?"

"Through my partner."

"And his name is ..."

"He'll contact you."

Maybe his partner planned to use an alias, one Brick didn't know. Maybe he was withholding her contact's name because the Romanians might get to her first and make her talk. "And if I see them before he contacts me, what do I do, send up smoke signals?"

"How about whistling 'Dixie' instead?"

Glaring at him, Riley snagged her purse from the desk. "How about 'The Eyes of Texas Are Upon You'?"

Brick chortled. "That ought to work fine."

"We won't be laughing if I don't spot the Romanians before the bioterrorists get hold of Agent *X*."

FIVE O'CLOCK. Time for her first performance. Cradling Frénie's musical-theater songbooks in one arm, Riley paused at the entrance to the lounge and straightened the hem of her beaded turquoise evening gown. The familiar flutter of pre-performance excitement galloped through her veins.

She nodded at Johann, Frénie's accompanist, setting up his electric keyboard at the front of the dance floor.

Flashing her curtain-call smile at the passengers chatting and sipping cocktails, she headed toward the front-row guests, seated eight inches from the baby-grand piano. Nothing like having an audience close enough to count the fillings in her teeth.

Seated in the middle of the couch, a mid-fiftyish woman was stuffed into a lamé sheath that would've been stunning on a svelte figure. Diamond bracelets climbed her arms, rock-sized rings weighted every finger. The spotlight glinted on a jeweled hair ornament stuck through her blonde beehive hairdo. Texas hair, they called it back home.

A balding man, his paunch ill-concealed by his jacket, sat beside her. He seemed unfazed by her relentless flirting with the silver-haired gentleman standing next to her.

"Good evening, mademoiselle." The silver-haired gentleman stroked his goatee and bowed toward Riley.

"Evening, sir." Given his cement-thick consonants, she placed him from a Slavic country. She set the music books and her beaded clutch on the piano and adjusted the height of the bench. The lid had been raised, but someone had messed with the bench since her practice session.

She opened the music book, fringed with numbered purple sticky notes marking tonight's selections, and began her first set with "I Could Have Danced all Night," from *My Fair Lady.* A great warm up for the voice that ended with a fun high note.

Applause erupted as she finished the song. Nodding her thanks, she creased the book open to the second sticky note. A shadow settled near her left shoulder. She startled.

"Was that one of those colora-what's-it notes?" Balancing a tray of canapés and a glass of water on his left hand, the blue-eyed Hunk set the glass on a napkin at the end of the keyboard, giving her that annoying assessing look.

"Sort of." The words came out stiffer than she'd intended. "Thank you for the water." She played the keyboard introduction, improvising while Blue Eyes offered his tray of hors d'oeuvres to her front-row fan club.

Six songs later, Riley stacked her books on the piano and acknowledged the applause with a single bow. Best keep still during her break, keep her voice fresh. She went upstairs to the staff's designated part of the sun deck. The salmon-colored sky stained the cityscape and bled across the Schelde River. She took her glass vial of liquid breath mint from her beaded clutch, dabbed a drop on her tongue, and closed her bag.

Footsteps sounded behind her and she turned. The silver-haired gentleman who had greeted her at the piano had entered the chained-off portion of the stern. Passengers weren't allowed in this area but she hated to be rude.

"An enchanting performance, mademoiselle."

"You're very kind. Musical theater's not really my forte. Opera is my field."

"Ah, I thought so." He fingered his silver mustache, his goatee. "I have many friends in the opera world. General managers of houses, conductors. Perhaps I could be of assistance to you."

"How kind of you." His offer might determine her future. Paid-up rent or singing on the streets.

"Riley, Captain Lundstrom wants to speak with you." Blue Eyes stood at the head of the stairs, arms crossed like the pasha of a harem.

She blasted him with a stream of eye missiles. What was it with Blue Eyes? Always showing up at the worst possible moment.

The gentleman chuckled, covered it with a cough.

"Excuse me." She swept past the Hunk and went to the lounge.

In the middle of the dance floor, Captain Lundstrom held court, surrounded by men in tuxes and women dripping with more jewels than Tiffany's vaults. The captain lifted his glass toward her. "Bravo, Miss Williams."

With a slight bow, she nodded her thanks.

Within seconds, the Hunk had joined her, his breaths warming her neck. She elbowed his ribs. "You and I are going to have a chat."

"You're right. We are."

"No. I mean a serious talk."

"You have no idea how serious."

"Listen, Blue Eyes. You just botched a career advancement for me."

"With Sugar Daddy?" He snorted. "I'm glad you're alive to talk about the future."

Her jaw slacked. "What do you mean?"

"There may be a bioterrorist onboard this boat."

"How do you know about that?"

"My pal Brickley."

No. Surely the Hunk wasn't her contact. "I can't keep calling you—" She glanced at his nametag. Jacob.

"Blue Eyes? I kinda like it." He planted his hand on the wall beside her. "Although I'm no crooner. But the name sorta has a Southern ring."

She inhaled his aftershave. Crisp. Elegant. And unlike the man, not overpowering. "You're invading my personal space."

"Sorry." He stood upright, his gaze roving the room. "Listen for my knock at your door tonight."

She rolled her eyes. Right. Let this blue-eyed wolf inside her den. "How will I know it's you?"

"I'll tap 'The Eyes of Texas Are Upon You.'"

"Sure you know it?" She let her voice drip with sarcasm.

The hint of a taunt gleamed in his eyes. "I'm a Victoria boy, Miss Cuero."

"A Texan. I don't believe you."

"Suit yourself." He flipped his white dish towel over his forearm and descended the stairs.

The nerve of the guy. Just when that charming gentleman wanted to get her more opera auditions. She sat at the piano and opened Frénie's *Cole Porter Songbook* to her next song, "Night and Day." A yellow sticky note fluttered to the carpet.

Leaning over, Riley picked up the paper and stared at the block-lettered message: 'Be careful, Miss Williams. An imposter claiming to work with Interpol may contact you.' Shudders rippled across her shoulders. Someone onboard knew she'd been to the police. Knew what she'd overheard at the café.

Inhaling on a slow count of four, she positioned her fingers on the ivory keys. But the vise gripping her throat muscles refused to budge.

On the opera stage, people only pretended to kill.

6

Heat firing in his chest, Jacob removed the appetizer plates from his other two tables. Riley was as innocent as his kid sister. Neither of them should be left alone with a woman-chasing fox like János Molnár.

He took the tray of dirty dishes downstairs to the kitchen then dashed upstairs to check on his third table. Dieter's incessant supervisory checks hadn't elicited any comments. Yet.

The Ackelroyds, a British couple, sat next to Molnár, Riley's wannabe Sugar Daddy. Just as they had during each of Riley's sets. He could understand why. Although she didn't sing country-western ballads, her voice gave him chills.

One more massive bite and Mrs. Ackelroyd polished off her trio of bruschetta. To her right, her husband, Alfred, wiped bits of smoked salmon from his chin. As she spooned her caviar onto toast points, Mrs. Cochran's gnarled hand screamed her true age, her glossy facial skin courtesy of too many cosmetic surgeons. Probably not the terrorist type. The two vacant places at the table he'd reserved for the Hossenis.

Resting her multi-ringed fingers on Molnár's hand, Mrs. Ackelroyd lifted her head toward the ceiling and cackled. "My dear man, you are too droll." Her bejeweled arm traveled up Sugar Daddy's sleeve.

Molnár gave her a reptilian smile. Hooded eyes, rigid mouth. Then he nodded Jacob to the table.

"Yes, sir?"

"I would like a memento of these charming people." Molnár gestured to the Ackelroyds, fumbled for the strap dangling from the back of his chair, and handed him a Minolta camera.

"Certainly, sir." Jacob stood opposite them and focused the lens on Molnár and the Ackelroyds. Strange, wanting a picture of a couple Sugar Daddy seemed to barely tolerate. Maybe he kept a dart board in his stateroom. "All right, on the count of three, everybody say cheese. One, two."

Mrs. Ackelroyd rested her head on Molnár's shoulder, the ridiculous jeweled flower in her mushroom hairdo obscuring his right eye and cheek. "You dear, dear man."

Between the hair doodad and her shiny dress, he'd forgo the camera's flash setting. For a nanosecond he almost sympathized with Sugar Daddy. Maybe she flirted because her husband couldn't keep his eyes off attractive young women. Like Riley when she sang. "Three."

"And another one, please." Molnár moved beside him and tucked a twenty-euro bill between Jacob's thumb and forefinger.

"Thank you, sir." He wanted to stuff the tip in Molnár's pocket. Who did Sugar Daddy think he was, buying him off?

"And now, just the lovely Ackelroyds." Molnár flashed her a diplomat's smile, polite, nothing too encouraging.

The man's acting skills rivaled Riley's. No wonder she was falling for the guy. Jacob jerked the lens open to F5, tweaked the lens angle. Why did he care? She wasn't his girl. "Big smile, please."

The snapshot caught Mr. Ackelroyd's face bland as a peeled potato, Mrs. Ackelroyd beaming Sugar Daddy a come-hither look. Jacob returned the camera to Molnár then positioned their first-course plates along his arm and stepped back from the table.

Someone shoved his dish-laden arm to his chest. "Hey." A foot hooked around his ankle, pulled him off balance. He braced his hip against Mrs. Cochran's chair as tomato sauce leeched through his shirt, dampened his skin.

Gasps rose from the other tables. Mrs. Ackelroyd and Mrs. Cochran clung to Molnár's arms. From across the room Captain Lundstrom shot him a pistol-whipping glare.

"My apologies." Sweat pricked Jacob's brow as he repositioned the plates along his arm. His first night on the boat and already his job was in jeopardy.

Smirking like a Cheshire cat, Dieter, the *maître d'*, stood a foot away. "Pay attention to what you're doing."

Jacob matched the steel-trap glint in the German's eyes. "Yes, sir." He scraped inky caviar and smoked salmon from his chest and onto the top plate on his arm.

Downstairs, he clattered the plates on the metal counter of the kitchen, then jogged to his cabin. Once inside, he tore off the soiled shirt, rinsed the tomato sauce from his chest, buttoned on a clean shirt and dashed back to the kitchen. As soon as dinner ended, he'd notify Interpol to recheck Dieter's background.

"Where's Mr. Ackelroyd's turbot?"

The cook shrugged his white-coated shoulders. "The plate was there two minutes ago."

"Someone must have taken my order by mistake." *Or on purpose.* "How long will it take you to plate me another?"

"Twenty minutes."

"Twenty—" Ackelroyd's dinner would be ready in time for dessert.

RILEY IMPROVISED a few phrases in the postlude to her final song, modulated to a new key, readied her body to repeat the chorus, but Johann strutted across the dance floor to his electronic keyboard. Her hands went clammy. *Oh. No. Time to dance.* She segued to the original key and ended the song.

Maybe if she paid him not to play the dance styles she didn't know—no, that would never work. She'd lose Frénie her job for certain. Riley closed the lid to the piano, forced a smile as flexible as rigor mortis, and acknowledged the applause.

Carrying a tray of after-dinner drinks, the blue-eyed Hunk stood near the entrance to the lounge.

She moved behind the piano bench, out of the spotlight. Seconds from now he'd witness every minute of her humiliation. She hugged the music books to her chest. The sticky note on the Cole Porter book grazed her chin. The sticky note from someone who knew she was working with Interpol. Someone she might have to dance with tonight. Someone she needed to identify.

A second Klieg light flicked on overhead. The spotlight glittered on Johann's rhinestone-studded jacket, reflecting the rubies and emeralds and sapphires on the parquet dance floor. He flashed the audience a toothy grin and swept his hand over his super-moussed hair.

"Uh one. Uh two. Uh one, two, three, four." Gyrating his narrow hips in time to his counting, he adjusted levers on the keyboard. His nimble fingers slid over the keys and a cha-cha poured from the instrument, complete with a percussion section.

Riley's stomach sank. She hadn't practiced the cha-cha.

Captain Lundstrom walked to the center of the empty dance floor and looked around the room.

Oh no, dear God, please don't let him ask me.

And then, just like her math teacher in eighth grade, the captain's searchlight gaze pounced on her. He sucked in his gut, tweaked his tuxedo jacket over his now-hidden paunch and extended his hand to her.

She gulped and laid her books on the piano bench. *Lord, get me through this without maiming him.* Pasting on her fake-it-if-all-else-fails smile, she walked over to him, her feet sweating inside her high heels. *Two-step, Johann, play a two-step.*

The other couples stood at the edge of the dance floor. Waiting. Watching.

Oh no, not an audience. After her Düsseldorf disaster, she'd sworn she'd never dance again in public. She should've refused the cruise job.

With the panache of Fred Astaire, Captain Lundstrom swept her into his arms. "You have a beautiful voice."

"Thank you, sir." Maybe her singing would save her job. Frénie's job.

He spun her into the cha-cha, her turquoise evening sheath straining at her calves.

She stubbed her toe on his shoe and a wave of surprise flickered across his face.

"Sorry, sir." With her free hand, Riley motioned other couples onto the dance floor. No one moved. "Frénie speaks very highly of you."

"She's a charming performer."

Riley mashed his instep. "Sorry."

Red streaks crept up his neck. "And a wonderful dancer."

Was he considering firing her on the spot? Telling him she was suffering from opening night jitters wouldn't help. Not once he saw how badly she danced every night.

"I presume opera singers don't have to dance onstage."

"Sometimes, in operettas."

"Ah, that's good. For you."

Heat flooded her cheeks. She should've set up a signal with Johann to cut the music short and end her misery. And her dance partner's. The toe of her shoe caught under the captain's heel.

Lundstrom startled.

"Sorry, sir." She wasn't making him look too good on the dance floor, either. "Frénie's very eager to return to the *River Nymph*."

"As I said in yesterday's meeting." His lips were thin as a garrote. "We bank on satisfied customers."

"Yes, sir." He couldn't fire her, he just couldn't. If only she could tell him about the sticky note, the Romanians, and Agent X. She had to keep this job.

As Johann finished the song with a Liberace-style flourish, the captain released her, an I'm-warning-you all too clear in his eyes.

One dance down. How many to go? Maybe she'd discover what it felt like to be the proverbial wallflower.

Lundstrom gave her a stiff bow then offered his hand to Mrs. Cochran who stood with other singles waiting nearby.

If only Frénie had coached her on what to expect. Riley retreated to the corner of the dance floor. Was she supposed to ask stranded husbands to dance? A hand touched her elbow and she turned. The silver-haired gentleman who'd spoken with her upstairs.

"We were never properly introduced." A thick accent overlaid his obviously British-trained English. "János Molnár. To you Americans, that is John."

"You're not Romanian." She slapped a hand to her mouth. "Forgive me. I like Romanians very much. Really." Apart from Hawk Nose and Eagle Eyes.

"We Hungarians have no love for Romanians." János bowed and kissed her hand, his warm lips grazing her skin.

She'd never get used to these European men, seven continents different from Cuero boys. Surely, he couldn't have left her the warning note. Besides, he'd followed her upstairs on her break. More than half a dozen men in the room fit the stereotypical description of Romanian men. Handsome, dark hair, and intense eyes wanting to undress her.

"May I have the honor of this dance?" Molnár's English sounded as if he'd learned it from a 1930s B-rated movie.

She glanced at his patent-leather shoes. Unscuffed. Unmarred. "Dance?" Her voice squeaked.

"I believe it's customary on this cruise line." Without waiting for her answer, he led her onto the dance floor where six middle-aged and elderly couples along with the captain and Mrs. Cochran were dancing.

A devilish grin splashed across Johann's face. He adjusted the dials and levers on his keyboard and lit into another song, plinking the keys with the bravura of a Las Vegas showman.

Listening to the rhythm, she counted the beats. Four. Not a waltz. Must be a fox trot.

"Shall we?" Molnár snugged her to his chest, his sweet cologne cloying. He glided her into the flow of dancing couples and stepped back with his left foot.

Riley lurched forward and tripped on his shoe. "Sorry, wasn't sure which way we were going."

"I believe it is customary for the man to lead." He chuckled, gave her an indulgent smile.

Oh, dear. Which one had she practiced in her room last night —leading or following?

At the base of her spine, his fingers massaged slow circles. "Try to relax."

Relax? With eleven nights of massacring passengers' feet and free massages in her future? Maybe after tonight no one would ask her to dance.

Molnár glided her past the bar where Blue Eyes waited while the bartender refilled his tray with fresh drinks. His gaze roved between her face and Molnár's hand on her back.

Hoping her aim was accurate, Riley jabbed her high heel into Molnár's ankle.

The pressure of his fingers loosened on her back.

"Sorry." She tried for a look of abject apology. "Dancing isn't one of my talents."

"Ah yes. Opera. I can be of great help with your career. Give me a copy of your résumé and I will arrange some auditions for you during the cruise."

"That's so kind of you." She tried to squelch the giddiness in her voice. Auditions. For a job she could ace. But Molnár's price might be too high. "Unfortunately, I'll be too busy." She'd be too busy cramming songs and dance steps in her head. Focusing on passengers most likely to have left her the warning note.

Someone in league with the terrorists.

7

R iley shrugged out of her evening gown and high heels and into a black T-shirt and exercise pants. What was it with these men? One dance after another, no matter how badly she bruised their insteps and scuffed their shoes. Ten dances with Mr. Ackelroyd.

After their dance, Molnár had excused himself and left the lounge. She sat on the bunkbed and rubbed her throbbing feet. Maybe Mr. Ackelroyd's insistence on so many dances was his revenge on his wife for flirting with Molnár tonight. But not once had she danced with anyone who seemed to be Romanian.

Soft knocks on her door tapped the rhythm of "The Eyes of Texas are upon You." Surely Interpol agents had more sophisticated means of communication than a corny old Texas song. If he really was an Interpol agent. She let him finish the first eight measures then opened the door.

The Hunk lolled against the jamb, looking even more handsome in jeans and a grey sweatshirt. "Thought you'd never answer."

"Just making sure you knew the ditty." She gave him a sarcastic grin. "These days a girl can't be too careful." The sticky note message flitted in her mind. "Better come in."

"What's up?" He stepped into the room and shut the door behind him.

"Found this waiting for me when I returned to sing my second set." Riley peeled the yellow sticky tab from the Cole Porter book and handed it to him.

The color drained from his face as he put a finger to his lips.

Every curl around her face shook as she nodded. He suspected someone had been in her room.

Once again, he tapped his lip, then mouthed, "One moment," and let himself out of her room.

The walls closed in on her. How had they gotten in? Had they bugged the place? Electronic surveillance hadn't been uncommon in Romania. Not if the security police suspected someone of a crime against the state. Once Radu was on their radar, they'd tailed her, watched her every move, bugged her apartment.

A minute later, Jacob returned with a small zippered case. He put a warning finger to his lips then took out a small electronic wand. Working slowly, he traced it over the walls, the bed, the closet, the bathroom, the dresser, the lights and mirrors.

She trailed him like a frightened kitten as he wanded behind the TV on the desk. *Whoozhee, whoozhee.* Red lights flashed on the detector. She pressed her knuckles to her lips. Who on the boat knew about her run-in with the Romanians, her visit to the police?

With a Swiss knife from his pocket, he pried the tiny disk from the wall, crushed it beneath his shoe and flushed it down the toilet. "Not good. The terrorists may be on to both of us."

"And Brick?"

"Sure hope not." The Hunk paced the narrow space beside her bunk bed.

"I thought you guys tapped phones, hacked into computers, you know, that sort of stuff. How come Interpol doesn't have more on these madmen?"

"Because whoever is in charge of this operation is extremely clever. We think he's not communicating via phone or email with the terrorist bidders. He's—"

"Or she."

"Yeah ... she, that's possible. He or she's probably doing it the old-fashioned way, contacting them in person."

"Brick thinks they plan to make contact in our ports of call. So, we go ashore and follow the Romanians."

"If we spot them."

"You mean, if *I* spot them."

He whirled toward her. "This is no business for an innocent woman, a civilian. These people are killers. No one who's on to them lives." He pinched the inner corners of his eyes and swallowed so hard she almost felt it in her throat. "No one."

"I'm sorry." She touched his arm. "I wasn't making light of the situation. I want to help, and whether or not you like it, you need me. No one else can identify Eagle Eyes and Hawk Nose." She leaned against the built-in dresser. The knobs dug into her back. "Maybe whoever left me the note isn't certain you're with Interpol."

"It's a classic divide-and-conquer tactic. Spread a carpet of innuendo and deception. If someone approaches you, says he—"

"Or she."

"Or she works for Interpol, play dumb. Demand ID."

"Speaking of identity, who are you? What do I call you?"

"Jacob Coulter."

"Is that your real name or an alias?"

"It's real enough."

Nice. He'd mastered vague. "All right, Jacob—or do you go by Jake? Or maybe the name is so new you haven't decided. How do I contact you?"

"I'm in room thirty."

Great. At the far end of the staff's quarters, not exactly nearby.

"Give me your cell. I'll program a speed dial to my number."

She fished her phone from her purse.

"Watch what you say when you make calls." He punched in his number, added hers to his cell then returned the phone to her. "Your conversations can be monitored with or without your phone activated."

Just like Romania. "Is 'The Eyes of Texas' our theme song?"

"No, choose a new one every day. Tell me at breakfast, or the night before."

"How extensive is your musical knowledge?"

"Mom and Dad are missionaries. I've got a pretty good repertoire of old-fashioned hymns in my head."

"Finding a hymn won't be a problem. I grew up on them, too." So that's why he had no trace of a Texas accent. What did his parents think of his career choice? "Since you're new to the cruise staff, you must've known about this plot before I stumbled into the picture."

Jacob went still. "Yes." His whisper guttered in his throat.

She shouldn't have been so flippant with him earlier. The guy was hurting. "I'd like to know which crew members you suspect, so I can avoid them."

"Steer clear of Dieter, the *maître d'*. Although he wasn't on our original list of suspects, he's working overtime to get me fired in the dining room. Mr. Atlas speaks with a German accent. Wouldn't surprise me if he bursts into 'Deutschland über Alles' at breakfast."

"He sounds charming."

"Yeah. Watch out for the new steward, Manuel Rodriguez, a last-minute hire for a slacker who quit unexpectedly. He's billeted in the cabin next to yours. With Dieter."

She gulped. "Lucky me. Any other possibilities?"

"You."

"Why me?"

"You were the latest and most suspicious hire of all. Seems you were a busy girl in Romania. Their secret police have quite a file on you."

Her shoulders sagged. She'd never escape her past, recover her reputation. "Please believe me. I was innocent."

"Not according to their records. Your boyfriend was one shady character. Connected with terrorists. How about you?"

"Haven't you ever trusted someone you shouldn't have?"

"Yeah." His eyes impaled her.

"I didn't know what was in those envelopes he told me to deliver." So many times she'd been burned, trusting men. The wrong men. At least Jacob's feelings were plastered on his face. She crossed her arms. "Well. Looks like I'm all you've got. Does Interpol want my help or not?"

"Tomorrow an Iranian couple joins the cruise, Khalid and Sora Hosseni." A haunted look clouded Jacob's eyes. "That sticky note confirms you're in grave danger. We need to get you off the ship and into a safe house."

"No. I'm not jeopardizing Frénie's job." Riley locked her hands inside her elbows. "I can't let her down. Besides, you need me as bait for the Romanians."

Jacob looked as if he might get sick. He closed his eyes and rubbed the bridge of his nose. "You'll need constant protection, constant surveillance."

"Seems I'm already getting coverage from both sides."

He blanched. "How am I going to keep you safe?"

When would she learn to keep her mouth shut? Riley wanted to tell him everything would be okay. She softened her voice. "How about 'The Star-Spangled Banner' for tomorrow's Name That Tune?"

"May she ever wave."

"May we catch these terrorists before Agent X hits the air waves. Or do you use the substance in water?"

"Riles, your way with words ..."

She smiled at his nickname. "It's a singers' trait."

"Keep your door locked at all times. Don't answer unless you hear the day's signal. Otherwise, with no peephole, you could be opening the door to an assassin."

8

Day 3: Cologne

Jacob put his empty oatmeal bowl on the tray and slid his arm along the back of Riley's chair. She'd dressed in the black top and slacks again. Probably her idea of a Ninja.

From their corner table at the back of the dining room, he'd gotten a good look at everyone who entered. Two no-shows, Manuel, and Jhun, the new cook. Dieter had grabbed a roll with cheese and left the room. "Aren't you glad you're having a nutritious breakfast to see you through the day?"

Riley eased away from him. "I'd rather have had an extra hour's sleep."

"Five-forty-five is pretty early." From now on she was eating with him. Then he'd know she was safe. "Tomorrow I'll knock fifteen minutes earlier."

"That won't be necessary. I have an alarm clock."

Funny, she didn't have the diva attitude he'd expected from an opera star. Riles looked super without the face paint, her hair in a ponytail.

"And we're meeting at this hour because ..."

"Had to make sure you don't leave the boat unescorted." He longed to finger the curls framing her face.

She sighed. "Surely all those hungry-eyed men on the dance floor have come to their senses."

"Yeah, I noticed." The memory of her in Molnár's arms still irked, Sugar Daddy's fingers doing a chiropractic dance on the end of her spine. He'd wanted to punch the guy in the nose, sweep Riles into his arms, and dance her out into the sunset. Maybe she preferred older men. "You stay with me today."

"You think that's wise?"

"It's a lot better than you waltzing on Molnár's arm."

"I wasn't waltzing. I was tromping on his feet. And every other unsuspecting man who requested a dance."

"I'd like to keep Brick's identity secret as long as possible. We need an ace onshore." Not another dead undercover agent.

She shoved aside her half-eaten oatmeal and picked at her omelet.

For a slender woman, she had a gorilla-sized appetite. "Sleep okay?" He squeezed her shoulder, her muscles tight beneath his fingers.

"Chased Hawk Nose all night." She lasered his hand with a pointed look. "Would you mind?"

"Part of our cover. Let people think I'm, uh ... we're an item."

"We're an item all right." She plopped her oatmeal bowl on top of the barely eaten omelet. "A bull's-eye on a target."

"Which is why you're sticking with me today."

She gave him a suspicious squint, like his mother's, ferreting out his kindergarten escapades.

"As long as you remember this is strictly business."

"I thought opera singers were skilled actors."

"We are. And another thing. Singers need their sleep. It's critical to a good performance."

"I'll be sure to let Hawk Nose and Eagle Eyes know you gotta have your beauty rest." Jacob risked tucking a curl behind her ear. "Be a good girl. Stay in your room until I finish breakfast duty for the passengers." He smooched the air.

Her sugary smile could bankrupt all the artificial sweetener manufacturers overnight. "Right."

"Aw, c'mon." He buffed his knuckles on her chin. "I thought a coloratura could do better than that."

"You giving out the Oscars this year?"

"Nope." But he'd sure like to get to know Riles better. Off duty. And when she wasn't a morning grumpus.

What was he thinking? How could he forget Christine's face when he'd told her about Noel's murder, her infant son wailing in her arms, the questions he couldn't answer for her. *Who killed him? Was he betrayed? How will I survive without him, Jacob?*

He stacked their dishes and took them to the kitchen. No way was he going to leave a woman vulnerable. Widowed and afraid, a child to raise without a father.

EARLY MORNING OPERA rehearsals were so not her thing, but a five-thirty breakfast call. Riley double-bolted her cabin door then took a cold shower, hoping the icy needles would jolt her awake. Sparring with Jacob at breakfast hadn't done the job.

Maybe she could catch a few historical sites today. For once. Two trips to Antwerp, and she had yet to see the sights. She slapped the bath towel around the metal bar, then dressed in a navy linen skirt, white blouse, and mesh slip-ons.

As Riley tried to close the closet door, it lodged against her suitcase. Yesterday she'd tucked the bag against the back wall of the closet.

Jacob's warnings flashed in her mind. Had someone returned to her room while they were at breakfast? She laid the suitcase on the bed and unzipped the main compartment. Two stage wigs protruded from their protective wrappers and boxes. Her blood pressure *whomped* into overdrive. Who'd damaged her precious babies?

Almost afraid to check, Riley opened her dresser drawers. Someone had skewed her neat rows of bras and bikini panties, mussed her pajamas and pantyhose in the middle drawer. The skin on her arms crawled. Who'd violated her privacy—Manuel or Dieter? She punched in the code on her room safe and checked her cash, her jewelry. Nothing missing.

She grabbed her purse and hurried upstairs to the dining room.

From the tray in his hand, Jacob served Mrs. Ackelroyd a croissant.

As she caught his eye, Riley nodded toward the door. Without acknowledging her gesture, Jacob picked up a pot of coffee and poured fresh cups for his guests. She waited outside the dining room for him.

"You rang, madame?" His tone was mock-serious, his eyes alert.

"Someone searched my room."

"How do you know?"

"My wigs."

"Your ... wigs?"

"I came to Antwerp from a gig in Düsseldorf. I prefer to wear my own wigs in performance. They're cleaner, no cooties. The eighteenth-century one had been moved to the center of my suitcase, and the curls were sticking out of the protective bag. Strands of hair were bent out of shape on my china-chop wig."

"You sure you didn't ..."

"Wigs are expensive. Believe me, I take care of mine."

"Your room may have been bugged again."

"So soon?" The words strangled in her throat.

"Shh, keep your voice down."

The Ackelroyds emerged from the dining room and walked toward them.

"Enjoy your day." Jacob stepped aside and let the couple pass.

"Lovely voice, my dear." Mrs. Ackelroyd patted Riley's hand.

"Thank you."

Mr. Ackelroyd's gaze did a slow zigzag from her face to her torso, then he winked.

Old men on the prowl. Riley ground her teeth. Another thing Frénie hadn't warned about. Riley pressed her back against the wall, giving the lech more room to pass by.

Moments later, the Ackelroyds entered their suite down the hall.

"Give me your key card." Jacob held out his hand. "Hang out near the piano, anywhere there's a group of people, until I come for you."

She rubbed her arms, unable to dispel the chill that coursed through her. Whoever had searched her room must have a key to it.

9

J acob waited until Manuel entered the laundry room at the head of the corridor, then let himself into Riley's cabin. Since last night she'd settled in. Makeup bottles spread out on the dresser, a Bible beside her impeccably made bed, clothes hung by type in the closet. One very organized lady. A lady who needed her beauty rest.

Using his surveil kit, he swept the room for bugs and almost missed the small disk in the corner of the wall above the lintel.

He pried out the device and crushed the Chinese-made disc. Another listening device was burrowed in the wall behind the television again. A third one hid above the wall clasp at the top of her dresser mirror. Hoping he'd find nothing, he swept her bathroom. Air whooshed from his mouth. No listening devices. No minicams where she'd feel most vulnerable.

Once inside his room, he re-swept it. The detector went wild near the bed. He ran his hand behind the headboard, dug out two state-of-the art miniature listening devices. Someone had been busy while he and Riley were at breakfast. Last night, his room had been clean.

Whoever was surveilling them now knew he was with

Interpol. Question was, was it Jhun the cook, Manuel, or Dieter? Manuel had a steward's passkey.

Jacob retrieved his earbuds and tuned his mini-receiver to the frequency set for Manuel's room. Dead. Manuel or Dieter may have found the bugs and destroyed them. Meeting with Riley in a secure spot onboard was going to be difficult. And far too public. He ought to let Schwarz know their cover had been blown. But if he did, would Schwarz take him off the case?

As he entered the main lounge, Riley was seated at the piano, her fingers racing in double-octave scales up and down the keyboard. "Ready to go, doll?" He nuzzled her neck, and she flinched. "Someone did a real number on your room. Play along, okay?"

"Sure." She brought her shoulder to his cheek, switched from scales to chord progressions. "Any minicams?"

"Thankfully, no, but no whisper would go unheard." The scent of her perfume, Chanel No. 5 filled his nostrils. "Just in case they change their MO, don't undress anywhere except in the bathroom with the door closed."

Riley hit a wrong note and the chord soured. "What do we do?"

"Not sure yet. Try meeting openly on the boat, maybe." If she weren't critical to the identification of the terrorists, he'd pack her bags himself and personally escort her to a safe house.

Easing away from him, she shut the lid over the keyboard. "I can't sit here all day, and I refuse to hide in my room. I'm getting my sweater and going ashore and playing tourist for a day."

"Not without me." Jacob clasped her hand and walked her to her room. Beneath his grip, her fingers were blocks of ice. He wanted to warm them in his hands. Instead, he waited in the doorway while she touched up her lipstick and grabbed a navy sweater from her dresser.

She joined him in the hall, her face pale.

"Everything will be all right." Jacob squeezed her arm. Surprisingly, she didn't resist.

Riley fiddled with a button on her sweater, twisting the disk until he thought it might pop off. "You really think you can catch these men?"

"Yes." He thrust a phony confidence in his tone and escorted her up to the sun deck.

Apart from Molnár, Mrs. Cochran, and the Ackelroyds, who were sitting in the bow, most of the passengers had disembarked and were strolling up the hill toward the cathedral. Maybe repeat passengers didn't care to see the sights at every stop.

At the head of the gangplank a slender olive-skinned man in hand-tailored slacks waited to be admitted onboard. Khalid Hosseni.

Adrenaline thrummed in Jacob's veins. Only ten feet between him and one of the most notorious assassins in Europe.

Khalid's outfit was pure GQ, casual yet commanding. The sweater, knotted around his neck over a silk polo shirt, and handmade Italian shoes reeked of megabucks. Sora waited a few feet behind Mr. GQ.

If he didn't know better, he'd peg her as a model on a Vogue photoshoot, dressed in white from turban to high-heeled boots. The file photos of Khalid and Sora failed to capture the evil that emanated from them in almost palpable waves.

With questions riddling her eyes, Riley sidled against him.

The security officer and the staff captain, Lundstrom's second-in-command, blocked the entrance to the boat.

For an eternity of seconds, Sora's predatory gaze settled on Jacob then scoured Riley.

Instinctively, he moved in front of Riley. Her rapid breaths feathered the hairs on his neck. Hard to tell if she were irritated with him or fearful, but he held his ground. It was possible Sora had been Noel's killer. She was the right height, the right build. If she'd done the deed, she might have gotten a good look at him that night.

Khalid handed the staff captain two burgundy passports stamped with the Iranian coat of arms. He flipped through them then handed them to the security officer. A few feet away, Manuel waited by the railing.

"Welcome to the *River Nymph*, Mr. and Mrs. Hosseni." The security officer handed the documents to Khalid.

Giving the officer a curt nod, they boarded the boat, Louis Vuitton shoulder bags and suitcases in tow. Manuel stepped forward and took their luggage to the X-ray machine. The Ackelroyds disembarked and headed toward the cathedral.

What he wouldn't give to search those suitcases. And he needed to monitor the Hossenis' conversation. "Riles ..." Jacob nuzzled her neck and she stiffened. "How about some time in my room, strictly business."

"Yeah, right, Mr. Bond." She edged away from him.

"I assure you, I'm no 007." She needn't know her bodyguard was a rookie field operative. "You can't go ashore unescorted, and our best bet for bioterrorists just stepped onboard."

"What about Eagle Eyes, Hawk Nose?"

As much as he didn't want her in on his surveil, freaking out over what someone had done to her room, he had to stay onboard. "Sorry, hon, this isn't a multiple-choice quiz."

"Oh yes, it is. I'm going to the cathedral." She pulled from his grasp. "The sooner the Romanians are caught, the safer we'll be onboard."

Tucking his newspaper under his arm, Molnár rose from his deck chair and headed toward them.

"Riles." Jacob lowered his voice. "I can't protect you if you aren't with me."

"I can't live like this, terrified of every shadow, of everyone who approaches me. Let's force them to make a move in the open." She headed for the gangplank.

She was one gutsy lady. "Riles, wait." He hurried after her.

But Molnár reached her first. "May I have the pleasure of accompanying you?"

"Yes, you may." She flung her sweater around her shoulders and tied the sleeves around her neck.

Jacob wanted to shake a fist at Molnár and tell him to keep his fat paws off his girl. Instead, he gave Riley his best hurt look and stuck out his hands, palms open. "Hon, please." He almost barfed, pleading in front of Molnár like a lovesick puppy.

Molnár watched them as if this were game point at Wimbledon.

"Riles, please." Jacob gave her his best aw-shucks-ma'am smile, hoping he'd masked his urge to throttle Sugar Daddy and give Riley a good spanking.

"Pardon me." Molnár cleared his throat. "I do not wish to intrude on a lovers' quarrel."

"Lovers'—"

Jacob pressed two fingers over her mouth. "Now, honey ..." He turned to Molnár. "Excuse us please." Jacob gripped Riley's elbow and steered her toward the stern.

"What do you think you're doing?" Venom riddled her whisper.

"Trying to keep you alive."

"That's right. By finding the Romanians. Unless there've been some new developments you haven't mentioned, I don't think I'm going to find them on the boat."

"Thank God for that." Because until he figured out who had bugged their rooms, protecting her would be difficult enough. For Molnár's benefit, Jacob slid his arm around her shoulder, toyed with the strap of her purse. "Perhaps you didn't know, but civilians are subject to the demands of Interpol's police officers. Think of me as your friendly neighborhood cop."

"Ha."

Nice guy, good cop wasn't working. "Riles, here are the facts. As an Interpol police officer, I can have you arrested and thrown in jail for obstructing a case. Got it?"

She wrenched her shoulder strap from his fingers. "Aye, aye, sir."

"That's better. We both might live longer if you drum up the acting chops and pretend we're in a serious relationship. As in you don't go off with Molnár or any other Tom, Khalid, or Alfred from this boat. Think you can do that?"

"So, if I slap your face right now, we've just had a lovers' tiff." She tilted her face up to his. "It doesn't count as striking an officer of the law, right?"

He dropped his hand from her shoulder. "While we stand here arguing I'm missing out on the conversation of two terrorist assassins. Care to join me?"

"Do I have a choice?"

"Nope."

RILEY SHIFTED her weight on the plastic chair in Jacob's cabin. A Bible, two bottles of water, and an ice bucket stood next to the television on the desk. No family photos. No other books. Maybe because she lived out of a suitcase much of the year, she indulged her nesting instinct in every hotel, even for a one-night gig.

With his earbuds in, Jacob hunched on the edge of his bed.

It was her fault he'd missed the Hossenis' arrival in their room. She'd embarrassed herself in front of Molnár and made things worse for Jacob. But nabbing the Romanians was important, too. She wasn't anxious to spend time with Molnár, but Jacob's persistent micromanaging her life had pushed her don't-you-dare buttons into her atomic-war zone.

She picked up Jacob's Bible and leafed through the pages, looking for verses he might have underlined. He didn't seem like any MKs, missionary kids, she'd ever met. Maybe she shouldn't be so feisty with him, but his debonair style and self-assured air scared her.

Scared her because she couldn't shake off the attraction she felt for him. An attraction she wished would go away. An attraction that could derail her determination to stick with

Lacy's—no—*her* goal. The career. The career. She must think about the career.

Jacob pulled out the earbuds and stashed the monitoring equipment in his safe.

"Get anything?"

"Just lunch plans, a tour of the cathedral. The door shutting as they left."

"I'm sorry I made a scene."

"That's okay. Hopefully, Molnár bought our act. I understand, you're frightened. Probably the first time your life's been in danger."

"Yes." He'd seen through her defenses so easily. Why couldn't Jacob be bald and paunchy and already married?

He checked his watch. "I have an hour until time to play waiter. Want to see the cathedral?"

"Yes. Shall I grab your water bottles?"

"Sure, why not." He let her stick the bottles in her purse then he took her hand. "Maybe we'll catch us a couple of Romanians."

RILEY LET Jacob hold her hand as they strolled through the cavernous sections of the cathedral. The tension emanating from his body fused with hers. A few yards ahead, Mrs. Ackelroyd was pointing her jewel-laden fingers at various objects, her husband engrossed in a brochure, oblivious to her chatter.

Since they were pretending to be an item, she could pretend Jacob was one of her leading tenors, a man for whom she feigned feelings of ardor, an ardor faked solely through body language and her eyes. If that convinced the passengers she and Jacob were dating, she might be able to undo the damage she'd caused this morning. And protect her heart.

"Did you know the cathedral was the tallest building in the world until the construction of the Washington Monument in 1884?" Jacob's voice sounded almost robotic.

"No, I didn't." The walls stretching toward the vaulted Gothic ceiling made her feel as inconsequential as a gnat. Perhaps that had been the architects' intent—for man to be in awe of God's majesty. Sunlight streamed through the stained-glass windows, igniting their rich colors like embedded gemstones, temporarily tinting the furniture and floors.

"It's still the largest church façade in the world."

"You should be a tour guide."

"I was once. For a few summers."

"Anything else I should know about you?"

"I'm a great dancer."

"Well, goodie for you." That was something they'd never have in common. Not that it mattered, of course.

At the Chapel of the Virgin, Molnár was kneeling at a prayer stool in the middle row, fingering the beads of a rosary.

Her heart sank. If only she could've avoided him, so soon after her tiff with Jacob.

Molnár walked to the aisle, genuflected in front of the carved triptych of the cathedral's patron saints, and made the sign of the cross.

With his hands steepled as if in prayer, a small, grey-haired priest in black robes crossed to the altar and bowed. After a few minutes he turned to leave. Molnár scurried to his side and said something to him.

The priest pushed his wire-rim glasses up his nose and nodded. He gestured toward the confessional in the far corner. Following him, Molnár stepped into the penitent's booth.

"Good." Jacob muttered under his breath.

"What was that?"

"I hope he's repenting for the sin of lust." Coals of righteous indignation burned in his eyes.

If she weren't careful, he could become her twenty-first-century knight in shining armor.

Just then, Molnár stepped out of the booth and turned toward them.

Nestling against Jacob's side, Riley gave him the adoring smile she mustered for a besotted-with-himself tenor.

His head jerked back. "Huh?"

"Play along," she said without moving her lips. "You've got an audience."

"Okay, babe." He snugged the small of her back to his waist, bent his head over her mouth, and kissed her. Quick, chaste, appropriate for a church.

But her heart zinged like a pinball machine gone crazy. What had she been thinking? If she were to keep her promise to Lacy, she had to shield her heart from this guy. "Here." She fished the water bottles from her purse and shoved one in his hand.

"Thanks." Jacob's neck flushed. His chest heaved as though he'd barely survived a two-hundred-foot deep-sea dive. In one long swallow he swigged half the bottle.

As Riley uncapped her bottle, her hand froze mid-air. "Over there, to your left. Hawk Nose."

10

Jacob could almost taste the capture of the man. He scoped the naves, the transepts of the cathedral. The people scattered among chairs facing the altar. The groups of tourists gawking at the artifacts and stained-glass windows. Half a block away, a short man in jeans and a black hoodie concealing his head, ambled along the aisles. The guy peeked over his shoulder.

From Riley's description, he'd recognize that nose anywhere. "The short guy walking like he's on a ship in a typhoon?"

"Yes."

Jacob snapped a photo of him on his phone then speed-dialed Brick.

"Yo."

"Got Hawk Nose in sight." Jacob described him and clicked off.

Seconds later Hawk Nose cleared the last row of wooden chairs and headed toward the main exit.

Riley's weight shifted to the balls of her feet.

Would she be safer alone in the cathedral or with him? "Go sit in one those chairs and pray."

"I'll be praying." She glanced around the church. "But what if Eagle Eyes is here too?"

This was insane—taking her into more danger. The sooner he could work this assignment without her, the easier he'd rest. "Okay, come with me. Do exactly what I tell you."

"Yes, Officer."

Ignoring her impertinent tone, he grabbed her hand and headed for the main doors. "Maybe he won't realize you spotted him."

Almost as if he knew he'd been seen, Hawk Nose doubled his pace and exited through the massive cathedral doors.

Jacob hurried after him, Riley matching his stride. Outside, crowds lined up to enter. But Hawk Nose had vanished. Jacob redialed Brick. "Just lost him. Where are you?"

"On the northwest side of the cathedral. With a good view three directions. No sailor-types in sight."

"We'll search up here." Jacob clicked off, tossed his water bottle in a trash bin.

"Let's split up. You take the left, I'll take the right." Riley headed for the steps.

"No way." He pulled her to him. "We may have been set up, to separate us so they can take you out."

"Oh." She chewed her lip. "Too bad you don't have a drone."

A drone would've been Schwarz's call, probably Brick's assignment. Why hadn't they seen to it? "There're so many places Hawk Nose could've gone." The elevator between the cathedral entrance and the street levels below. The ramp to their right. The steps that led to the square below. The Hauptbahnhof, the train station, that bordered the rear of the cathedral. He chose the ramp. "You see either of the Romanians?"

"No, just the Ackelroyds and Mrs. Cochran." Riley pointed to a bench near the steps that led to the train station.

With that ridiculous doodad in her hair, he'd know Mrs. Ackelroyd anywhere.

She looked up from her ice cream and waved as if she hadn't seen them in a decade. "Yoo-hoo."

Giving her a wave, Jacob whispered, "Let's head for the square, the train station." He took the steps, shoved past people sitting, standing, and traipsing up and down the staircase.

"*Verzeihung, bitte.*" Riley apologized for their rudeness in German. "In Antwerp, Hawk Nose escaped on a tram."

The sleek, red-nosed Thalys train, from Paris and Brussels, glided along the elevated rails behind the cathedral, and headed into the train station. Jacob sent out an alert to surveil departing trains.

Chances were, he and Riles would never find Hawk Nose within the myriad of departure platforms. A slew of green bikes and scooters, free for the borrowing, were tucked between support bars outside the hotel. If Hawk Nose had chosen that route, they'd never catch up with him. He dialed Brick. "Meet us outside the train station."

Moments later, Brick exited the elevator and walked over to them. "No luck?"

Jacob scrolled through his photos of Hawk Nose. In the cathedral's half-light, he was hard to ID. Jacob passed the phone to Brick. "Managed to get the guy's backside, twice."

"Sad, bro." Brick handed the phone back to Jacob. "I fear your future holds no Ansel Adams prize."

"Yeah. Forgot to ask Hawk Nose to primp for his close-up." But after today, Jacob would know the Romanian anywhere. Now he could ask Schwarz to send Riley home. No more spy games for her, no more danger. She could return to her career. And be free from him.

Then he'd be out of danger too. Danger from letting go of his own vow—no marriage, no kids. No one to worry about every day on the job. If he could forget their kiss. The sensation of her lips on his.

"Schwarz wants you to search and rebug Manuel's and the Hossenis' rooms ASAP," Brick said. "As in today."

"Consider it done." A wave of nausea rolled through Jacob's gut. Cramps wrenched every inch of his intestines. Within seconds, sweat beaded his forehead. This was no time to be getting sick. He grabbed Riley's arm. "Let's get back to the boat. I've got lunch duty in twenty minutes." As soon as he'd finished serving lunch and set up for dinner, he'd talk to Schwarz then tell her she'd been relieved of her Interpol service.

RILEY HALF DRAGGED Jacob from the dining room toward the staff elevator. His pasty face, gleaming with sweat, looked like raw dough. Moisture from his sodden shirt seeped through her blouse, slicking her skin. Gritting her teeth, she hauled him inside the elevator and punched the button. The doors closed around them. "Think we should get you to a hospital?"

"No." His voice was hoarse. "You heard my orders."

"If your supervisor knew you were too ill to stand, he'd tell you to move on to Plan B."

"And what might ... that be?"

"I'll do it for you. Think of me as Kemosabe. You know, Tonto, the Lone Ranger's sidekick."

"No. It's too dangerous." He clutched his side and doubled over. "Must be something I ate."

"Or something someone put in your food. What have you eaten today?"

"No lunch, same breakfast as you."

"It couldn't have been in the scrambled eggs. We dished those from the warming tray. Probably wasn't the toast, or in the bowls of jam."

"Oh please. "He gagged. "Stop talking about food."

"Wait. I never drank my water at the cathedral. Someone must've tampered with the water bottles."

The haze clouding his gaze lifted. "Oh?"

Her pulse shot into overdrive. Had someone poisoned him

with Agent *X*? His eyes looked glassy. His chest rose and fell with short, sharp heaves. *Dear God, please, please let him be okay.*

"If you're thinking they were trying out Agent *X* on me, you can relax. After the central nervous system shuts down, death is almost instantaneous. For the lab rabbits."

"How comforting."

The bell dinged and the doors glided open. With his hand propped against the wall, she propelled him down the hall to his cabin.

"Your key, please." She held out her palm.

The card palsied in his fingers and fell to the floor. She retrieved it, opened his door, and helped him to his bed. Who could have done this to him?

Jacob flopped on the mattress, arms and legs flung out in snow-angel formation. A half-dead angel.

"I think you ought to call your office." Riley lifted his legs onto the bed, unlaced his shoes and put them in his closet. "And let them know you've probably been poisoned."

"You're a bundle of cheer." He turned pale green, gagged a couple of times.

As soon as Riley set the waste basket beside his bed, he threw up. When he was finished, she cleaned the basket in the bathroom then bathed his face and neck with a wet washcloth. "Maybe Brick can get my bottle analyzed." She pressed her palm to Jacob's forehead, his cheeks. His skin felt like hot coals. "You're feverish. I'll be back in a minute."

The corners of his mouth quirked. "I haven't been mothered like this since I came down with bronchitis at the age of five." His gaze wandered to the wall. "The only time I recall my mother sitting by my bed, holding my hand, watching over me."

"Oh." What could she say to heal his hurt? She couldn't imagine her own mother not being there when she needed her.

Once inside her room, Riley drew a star on the label of her water bottle then hid it in her bottom dresser drawer. No point risking a drink by mistake. She took a thermometer from her toiletry bag and filled her ice bucket in the laundry room. Frénie's symptoms had been similar. The bucket shook so hard in Riley's hands, ice cubes tumbled to the linoleum. Had terrorists poisoned her friend and planned to insert their own performer?

Riley let herself back into his cabin. Somehow, he'd managed to hang his waiter's uniform over the chair, put on his pajamas, and pull out his surveil kit. "How did you manage to debug the room?"

"I didn't. You're going to learn how to do it." He removed the wand from the case, showed her the power button and gave her the device. "Run it around the walls, the furniture, just like you saw me do your room."

"Okay." Moving slowly around the room, she checked for hidden microphones. For once, their space hadn't been invaded. "Clean." She grabbed the pillow from the top bunk, scooched the cushion behind his neck then shook the thermometer and popped it under his tongue. "Singers always come prepared. For us, a cold can be a disaster. No high notes, no voice. And presto, no pay."

A couple of minutes later, she checked the thermometer reading. "One-hundred-three degrees. You're not waiting tables tonight."

"Oh, yes I am." He gagged and hunched over the waste basket.

When he was finished, she cleaned the basket in the bathroom, then wrapped a few ice cubes in a clean washcloth and whacked them with the heel of his loafer. Frénie had been ill for days. Too weak to get out of bed. Too ill to be released from the hospital. The ice chips clinked as she poured them into a glass, then returned to his bedside and held the cup to his lips.

"Try sucking on a few of these. You're dehydrated and we need to get the fever down." They'd have to start praying in a miracle. She couldn't do this job alone. There were less than nine days left on the cruise.

"You do this as if you have experience." The hint of a quiver quirked his smile, stirring places in her heart she'd tried to bury.

"I—I used to do this for my twin sister. She had leukemia. During chemo we'd talk about becoming opera singers when we grew up." Struggling to squelch the flood of memories, she rearranged the top sheet over him. "Lacy was a mezzo-soprano. That's a voice with a richer color, lots of low notes, and often less high range." Riley fiddled with the edge of his pillowcase, now damp beneath her fingers.

"Her dying wish was that I'd have that career for us and become an international opera star. I promised her I wouldn't let her down."

"I understand." He covered her hand with his. "My best friend, Noel, was like a brother to me. He died a few weeks ago." Jacob's Adam's apple plunged twice. "In ... in my arms."

Tears sprang to her eyes. Blinking at them, she rested her other hand on top of his. "I'm terribly sorry." Her throat constricted her voice into a whisper. She'd been curled beside Lacy in her hospital bed when her sister died.

Moments later, Jacob's eyes closed. She waited until his breathing was less ragged then slipped her hands free and moved to his chair. If only she had a number for his Interpol supervisor, someone she could call to send a doctor who wouldn't ask too many questions.

In the hall, footsteps seemed to pause outside his door. If anyone snuck in while she was performing tonight, Jacob would be too feeble to fight off his killer.

UNTIL SHE'D LEFT to shower at four, he'd vomited almost every twenty minutes. Riley bent over Jacob's bed, felt his forehead then his cheek. "You sure you'll be all right?"

His nod was limp as a rag doll. Sweat still glistened on his face and neck, matted his pajama top to his chest.

If only she could cancel the performance and stay with him until he quit vomiting and could keep down some ice chips. "You're flushed. Probably still feverish."

"Must be your touch."

She dropped her hand to her side. "Wouldn't do to excite the patient."

"Don't worry. You won't." But the look in his eyes seemed to dare her to try. "Although I expect every male on the passenger roster will be vying to dance with you." His gaze trawled her from head to toe. "That dark blue gown against your red hair ..." He let out a low whistle, but the sound cracked and died from lack of air pressure.

Ducking her head, Riley suppressed her smile. She shouldn't let his approval get to her, but he made her feel so feminine, so —The career. The career. Don't forget the career. No way would she break her vow to Lacy. Riley hunted for a safer topic. "Are you still planning to search Manuel's and the Hossenis' rooms?"

"Yes."

"What do you expect to find? A map with directions to Agent *X*?"

"Evidence against Manuel. Most likely a member of the crew poisoned your girlfriend. And right now, he's *numero uno*."

"And maybe your water bottles, too. At the moment it's not worth risking your life for."

"It's bad enough watching Molnár paw you on the dance floor." Jacob inched himself to a sitting position and the color drained from his face. "But stay away from Khalid and Sora. They're known assassins."

Tonight's performance couldn't be over soon enough. "Then why don't you arrest them?"

"Because we have no proof." Another shallow breath heaved his chest. "Some of us still play by the rules, the laws of the land."

"I'm glad you're one of the good guys." She stroked a damp strand of hair from his forehead. "But you're much too ill to be up, snooping." Then she straightened the pillows behind him, and he settled back against the headboard. "What if the Hossenis return to their cabin early and catch you?"

"They won't. Stop by after you're finished tonight. I'll walk you to your room, make sure no one's been in there."

"Right, Ranger Bob." He didn't look strong enough to walk to the bathroom, let alone escort her to her cabin. "By the way, tonight's theme song is 'Standing on the Promises.' You know the hymn?"

"Yep."

"Get some rest."

"Thank you. I had no idea divas could be so nurturing. Kind. Caring." He shook a finger at her, the gesture as feeble as Methuselah. "You be careful. If Sora or Khalid knew you were on to them, they wouldn't hesitate to kill you."

At his warning, her stomach clenched. "Right. On that uplifting note, I leave you."

11

Riley almost choked on the lyrics of "I've Got You Under My Skin." What had she been thinking, choosing such a song with a row of predators eight inches from her bench? As usual, Mr. Ackelroyd seemed blasé to his wife's fawning over Molnár, whose attention seemed fixated on her every move at the keyboard. A pity Broadway lyricists couldn't pen something besides love songs.

Seated on the loveseat next to them, Khalid's eyes undressed her, stitch by stitch. Sora's red talons clawed the armrest, her glower roving between her husband and Riley.

Flashing her thousand-watt theater smile around the room, Riley shut the piano lid. Thank heaven she hadn't picked Ado Annie's "I Cain't Say No." Applause erupted from her front-row fan club. She rose from the keyboard and bowed.

"Most enchanting." Khalid blocked her escape from the piano. Within two seconds his musky cologne overpowered the last vestiges of her Chanel No. 5. "May I get you something to drink?"

"No, thank you." She glanced away from the penetrating forcefield of his gaze. "If you'll excuse me, I need to prepare for my last set." And check on Jacob.

The half-step back he took barely allowed her to clear his body.

"Pardon me." But her shoulder still grazed his tuxedo. With every stride, her form-fitting gown tugged at her legs. She took the stairs to the staff's quarters, tapped the first four bars of "Standing on the Promises" on Jacob's door, then let herself inside with his key.

His pajamas lay wadded on the bed. The light was on in the bathroom, but no sign of Jacob. She hurried to Manuel and Dieter's room and tapped on the door. "Jacob?" What if he'd fainted inside their room? Pressing her ear to the doorjamb, she knocked again. "Jacob, let me in." With her skirt lifted to her knees, she took the stairs to the passenger-suite deck.

Halfway down the hall, Jacob, dressed in his steward's uniform, cradled a stack of clean bath towels in his arms. Zigzagging from wall to wall, he lumbered toward the Hossenis' suite.

As weak as he was, he'd never make it. The Hossenis would find him and kill him. She'd be on her own, trying to track down the bioterrorists. Hitching her skirt to her thighs, she race-walked toward him. "Steward. Oh, Steward."

Jacob swung toward her, his head lolling on his chest. "What are you doing here?" The slur in his speech surpassed the soused guests she'd heard in the lounge.

"Trying to keep you from getting us both killed." With his arm wrapped over her shoulder, she walked him back to his cabin, groaning under his weight.

Grunting like an outmatched body builder, she maneuvered him inside the room. "I'm taking your passkey with me." She turned away from him, stashed the piece of plastic inside her bra and adjusted the keycard so its outline didn't show through her gown. Sweat from his body had stained her satin bodice.

From her room she snagged a white silk shawl and tied it over her shoulders to cover the wet spots, then checked the time. She should've been at the keyboard five minutes ago.

Hopefully Captain Lundstrom wasn't there, clocking her arrival. Once she'd finished her third set and the guests were at dinner, she'd change into a new evening dress.

SHORTLY BEFORE EIGHT-THIRTY, she zipped her white chiffon evening gown then checked on Jacob. He was sprawled on his bed, light snores coming from his open mouth. If only he wouldn't try to bug the rooms again tonight. She took the elevator upstairs. As she entered the lounge, the rhythm of a cha-cha rippled from Johann's keyboard.

Four couples were shimmying through the moves. In a classic GQ pose, Khalid leaned against a marble pillar at the edge of the parquet dance floor. She wished she'd taken the stairs. Then maybe Johann would be playing a waltz or a two-step. As if he'd read her mind, he plinked out the final cha-cha-cha chords. *Make it a two-step, Johann, a two-step.*

Khalid nodded to Johann then strode toward her across the dance floor. Giving her a mischievous grin, Johann lit into a tango.

Good heavens. She could barely two-step and waltz. But a tango—she hadn't a clue which foot to move first. No doubt he'd bribed Johann to play this wretched piece.

"I believe this dance is mine." With a haughty tilt of his head, Khalid held out his hand, a man certain he won't be turned down.

"You're too kind." She was about to dance with a murderer. How had he killed his victims? Squelching the thought, Riley allowed him to take her in his arms.

With the prowess of a professional ballroom dancer, Khalid swiveled her into position and shifted his weight to his right side. He bent his knees beside hers, pressed his right hand into her palm and glided backward.

She hesitated and her knee rammed his. "Sorry."

Somehow, she made it through the next two steps. In one suave move he tilted her backward, his fingers drilling her spine, his chest grazing hers. Her heel caught on the chiffon hem. "I'm such a klutz." He'd probably kill her for her lousy dance skills, not because she was working with Interpol.

Deftly he maneuvered her off the hem and back into the dance. "You seem very nervous."

"I—I don't do the tango."

"Isn't it customary for cruise entertainers to be expert in ballroom dancing?" He whipped her the opposite direction.

"Yes, but—"

"You must be a new employee. One, who for some reason, wasn't required to meet the job requirements."

"I'm subbing for my friend who was taken ill."

"Perhaps this isn't your real profession." His fingers probed her vertebrae.

"I'm an opera singer. As you can tell, dance wasn't my best class in school." Her giggle came out more like a whimper. Maybe someone on the boat had set him up to interrogate her.

"Your palm is sweating."

"Really. I go through this every night." She attempted a smile, but cement boots had encased her lips. "The only men who dance with me more than once are lech—brave."

Across the room, Sora was holding court from the middle of the couch. Seated on the armrests, Molnár and Mr. Ackelroyd ogled her, men old enough to be her grandfather. But Sora's bullet-ridden gaze was riveted on Riley and Khalid.

"I think your wife wants this dance with you."

"Tonight, I prefer to tango with you."

"I can't imagine why." Odd, Sora letting him live so long. Maybe détente was understood in marriages between assassins. "What do you do for a living, Mr. Hosseni?" Maybe if she got to know the Hossenis it might help Jacob. Who was she kidding? She was babbling like an idiot.

"Khalid, please." He swung her in the opposite direction.

"Khalid." Sheesh, she'd never been on a first-name basis with a killer.

He laid his cheek against hers, his skin as hot and rough as desert sand. "Perhaps you have other talents."

If he pulled her any tighter, they'd be Siamese twins. She tried to ease from his embrace. "Nope. Nope. Just opera."

"I think I'd like to discover your secrets for myself." He yanked her so close the diamond studs in his shirt bit into her chest. "For an opera star, you seem more like a rabbit cornered by a jackal."

"I told you, I'm not a dancer. The cruise was departing. They needed a singer."

His eyes hooded. "I am very good at extracting secrets."

She gulped. "I'll take your word for it."

"Your cabin shouldn't be too difficult to find."

Assassins probably carried lockpicking kits. If only she had a can of mace, a stun gun. "Guests are forbidden to enter staff quarters."

"That's hardly a deterrent." He pressed her palm backward until fiery shards shot through her wrist. "What I want from you won't take long."

No way was she spending the night in her room. Riley stepped out of her chiffon gown and threw on sweatpants and a top. Tonight, she could've kissed Captain Lundstrom for rescuing her from Khalid. For the next six dances Lundstrom, his staff captain, or the purser had endured her foot fumbles on the dance floor then escorted her to her room.

Her cell phone buzzed, and she checked the caller ID. Oh no, Frénie. Tucking the phone between her shoulder and her ear, Riley sank on the bed.

"How did it go, *chérie*? Did the men survive dancing with you?" If Frénie's laugh were any more forced, it would crack.

"Fine, just fine." Riley massaged the balls of her feet, a tender spot on her instep. "How's the patient?"

"Tomorrow the doctor may release me, but he said I am not yet well enough to work. Perhaps in a few days I can catch a train to your next stop and take back my job."

"Don't even think about it." The words rushed from Riley's mouth. "I'm splitting the paycheck with you." If Frénie showed up, there'd be no way to stay onboard and help intercept the terrorists, the vials. "Stay home and rest. I stocked your pantry. Broth and rice, soup and eggs. And chicken in your freezer. You won't have to go up and down all those stairs every day until you have your strength back."

"Ah, *chérie*, you are such a good friend. Now tell me the truth. How is the singing, the dancing really going?"

Riley shivered. Surely Frénie had never danced with an assassin. "For a girl from Cuero, Texas, it's been pretty exciting." Not to say humiliating, but she'd spare her that piece of information.

"Hmm ... we'll see if they dance with you tomorrow."

If only they wouldn't. Especially Khalid. "Shall I keep a scorecard of repeat requests?"

"Ha ha, very *drôle*."

"Did the doctor say what caused your food poisoning?"

"*Oui*. It was some name I can't pronounce."

"Can you find out and call me back? There's a waiter onboard who has the same symptoms. I'm very worried about him."

"Ah *chérie*, is he interested in you? What does he look like?"

"Blue eyes, blond hair. He's very ill at the moment, and his interest is purely professional."

"*Non*, this I do not believe. No man's interest in you is purely professional."

"Don't be silly. This is strictly business."

"What kind of business?" Sharpness edged Frénie's tone.

"Uh, well ... subbing for you."

"I think you are not such a good liar. With all the food you left me, I should be able to return to the ship in a few days." Frénie yawned into the phone. "I will call you soon. And I want to hear all about him. Every eensy-weensy detail."

Riley blew a kiss into the phone and then disconnected. She grabbed a pillow from the bed and hugged it to her chest. In less than a week, she'd come under the scrutiny of terrorists onboard, on land, and now her best friend. A friend who knew how badly things had gone and insisted on playing Cupid while the world was falling apart around them.

12

Day 4: Coblenz

Opening one crusted eyelid, Jacob peered at his watch in the half light. Nine a.m. If he had to endure another night of dry heaves, chills, and abdominal cramps, he'd die. Vague recollections of Riley cleaning out his waste basket during the ordeal and debugging his room again, flitted through his mind. Everything seemed like a nightmare on auto-replay.

He opened his other eye. Across from him, Riley sat with her elbow on his desk, her chin propped in her hand. "How long have you been here?" His voice splintered on every word.

"All night." She stifled a yawn.

"Thanks." He hiked himself to a sitting position, stifled a grin. She'd sacrificed her beauty rest to take care of him. "Heard from Brick while you were hoofing it on the dance floor. We're bringing Manuel in for questioning."

"Great. One less terrorist on the boat." She stared at the floor, nibbled her lip.

"Everything go okay last night?"

"Yep." She crossed her legs. Uncrossed them. Fiddled with a curl at her shoulder. "Every male guest is probably wishing there were a shoeshine boy on the boat." Although her eyes seemed puffy from lack of sleep, her mouth had compressed into a taut line.

"You sure there isn't something you want to tell me?"

She shook her head, rose, and paced the room.

"Gotta bug the Hossenis' room." Jacob moved his feet over the side of the bed. "Interpol agents are like the postman." On an inner count of three he hauled himself upright. "Neither rain, nor snow, nor—" He took one step and his ankles wobbled like a little girl trying out Momma's high heels. Nausea curdled his gut, threatening to erupt. As he tried for a second step, his legs gave way. He grabbed for the bedpost and plopped on the mattress.

"You were saying?"

"Maybe ... later."

"Uh-huh." She tucked the sheet around him. "I'll bug the rooms."

"No."

"If the Hossenis catch you, Interpol loses their spy onboard. Face the facts, Jacob. You're too ill to do the job. They'll kill you, and where does that leave me?"

"Alone. Defenseless." The words choked off in his parched throat. He couldn't let anything happen to her.

"How hard can bugging a room be? I'm teachable."

"You're a civilian. Not an agent."

"You think these terrorists are buying that logic?"

She was right. Riles was in as much danger as he was. But right now, he couldn't protect her. "You're not ... bugging ... those rooms."

"Oh, yes I am." She pinned his shoulders to the pillows then hooked her hand beneath his knees and swung his legs onto the mattress.

MIDMORNING SUNLIGHT FILTERED through the gap in Jacob's curtains. At his mirror, she patted her China-chop wig into place, fingered the holes in her earlobes where her earrings ought to have been. Wearing them today would increase the risk of being recognized. They'd be safe in her room. Drawing a deep breath, she blew it out. She had to make herself do this. If she and Jacob didn't go on the offensive, Khalid and Sora and the other terrorists might win this battle.

If she pretended this was an opening night performance, a new production, she could do it. Wearing Jacob's too-large white jacket, his slightly tight white slacks, and her own athletic shoes, Riley pirouetted beside his bed, her hands out for balance. "How do I look?"

He rolled his eyes. "Great, just great. Best-looking steward I've seen. Even without makeup."

One hand circling near the side of her head, Riley hummed a vocal siren, slurring the pitches as she connected them from low to high. She drew a deep breath and started a new sequence a step higher.

His jaw fell open.

"Just warming up." Peering in his dresser mirror, she tucked in a few stray hairs of her black-bobbed wig. Hopefully the wig would bring her better luck than last month as the too-tall Mi in Düsseldorf. "Think I'll pass inspection?"

"Yeah, if they're blind."

"Aw, c'mon. Performers psych themselves up before they go onstage. Helps them cope with nerves." Or sheer terror.

"For heaven's sake, Riles." Jacob dug his elbows into the mattress, struggled up against the pillows. "This isn't an opera gig. If the Hossenis catch you in their room, they'll kill you and toss your body overboard."

"Thank you, Mr. Positive Reinforcement." The guy just didn't get it. "Singers can't afford to hang around worriers, people who set you up to fail." She jabbed a fist on her hip. "In case you didn't know, it takes courage to go onstage, deal with the unexpected, cope with the cracked high note in the middle of an aria." She extended her palm toward him and wiggled her fingers. "Give me the bugging devices, O fearless leader." Before she chickened out.

"You can't do this." He sank into the pillows, clutched his forehead. "It's too dangerous. I won't let you."

"Wanna bet? Now hand over the bugs so I can get back to work on my songs for tonight." And pretend this nightmare wasn't reality.

"Okay." He blew out his air. "Bring me the dop kit in my duffle bag, please."

She unzipped his luggage and handed him the leather kit.

"Assuming you can get in their room, you may not have much time." He unscrewed the bottom plate from a large can of shaving cream and shook the contents on the bed. A two-pronged white electrical converter, two slender devices that looked like ballpoint pens, four black cylindrical devices about the size of a quarter, a USB flash drive, and a black computer mouse fell on the sheets.

"We'll choose a few of these." He activated a tiny switch then handed her the white converter. "Might try plugging it behind the desk. Drop a pen in the back of the desk drawer. Maybe roll one under the center of the bed where they can't vacuum it up. Plant a couple of the small disks under the bottom of the bed, the desk, or sofa, places like that."

"What happens if Sora tries to use this?" She bounced the converter in her hand.

"She'll probably ruin her appliance and blacken the wall outlet." He activated the pens and several disks. "And blow out my eardrums. They're sound activated. I'll be able to track your progress."

All he'd hear was her heart pounding. "I'll tuck the converter between the towels." Riley stuffed the smallest devices in her pants pocket.

"Good thinking." He handed her the passkey.

She started another vocal slide in chest voice, and gestured her way through it, hand in front of her chest then arcing it over her head as the pitches climbed, focusing on the vibration in her facial bones.

"What. Are. You. Doing?"

"Testing my high notes, the resonance."

"You won't need 'em. Today, you're not a singer. You're a spy. Think stealth, silence, speed." Jacob thrust his fist in the air. "Survival."

She flicked a piece of lint from her uniform jacket. "You'd be the last person I'd want backstage before a performance." Good thing she'd never have to worry about that.

"Will you listen to me?"

"I am, I am."

"No, you're not. You're like a racehorse, pawing the start line, waiting for the gun to go off. What if they catch you, how will you handle that, what will you say?"

"No idea." She shrugged, arms spread, palms out. "One thing you learn as a singer—never play the what if game. What if my high notes crack? What if I freeze and they come out flat, or sharp? What if I slur my runs?"

He slapped the mattress. "No agent goes in without a Plan B."

"I haven't got one, so if you hear a high *F* shrieking through the woodwork—"

"Listen to me." He grasped her wrist and pulled her to the bed. "Today. You're not a singer." The snarl in his voice matched the coals smoldering in his eyes. "You're a secret agent on a mission, a potentially deadly mission."

"Right." She glared at him. Working with a secret agent was almost as bad as working with a tenor.

"Go over your plan once again."

What plan? She was an agent with no training, no backup, no Plan B. Knowing her, she'd probably need Plan Z^3. "Take two sets of clean towels from the linen closet. Let myself in the room, plant the bugs and leave." If she were lucky.

"I can't let you do this. It isn't right." He raked a hand through his hair, leaving the ends sticking up. "You're not qualified."

"I'm all you've got." If she didn't go through with this insane plan, the terrorists might succeed in using Agent X.

His chin dropped to his chest. "I'll be praying for you." He held out his hand and she clasped his icy fingers. "God, forgive me. I shouldn't be letting—"

"It's okay, Jacob. I want to help. No matter what the consequences."

The two dark pools of guilt in his eyes nearly undid her. She slid her hand free before he could feel the tremble working down her arms and heading for her fingers. Last night she'd been safe in his room. But letting herself into the enemy's camp—no. She couldn't let her thoughts roam.

His face went pasty-green and he laid back against the pillows. Sweat dribbled down his cheeks and neck.

Riley ran cold water on a washcloth and dabbed his forehead, his cheeks, his neck. "Can I get you anything before I go?"

"Just come back safe." A sick look swept across his face.

"I intend to." She set an extra roll of toilet paper next to his pillow, moved the waste basket beside the bed. "See you shortly, chief."

He reached for her. "Riles—" Then grabbed for the waste basket.

Moving quickly, she let herself out of his room before he changed his mind about letting her spy.

13

Riley hid the converter between the two sets of towels clutched to her chest and knocked on the Hossenis' door. As she listened at the doorjamb, her heart drummed her sternum with a get-out-of-there rhythm. Unrecognizable in the uniform, she'd be safe. She'd be—

The door behind her opened. Her gut hitched. Holding her breath, she waited for someone to scream 'stop thief.'

"Oh, Miss, could I get two sets of clean towels?" a woman said.

The converter—what should she do with it? Drawing a breath, she turned around. Mrs. Ackelroyd. Riley's mind raced in a thousand directions, none of them logical. She snatched the converter, deactivated it with one hand, and thrust the towels into the woman's hands. "Here, take these."

"Hmm." Mrs. Ackelroyd eyed the converter.

"You didn't call for one of these, did you?" Riley held up the device. Please, please say no.

"No ... but I might need one." Mrs. Ackelroyd reached for the converter.

"I better get it tested first." Riley moved her hand behind her back. "We've had complaints about some of them not working properly."

"Is that so?" A finger to her lip, Mrs. Ackleroyd tilted her head, gave Riley a slow head-to-toe then squinted up at her. "I've seen you before ... haven't I?"

Riley's heart lurched. "No madame, I don't think so."

"Oh yes I have." Mrs. Ackelroyd drew the towels to her chest, tapped the fabric. "But it wasn't here ..."

"I'm filling in for someone today. I'd better get back to my work. Have a nice day." And don't think too hard. Riley walked back to the linen closet, her knees knocking like her first attempt on stilts. She'd been seen. If she had any sense, she'd hightail it back to Jacob's room and resign. Playing Emma Peele and Mrs. King was definitely not her gig.

Instead, she pulled two more sets of towels from the shelves and returned to the Hossenis' suite. If she knocked, Mrs. Ackelroyd might open her door. This time the woman might remember where they'd met.

Before Riley lost her nerve, she inserted the key card, let herself into the Hossenis' room and eased the door shut. The click into the doorjamb sounded like a gunshot.

Two large closets lined each side of the entry hall. A full-sized marble bathroom with a shower/tub to her left. Broad windows overlooked the deck and the outskirts of another medieval village. No sliding doors for a possible escape. The nightstands on both sides of the king-sized bed, a couch, several striped armchairs, and a coffee table fit easily into the space. So unlike her cabin or the rooms she'd glimpsed elsewhere on the *River Nymph*.

She wiped the sweat from her fingers on the towels and set them on the edge of the bed. Kneeling beside the bed near the headboard, she shot one of the ballpoint pens underneath the mattress. At the foot of the bed, she inserted a bug the size of a quarter beneath the box springs, another one beneath one of the armchairs.

Muted voices sounded from the hall. Her heart sprang into her throat. Was it the Hossenis?

The voices drew near.

She grabbed the converter and the towels from the bed. Spun around. No balcony. No way to jump overboard.

The voices seemed to be outside the door.

Clutching the towels to her chest, she ducked inside the closet, worked her way past Sora's clothing, and crouched as far from the open closet door as possible. A key card inserted in the lock. A click. Voices beside her. The door shut with a firm click. Oh, why had she hidden? Now if she were caught, there'd be no talking her way out of this. Stupid, stupid, stupid.

Every garment in the closet exuded Sora's rich perfume. A tickle rippled inside Riley's nose. She gritted her teeth against the sneeze, clamped her nostrils. *Help me God, please help me.*

She forced herself to concentrate on the Hossenis' conversation. Probably Farsi, but the undercurrent of their tone carried an unmistakable urgency.

Footsteps sounded then Sora blocked the open closet door, the hall light silhouetting her body.

Riley shrank against the wall. What if Sora chose a garment from this side of the closet? Jacob's warnings claxoned in her mind. *The Hossenis won't hesitate to kill you.* Could she pay them to spare her life? What was she thinking—she had no money.

Six inches from Riley, Sora grabbed a hanger with a paisley caftan from the rod. The jacket next to the caftan fell to the floor. Riley held her breath. Leave it, leave it, leave it. Heels clacked on the bathroom tile floor. The held breaths eked out her mouth. Metal clinked on metal, the sound of a hanger on a towel bar. Footsteps approached the closet, Sora's voice derisive.

From the nearness of Khalid's guttered whisper, it sounded as if he were close enough to touch Riley. She flinched. Held her breath again. Then a loud smooching sound. The crack of a slap. Khalid's voice, ferocious, furious. Sora spoke again, her words rapid-fire staccato. Seconds later the cabin door opened then slammed shut.

Riley's back ached from crouching. The breaths she'd held shuddered from her mouth. But the knots in her gut muscles wrenched a few more degrees. Was she alone in the room with Sora or Khalid?

Either way, she was still trapped. And he or she was still a killer.

Footsteps padded back and forth on the carpet.

Had Jacob heard the exchange? What if he tried to rescue her? Her arm went numb from clutching the towels to her chest. The humid air clung to her skin like an overheated sauna. Sweat trickled down her armpits.

Footsteps thumped on what sounded like tile. Water gushed from a faucet then switched to the faint pitter patter of the shower. Her chance to escape. Her only chance.

If the bathroom door were closed.

She squatted, nudged the converter into the back corner, then stood and edged past Sora's clothing, trying not to jostle the hangers. Shooting up a few more silent prayers, she tweaked her wig into place and stepped from the closet. Her stomach plummeted.

The bathroom door stood open.

Too late now. Her heart thumped so hard she could barely breathe. She crept past the fogged bathroom mirror over the sink. Five more feet and she'd reach the door.

"What are you doing in here?" Khalid's voice stabbed her like a knife.

14

Dear God, no. Jacob pushed the earbuds deeper. Riley was trapped. Somehow he'd lost her in the hall before she entered their suite. Now the Hossenis were fighting about her.

A ball of adrenaline burst through him and he threw off the sheet, staggered to his closet, clawed his extra steward's uniform from the hanger. The inside of his skull spun like an out-of-kilter gyroscope.

Balancing against his dresser, he shrugged out of his pajamas, his fingers shaking like a junkie. *God help. Please let me reach her in time.* With agonizing slowness, he fumbled the steward's uniform over his sweat-slicked skin.

Then he stumbled out to the hall, lurching from the left wall then to the right. *I'm coming, Riles, I'm coming.*

Dieter entered the staff corridor. "What do you think you're doing?" Giving him a once-over, his eyelids shrank to menacing slits. "That's a steward's uniform."

"Outta my way." Jacob flailed a hand in Dieter's direction.

The *maître d'* widened his stance, blocking the corridor. "I'm reporting you to the captain."

"Fine with me, bud." Jacob lumbered toward him. Sparklers burst behind his eyes and Dieter's face morphed into a grotesque smear. "Now outta ... my ..." Jacob's knees buckled and he crashed to the floor. Fiery arrows lanced his thighs. "Riles ..."

Dieter grasped him under the arms and dragged him to his room. He dug in Jacob's pocket, unlocked the cabin door and threw him on his bed. Ebony waves rushed through his head and claimed him.

RILEY'S FEET riveted to the carpet. Khalid would never let her go. With her pulse thumping against her throat, she turned toward the bathroom.

A bath towel wrapped around his hips, Khalid stood in the doorway. Drops of water slithered from his dark chest hair and trickled down his bare legs.

The moisture fled her mouth, leaving her tongue a dried out foreign lump. He'd been in the shower, seen her head to the door. What on earth could she say? "I—I brought you these." Not the best Swedish accent but hopefully he wouldn't know the difference. Willing her hands not to shake, she held out the towels.

He didn't take them from her. "Where were you?"

Focusing her gaze on any move of his hands, she ducked her head and jerked her finger at the stateroom door.

"Impossible." He lunged toward her, fists clenched, his body poised for attack. "I would've seen you enter."

"But sir, I knocked on your door. There was no answer." No point mentioning he hadn't been in the room when she'd entered. "I—I thought your wife was in the bathroom. I—I decided to leave because—" She tucked her head again. If only she could blush at will. "I—I did not wish to see a naked man." Riley tossed the towels in his face, darted toward the door, and threw back the bolt.

He tossed the towels on the floor, grabbed her wrist, and spewed words in Farsi she assumed weren't complimentary.

"Sir, let go of me, or I'll scream."

Muttering in Farsi, he released her.

Riley flung open the door and fled from the room. She forced her legs into a calm stride, while her mind yelled run, run, run. In case he was still watching her, she unlocked the linen closet and removed a clean set of sheets and towels from the shelves. Without turning to check his doorway, she headed up the hall, away from Khalid, away from danger. Away from death.

She hoped.

Moments later Riley swung into the stairwell and slammed into Sora. "Oh, pardon me, madame." Riley stepped back, keeping her head down.

Uttering something in Farsi, Sora swept past her.

Riley hurried downstairs to Jacob's cabin, rapped the first four bars of "Standing on the Promises," double the normal tempo. She let herself into his room and sagged against the door. Every muscle in her legs turned to mush. "Hope you had a pleasant and uneventful morning."

He lifted his head from the pillow, his face gaunt, his eyes hollow. "Thank God, you're all right."

"Catch anything interesting on the airwaves?"

"Yes." He reached for her hand.

As she sat on the edge of his bed, he wrapped her fingers in his, the touch so like her dad's when she'd skinned her knees as a child. She bit her lip. A good cry was what she needed, but not here, not now. Jacob didn't need to see she wasn't good spy material. After all, she was all he had.

"Man, I've never prayed so hard in my life."

"Me, too." She'd take arias with high *F*s any day over this secret agent stuff. How did he stand the tension, the constant danger? "Does your family know what you do for a living?"

"No." He picked at a loose thread in the sheet. "They think I'm a desk analyst for an international firm in Brussels. They're missionaries, posted to the Guatemalan jungle." A hardness crept into his voice. "I hardly ever see them."

"Oh. I'm sorry."

"I suppose your life is one glittering party after another."

"Nope. I pretty much live out of a suitcase nine months of the year, and if I'm lucky, I get home to Cuero every two or three years. Europe has been my home for five years, and I've yet to see the sights, do the tourist thing."

"Maybe you can take a vacation after the cruise."

"Not without some gigs in the basket. Last I heard, travel costs money." Best steer the conversation away from their personal lives. "What were the Hossenis talking about when they came in the room?"

"You."

"Me?"

"Sora's insanely jealous of you. She threatened to carve his flesh into ribbons and then yours—"

Riley held up a hand. "Okay, okay. I get the picture."

He grabbed her sleeve. "Do you think he recognized you?"

"I don't know."

"You'd better wear the highest heels you've got tonight, convince him you're too tall to have been the steward."

She wasn't sure her legs would hold her up tonight, let alone don a pair of stilettos. Or if she could sing a note. As a singer, tension was her number one enemy, especially for a coloratura's more delicate instrument. "You need anything?"

"No, thank you. Now that I know you're all right."

"Then I'll head to my room and clean up. I've got to find twenty-five songs I haven't already sung on the cruise."

He gave her a lopsided grin. "And practice those dance steps."

"Yeah, that, too." She groaned.

"Wish I could help you there."

"Trust me, you'd regret it. You'd be permanently invalided out of Interpol, unable to serve your country."

A twinkle gleamed in his eyes. "Oh, I don't know … I'm a pretty good dancer." A bit of color stained his cheeks.

"So is Khalid." Shudders worked across her shoulders. A welt had risen where he'd gripped her wrist only minutes ago. She'd given Khalid far too much to ponder—her lack of qualifications for the job, her presence in his room. "And all the other men I've danced with on the cruise."

"Trying to make me jealous?"

"No, just trying to protect your job." And keep him from entangling his heart because she would surely destroy him. Jacob needed someone to be there for him. Opera stars lived like gypsies. Here today, gone elsewhere tomorrow. A life utterly unfair to a husband and children.

15

Day 5: Cochem

Thanks to Mrs. Ackelroyd sending back her soft-boiled eggs, not once, but twice at breakfast, Jacob was twenty minutes late for his meeting with Brick and the team. He huffed up the sidewalk into the medieval town of Cochem. He'd hated leaving Riley alone in her cabin, even though she'd promised to stay locked inside and skip lunch, if necessary. But the fewer Interpol agents she could identify, the safer for all of them.

Rain-freshened air mingled with the scent of moist soil, the terraced vineyards carved into the hillside. He crossed the intersection to the cobblestoned marketplace and the yellow, half-timbered Alte Thorschenke Hotel. Yellow, red, and orange umbrellas shaded early-morning patrons at the outdoor café. To the left of the hotel, stood an ancient stone tower that once guarded the entrance to the city. If Brick hadn't given up on him, he should be waiting inside the restaurant.

He crossed the minuscule lobby with its suits of armor and entered the cozy, wood-paneled restaurant. Middle-aged guests were breakfasting at tables covered with red-and-white checked cloths. The smell of freshly brewed coffee hit him.

The few bites of toast he'd forced down at breakfast with Riley threatened to revolt. He focused on the beamed ceiling, the stags' heads and coat of arms lining the walls, willing his stomach to behave.

Brick sat at a small table in the back corner. He lowered his newspaper.

Good. Maybe the day's mission wasn't totally botched. As Jacob headed toward him, a barrel-chested man rose from a table in the second row.

"Son."

Jacob startled. "Dad. Mother, what are you doing here?" Decades in the Guatemalan sun had bleached his dad's hair and beard whiter than century-old bones. Two small suitcases were at the side of the table leg.

"We're here to see you." His mother's voice trembled.

Since he'd last seen them, streaks of grey now laced his mother's tight bun. Her faded floral-print dress had probably never been in style.

Brick picked up his newspaper.

"How did you find me?" Jacob couldn't keep the shock from his voice. He hugged his father, certain his dad would've preferred a handshake. Then his mother rose from her chair, her figure angular as a praying mantis. Unable to restrain himself, he wrapped her in his arms, longing to prolong the embrace, but she wouldn't approve.

"Good to see you, Mother." How easily he fell into the old pattern, emotions firmly in check, behaving as remote and stiff as his parents. He sat at the table, fought the urge to check his watch. The Interpol team was waiting. Brick was waiting. "How did you know I'd be here today?" No one at Interpol would've revealed his whereabouts.

Thunder mottled his father's face, probably rivaling Moses when he caught the Israelites cavorting around the golden calf.

"Son, you lied to us." His mother's cheeks drooped.

The hurt in her voice pulled the plug on his heart, and every drop of blood drained from his body. The day he'd dreaded since he signed on with Interpol had come. How much did his parents know and who had told them? Beads of sweat dampened his forehead. He glanced toward Brick, hidden behind his newspaper. Had he known about their arrival?

"I work in Brussels."

"You didn't tell us you work for—"

"Dad." Jacob held up a hand. "We need to have this chat somewhere else."

Understanding crossed his father's face and he nodded. "We wanted to see you before we leave for our new posting."

"Oh?" He was an adult. Why should a new posting tug at his heart like it had when he was a kid, wondering what country they'd leave him in, what strange boarding school he'd be sent to while they served the Lord? "Where's that?"

His father smiled. "Iraq."

An invisible fist punched Jacob's gut. "Iraq? That's a closed country to Christian missionaries. You can't go. It's too dangerous."

"Those people need the Lord, too," his mother said.

"Yes, they do." But they were his parents. He couldn't lose them, too. "You could be killed."

"So could you." His mother folded her hands on the table and fixed him with that steely expression he knew so well. Her I'm-right-and-you're-wrong look. "But we'd die doing the Lord's work."

They knew why he was here. Who had told them? As the guests at the next table left the restaurant, Jacob lowered his voice. "I have to know who told you. It could be a matter of life or death."

"Whose death?" his mother said.

"Yours. Mine." And Riley's.

For the first time he could remember, his mother blinked back tears. "We wrote you at your apartment, telling you we were coming, but you weren't there when we arrived. There was a note on your door, saying you could be reached at the number below. We called it, but no one answered. Then two days ago, this nice man called us on our cell phone, told us where you were and the names of the cities you'd be visiting, and—"

"Where you work and what you really do." The hatchet in his father's whisper plunged through Jacob's heart.

Someone was watching his apartment. Reading his mail, bugging his landline. "Did this nice man give you a name?"

"He said his name was Tudor."

"Tudor." The name the Romanians had given their boss, the one selling Agent X. "Can you describe his voice? Did he speak with an accent, a country you could identify?"

"Don't all Europeans speak English with an accent?" An aborted chuckle died in his mother's throat. "Unless they learned English from British teachers."

"His voice was deep, like a Russian bass. He spoke slowly, almost measured in tone." His father stroked his chin, his gaze miles away. "No ... I don't think I could place the country."

Tudor could've deliberately disguised his voice. But sending his parents here had been a warning and a threat. He had to get them out of there, before they became hostages, leverage against his assignment.

"The man who called you ... is most likely responsible for ... for Noel's death." Jacob squeezed the inner corners of his eyes. "Tudor blew my cover to use you against me and to put you in grave danger."

His mother jutted her chin at him. "He said you'd say that, justify the things you do. Killing people."

"I haven't killed anyone." Yet.

"But you will, son." The gravity in his father's tone cut through Jacob like an Old-Testament prophet. "I see it in your eyes."

"My job is no different from yours."

His mother went rigid. "How can you say that? We work for the Lord."

"So do I. Undercover. And when you go into Iraq, you'll be undercover agents, too."

"But for the Lord."

"What I do is no different from our soldiers, serving wherever they're sent."

"But our work saves lives."

"So does mine. Thousands of them."

"Find a good woman, son." His father thumped a fist on the table, rattling their breakfast dishes. "Marry, raise a family."

Jacob turned to him. "Like you did? Abandoning Tracy and me."

"We did not abandon you." Anger collided with hurt in his mother's eyes. "We sent you to fine schools."

"Abroad. Thousands and thousands of miles away from you. One school after another. I never saw you, never really got to know you, never had my mother around to—" He hated the bitterness in his voice but he'd pent up things he'd wanted to say to them far too long. Now he couldn't stop the flow of accusations.

With the newspaper tucked under his arm, Brick rose and left the restaurant.

Jacob wanted to dash after him. Why did this have to happen today, in the middle of a deadly op? He'd known all along what their reaction would be when they found out. Disapproval, rejection.

He'd lost them all. First Noel, now his parents. He swallowed over the fist in his throat. "You've got to get out of the country now. As soon as possible." His voice cracked. "This man Tudor is a vicious terrorist."

"That nice man?" She flicked her hand at him.

"Yes." He couldn't take them with him to the team meeting, blow the operation. Nor could he risk leaving his parents here, because Tudor was probably close by, watching.

16

Despite Jacob's don't-you-dare-leave-your-room warning, she had no choice. Interpol would need to analyze the other water bottle. Riley peeked over her shoulder for anyone following her then darted down the gangplank. Which way had he gone? She scanned the castle on the hill, the narrow, winding lanes of the Old Town square, the outdoor tables at the Alte Thorschenke Hotel.

Inside her purse, her cell pinged with a text message. She hefted her purse strap on her shoulder, checked the message. Frénie. Some incredibly unpronounceable name of the poison someone had used on her. Jacob would need this info, too.

But he'd been so secretive about his onshore meeting. If she couldn't find him, she'd have to take the bottle back to the boat. As she headed for the ancient tower walk-through beside the hotel, footsteps pattered behind her. She whirled around.

Brick caught up with her. "Could I interest you in a man in need of rescue?"

"You don't seem to need rescuing."

"No, but Jacob does."

"Oh?"

"Some old couple accosted him when he was about to meet

me. We're late for a team huddle. Judging from their body language, I'd say things weren't going too smoothly."

"What do you want me to do?"

"Turn on the charm. Do whatever it takes to get him out of there, ASAP. Say whatever you have to. Today's meeting is urgent."

"Where is he?"

"Inside the hotel restaurant you just passed. I'll wait here five minutes. If he hasn't come out, I'll try to get word to him later."

"Okay." She turned around and entered the hotel. Even from the restaurant window, strain emanated from Jacob's body, head jutting forward, hands splayed on the red tablecloth. The man and woman sat ramrod straight, arms crossed, faces hard as flint. Her steps faltered. How should she play this one?

With her ingénue smile glued in place, she waltzed through the double doors and crossed to the table. He'd better give her some clue how to greet him.

A kaleidoscope of emotions flooded his face—wide-eyed disbelief, a soldier on point in enemy territory.

She draped her arm across his shoulders and turned on the Texas twang she'd worked so hard to lose as a singer. "Sugar lamb, I hate to interrupt, but I was hoping you'd buy me a little prezzie from that shop around the corner. I'd really love to have a pitcher."

The man and woman gaped at her.

Jacob leapt from his chair and slipped an arm around her waist. "Mother, Dad? I'd like you to meet Riley Williams."

"His fiancée." Good grief, where had that come from? Too late to say she'd meant friend. Batting her lashes at him with Southern-belle innocence, Riley laced her fingers in his. She wanted to kick him in the shins, shake the glazed stupor from his face. Surely he realized they could become disengaged as easily as she'd engaged them. And she would, too, as soon as his parents left. "Hon, why didn't you tell me your parents were meeting you today?"

"Because he didn't know." His father rose and Riley extended her hand.

The man hesitated then clasped it in his calloused fingers. She shook his mother's hand, her skin equally rough.

Fifty chops with a butcher's cleaver wouldn't have severed the tension in the air. Had she worsened things for Jacob? He looked as if he wanted to bolt, but was unsure which way to run. She squeezed his elbow, dropped the phony smile, and let him read her eyes. "Hon, I'd love to stay and visit with your parents. Maybe I could take them sightseeing."

But her offer seemed to worsen his indecision. He was probably worried about what she'd say to them. So was she. "Just one piece of pottery." She looped her arm in his. "I promise I won't ask you for anything else."

Across the table his parents eyed her as if she were their next meal.

Too late now to back out of the charade. Riley tilted her head to the side and tapped her cheek with her forefinger. Hopefully Jacob didn't think she was pointing out a zit.

He glanced at his parents then pecked her cheek, the kiss as nervous as a boy on his first date.

"I forgot to give you this." She unzipped her purse and pulled out the water bottle. "It's the one left from our day in Cologne." Then she pulled out her phone. "And this came in for you." She showed him Frénie's text message.

"Yeah, thanks." He jammed the bottle in his windbreaker pocket, took a screenshot of the text message, forwarded it, then peered outside the windows.

"Do you want me to take your parents sightseeing?"

"Tudor sent them."

"Oh." Were they safer sitting at the café or sightseeing? Suddenly she wished Jacob didn't have to leave. But if she and his parents lagged a few yards behind him, they might lead Tudor to the Interpol meeting.

Mr. Coulter cleared his throat. "Miss Williams, our son seems to think we're in some sort of danger."

"You are, Mr. Coulter. If Tudor sent you, you are." They all were. She opened her mouth to say more, but Jacob's hint of a frown silenced her. Maybe they were safer indoors. "How about having a coffee here?"

"Then we can get acquainted." Mr. Coulter's frigid tone suggested this would be a one-sided exchange.

Jacob gave her hand a double squeeze. "Thanks. Hon." He choked out the endearment.

As soon as they got back to the boat, she'd have to give this boy some acting lessons.

"See you all later." He hugged his dad then lingered over his mother's embrace.

"Sit." Mr. Coulter jerked a finger toward Jacob's vacated chair then signaled the waitress over. Mrs. Coulter planted her elbows on the table, her gaze nailing Riley like a steel trap.

The edges of Riley's smile faltered. She sat on the wooden seat and faced her inquisitors.

Wow. Riley had said she'd marry him. Jacob strode through the tunnel of the medieval tower. He ought to be grateful to her for showing up, but hitting his parents with an engagement on top of finding out he was a spy—what worse trouble would she create for him now?

Standing outside the pottery shop, Brick checked his watch. "Let's go. We're late." He headed up the hill.

Jacob fell in step with him. "You think Riley was serious about the piece of pottery?"

"That's the least you can do for her after bailing you out."

"I'm not sure whether she bailed me out or dug my grave. Tudor called my parents, told them where to find me and what I really do for a living."

"Tudor? Man, your cover's been blown."

"Riley's life is at stake. And now, so are my parents'." Jacob gripped Brick's arm. "I'm not quitting this case."

Brick shook his arm free. "You won't have any choice once Schwarz finds out."

"That's exactly what Tudor wants—me pulled off the case, and Riley dead." Thank goodness he hadn't told Schwarz someone had blown their cover onboard the *River Nymph*.

Partners didn't rat on each other. Winded from two days of vomiting, Jacob plodded after him. "Hey partner, let's keep this between us. It's too late to replace me on the cruise. The terrorists might change their plans."

Brick said nothing.

At the end of the buildings on the street, Brick rapped twice on the side door of a white Eurocom van, and a man opened it a few feet. Jacob glanced over his shoulder, hopped inside after Brick and shut the door.

Perspiration from the walk matted Jacob's shirt to his chest. A haze of cigarette smoke clotted the air. Two men in headphones hunkered in front of a bank of computers, the screens glowing with the quivering red-and-blue lines of monitored conversations. Holding a green ashtray filled with half-smoked stumps, his police supervisor Helmut Schwarz perched on a stool in the corner. A fresh cigarette dangled from the corner of his lips. Unspoken questions filled his sharp gaze.

"Sorry. Had trouble getting away." Jacob handed Schwarz Riley's bottle of water. "The other one from my room, possibly poisoned."

"Analysis may take a couple of days." Schwarz pulled the cigarette from his mouth. Ash fluttered to his black slacks. "Might be interesting to see if it's the same poison used on Miss Fréneau." He stuck the bottle in the satchel at his feet. "We'll keep this brief. Latest intel indicates sightings of suspected terrorists gathering in Trier. There's a good chance that's where they'll sell Agent *X*. If not there, in Luxembourg. We'll need Miss Williams on site to make the identification."

Jacob shoved a hand in his windbreaker. Why couldn't they leave her out of this? "How many men will you have on the ground, sir?"

"Two teams of six, plainclothes."

"Any of them assigned specifically to Miss Williams?"

"We're there to catch the terrorists and confiscate the vials." Schwarz stubbed out the cigarette in his ashtray. "Which is your priority as well, understood?"

"Yes, sir." Jacob clamped his jaw to keep from lashing out at his supervisor. Schwarz was asking a civilian to risk death. And by the way, we can't offer you any protection because the good of the masses is more important than an individual. "Any other instructions, sir?"

"I believe the passengers are doing a tour of the American Veterans Cemetery in Luxembourg?"

"Yes, sir."

"Be on the bus."

"Yes, sir." Jacob moved to the door, turned back to Schwarz. "By the way, do we have any leads on who might have betrayed Noel?"

Schwarz lit a fresh cigarette and blew the smoke in Jacob's direction. "What makes you think he was betrayed?"

"He broke protocol. The night he died, he called me, not his case manager."

Schwarz's eyelids hooded.

"May I ask who his supervisor was?"

"Sir." Brick blocked the doorway. "We have a problem."

Jacob froze. *No, Brick. Don't do this to me.*

"Oh?" Schwarz pulled his cigarette from his mouth.

"Jacob's parents are on the scene, courtesy of a phone call from Tudor."

He whirled toward Brick. "I trusted you."

"Sorry, pal." Brick lifted his palms outward. "I didn't make the rules."

"Why didn't you tell me?" Schwarz cursed under his breath. Stubbed his cigarette in his ashtray. "This changes everything. You're off the case."

17

Cochem

R iley glanced from the Coulters' faces, brittle with suspicion and disapproval, to the tablecloth. They'd seen through her lie, her sin. She should've called Jacob her significant other, but she couldn't change her story. Why, oh why had she said fiancé, because not in a gazillion years would she marry him.

The waitress brought their coffees. Riley's stomach knotted and churned too much to risk a sip.

Mr. Coulter bowed his head and prayed over the drinks.

"How long have you known Jacob?" his mother asked.

"It seems like forever."

Mrs. Coulter cocked an eyebrow. "Really?"

"He's a wonderful man. Courageous, tender, caring. Witty, too." Oops. Judging from their thin-set mouths, they probably considered humor a vice. Riley opened the packet of spice cookies on her saucer and nibbled a wafer to fill the thick silence. She checked her watch under the table. Was Jacob planning to come back to rescue her?

"How long have you been engaged?" Mrs. Coulter's unwavering gaze drilled fresh holes in her.

"Much too short a time for him to have told you." Heat burned Riley's cheeks. Why didn't the woman just say what she was thinking? Liar, liar, liar.

"But he's given you no ring."

His mother should've been in interrogation. Maybe Interpol had a job for her. Then his parents couldn't hold his career against him. Riley pulverized the cookie over her coffee cup. "With our busy schedules on the cruise—"

Mrs. Coulter shot forward in her chair. "Oh, so you're with Interpol too."

"No, I'm an opera singer from Cuero, Texas, subbing as a performer on the boat for my best friend who's in the hospital." Amazing how fast the truth tumbled from her mouth. "I perform all over Europe." When she could get gigs.

"So that's how you met our son."

"Yes." Well, technically.

"An opera singer and a spy." Mr. Coulter drummed his fingers on the table. "What a marriage that will be."

At the improbable scenario, Riley almost laughed.

"When's the wedding?" He folded his hands over his chest. "Who's officiating at the service?"

"We haven't discussed that." Riley crumbled the last of her cookie over her coffee cup. She still needed to come up with twenty songs for tonight's performance and practice her dance steps. "Mr. and Mrs. Coulter, I have a problem. I don't know where Jacob is, and I can't leave you two alone. And frankly, a walking tour around the town is risky."

"We're perfectly capable of taking care of ourselves. Been doing that for decades in more dangerous places than a village café," Mr. Coulter said.

"Not with Tudor around."

"So where is this mysterious Tudor?" One side of Mrs. Coulter's mouth twisted into an uncharitable sneer.

"I wish I knew." Riley glanced at the square outside.

"Come, Myra." Jacob's father scraped his chair back. "Since

we're not wanted and our son obviously doesn't care to visit with us, we'll be on our way."

"Mr. Coulter, that's not true. Tudor lured you here to get your son killed." Almost hesitantly Riley touched his arm. "I know Jacob. He was utterly torn, trying to figure out a way to protect you from these terrorists. Please believe me. I'm telling you the truth."

"Yes, for once, I think you are." Mr. Coulter picked up their small suitcases.

"I'll walk you to your car."

"That's not necessary. We took the train." He nodded his wife toward the door.

"Jacob will want to know you got away safely." Watching for the Romanians, Riley walked them to the train station on the hill overlooking the Moselle River. She waited inside the station while Mr. Coulter purchased two second-class tickets to Brussels, his stentorian voice announcing their destination. Hopefully Tudor wasn't around to hear.

He pocketed the tickets then motioned his wife outside, beneath the portico. A few people waited on the sidewalk beside the railroad tracks. Moments later, a bell chimed over the PA, and a voice announced the arrival of a train from Strasbourg.

Without asking their permission, Riley sat beside them on the wooden bench. What if something happened to Jacob and their harsh words remained between them? How could his parents live with the guilt?

In the hour since she'd met them, their weather-beaten faces had grown haggard. She decided to try again. "Although Jacob hasn't talked much about you, the depth of his love for you is evident. What you think of him matters to him."

Staring off somewhere in the distance, the Coulters kept silent.

"Please find a way to keep in touch with him because he'll worry about you. Phones are vulnerable. A letter, perhaps." Riley leaned her head against the wall, wishing their train would come.

Yes, she'd lied. Something she'd been brought up not to do, something she knew was wrong. A sin she'd have to bring before the Lord. But she'd do anything to protect Jacob.

At the realization, shockwaves zinged through her.

ONE MORE CRISIS today and he could become a very dangerous man. Jacob circled the dining table, serving bowls of wild-mushroom bisque to Molnár, Mr. Ackelroyd, Mrs. Cochran, and the Hossenis. Thirty minutes of convincing Schwarz that Captain Lundstrom wouldn't permit a new staff member this late on the cruise had bought his boss's reprieve. For the moment.

A reprieve and a desire to ditch his partner. Brick didn't know the meaning of loyalty. The soup bowl nearly slipped from his fingers. Had the guy been involved in Noel's undercover work, had he betrayed him? But Schwarz's refusal to name Noel's case manager had been equally suspicious. Jacob wedged between the Ackelroyds and served Mrs. Ackelroyd's lobster bisque.

The pot light above glinted on the flower pin in her beehive hairdo. She fluttered her bejeweled fingers, playing to her audience around the table. "As I was saying, our steward didn't clean our rooms this morning. Beds left unmade, the bathroom a disaster zone. Why didn't that substitute steward—do you call a female steward a stewardess?" Mrs. Ackelroyd tittered.

Clearing his throat, Molnár paused his spoon over his bisque. "A woman ..."

"Well, anyway, that female steward didn't show up to take his place."

Across the table, Khalid squared his shoulders, cast a sideways glance at Sora.

Jacob's stomach flipped a one-eighty. Riley. The other day he must've been in the bathroom instead of at his earphones when she ran into Mrs. A. Why hadn't Riles told him about the encounter?

"If that stewardess expects a tip ..." Mrs. Ackelroyd elbowed her husband.

"Did you report this to the captain, the cruise director?" Molnár pushed his soup bowl aside.

"You bet your bottom shilling I did. Right before lunch."

Sidling between their chairs, Jacob offered his guests freshly ground pepper, ignoring their annoyed wave-offs. He needed to get downstairs and check Manuel's room. Maybe he'd gone ashore to pick up the vials of Agent X from the Romanians.

He set the peppermill on the workstation counter and headed for the doorway. As he drew near, Dieter blocked him, arms folded, legs spread in an over-your-dead-body stance. Jacob returned to his table and cleared the soup bowls.

"You know ..." Mrs. Ackelroyd tapped a multi-ringed hand on the tablecloth. "I've seen that stewardess somewhere before ... she denied it, of course."

Lowering his arm with the stack of soup bowls, Jacob angled between Mrs. Cochran and Mrs. Ackelroyd.

"I'm positive I'm right. And I'm certain she wasn't a—"

Two bowls fell on her lap, spilling the orange and brown remains of soup across her white skirt. She screeched, and Dieter snapped his head in their direction.

"I'm terribly sorry, madame."

"Why you—" She dabbed the stains with her napkin. "The quality of the help on this cruise is deplorable."

Seated at the other side of the table, Sora and Khalid watched him, her lips pursed in disgust, the almost visible wheels of logic turning clog by clog in Khalid's eyes.

Riles was in danger. Jacob went to the kitchen, stacked the lunch entrée plates along his arm then served his guests.

JACOB RESET his lunch tables for dinner then retrieved his surveil kit from the safe in his room. Checking the hall first, he knocked on Manuel's door. "Hey Manuel, you in there?"

There was no answer. Using the captain's passkey, he let himself inside the room. He'd have to work fast. Dieter might return any minute.

Both beds were neatly made. No personal items on top of the dresser. On the back of the chair lay a discarded black shirt and pants, too small to be Dieter's clothes. A clean steward's uniform and a couple pair of jeans and T-shirts hung in the closet. White sports shoes and a soft-sided carry-on suitcase lay on the floor. Jacob searched the luggage but found only dirty laundry. Working swiftly, he went through Dieter's closet. In the bathroom, the usual men's toiletries.

He punched the pound sign twice on Manuel's safe and entered the ship's four-zero administration-access code. Since the last search, Manuel had added a stack of fifty-euro bills, possibly a hundred of them, and a new passport in the name of Juan Hernandez, with Manuel's picture. Jacob locked the safe, activated a pen-style listening device, rolled it under the bottom bunk bed then placed a small disk at the back of each man's closet shelf.

Jacob snuck into the hall, pounded the rhythm of today's signal hymn, "Turn Your Eyes Upon Jesus," on Riley's door with the fierceness of a police raid.

Inside the room, the counting one-two-three-four ceased, and she opened the door.

Without waiting for an invitation, he entered her cabin and shut the door. He shoved his face inches from hers. "Why didn't you tell me Mrs. Ackelroyd saw you outside Khalid's stateroom?"

She stepped back from him. "So that's what's eating you."

"Eating me? Do you have any idea the trouble you're in?" He closed the space between them.

"For one, I knew you'd worry. And two, there wasn't anything I could do about it. The job had to be done, right?"

"But not at the expense of your safety."

"I'm safe, aren't I?" She spread her hands.

"Not for long. At lunch today, Mrs. A blabbed about seeing a female steward, someone she's sure she's met before who isn't a steward. And Khalid, whiz kid that he is, suspects it was you."

Riley sagged against the dresser. "Great." She snapped her fingers. "Hey, I could go blonde tonight."

"Yeah, and they make the mental hop from Riley the blonde diva to a six-foot, black-bobbed steward."

"I'm five-foot-ten."

"Close enough."

"What do we do now?"

"Get you off the boat. Permanently."

She jerked away from the dresser. "Oh no, you don't. I can't cost Frénie her job." She shoved her face nose-to-nose with him. "Unlike you, I signed a contract for this job. And I never break my promises."

"I'm not letting you risk your life anymore."

"It's too late. The minute I followed those men at the café in Antwerp, I made my choice. You think they'll let me live if I leave the boat and return to Vienna? Wouldn't you say I know a bit too much?"

Jacob sank onto her desk chair. She was right.

"There, see? You do need me."

"Manuel's missing. And you could be next."

"Missing? Since when? The Hossenis' bed was made yesterday morning."

"Mrs. A said he didn't show up for work this morning. I just searched his room. No sign of a hasty departure from the boat."

"He could've gone into town to meet a terrorist contact." She sat on the bed, toyed with the square gold stud in her earlobe. "Maybe someone warned him you planned to arrest him today."

"Yeah, maybe." Riley was the only one on the boat who knew about that plan. "Wonder how he found out?"

"How would I know?" She crossed her legs and drummed her manicured fingernails on the mattress.

She'd be the perfect plant inside Interpol's ground team. Her singing gigs enabled her to travel around Europe. Maybe she was the terrorist Noel had tried to tell him about. The incident at the Antwerp café could've been an elaborate ploy to gain Interpol's trust. Her fingers danced on her leg, her auburn curls falling around her shoulders like a vision of Botticelli. Whoever invented honey traps must've had her in mind.

Maybe his parents were better judges of character than he gave them credit for. He paced the narrow confines of her room. Maybe she'd written the warning sticky note she claimed someone had placed on her music. Suggesting Tudor could be a woman had been her idea. In Cologne, she'd brought the poisoned bottles of water with them.

Raking his hand through his hair, he did another circuit of her room. Once again, he'd let her beauty and her quirky personality warp his judgment, rip the shield from his heart. No more. He yanked open her door.

"You haven't told me what our next plan is."

"There isn't going to be any plan."

"What do you mean?"

"You're out of the picture."

"Jacob—"

He let himself out of her room, shut her door before he caved into her plea.

RIGHT NOW, she'd like to strangle Jacob. The Lone Ranger rides again. Did he leave Brick out of the info loop, too? Riley grabbed her floor-length slip and a pair of stockings from her dresser, whacked the drawers shut, threw the underwear on the bed. He hadn't even asked about her time with his parents. Not that she'd tell him she'd tried to salvage their strained relationship, nor that she'd seen them safely on the train to Brussels.

Thrusting her fingers inside her jewelry pouch, she dug out her evening earrings and laid the diamond-studded disks on the dresser. Instead of agonizing over Mr. High and Mighty Super-Spook, she ought to be reviewing her songs for tonight, warming up her voice.

Inside her purse, the phone rang several times. Hoping it wouldn't be Frénie, she checked the caller ID. Her agent in Vienna. Unable to restrain the giddiness in her voice, she answered the call.

"I'm sorry Miss Williams, but none of the German and French houses you auditioned for offered a contract."

"I see ..." The airline ticket she'd already bought was non-refundable. "Thank you for letting me know." She jabbed the ringer off, tossed the phone on the bed. Her parents were counting on her visit, her first one in three years. If she didn't get performance contracts soon, she'd have to give up her apartment and move back home. Surely that wasn't what God intended for her, was it?

Riley took several deep breaths, trying for calm, then began a vocal siren, low to high pitches. Her throat was so tight, she barely reached middle *C*. Great. Less than three hours until her performance, and her vocal folds were tied in sailors' knots. She started another siren and rolled her shoulders, but the muscles still felt taut as piano wire.

Choosing her gown and shoes always relaxed her before a recital. Perhaps she'd wear her red silk dress tonight. Humming a few pitches, she focused on the vibrations in her facial bones, started a vocal siren, and opened the closet door. Manuel's body hung from the clothing rod. The pitches rose into a full-blown scream.

She stumbled away from the closet, sank weak-kneed on her bed.

Seconds later her door burst open. Jacob rushed inside her

room. "What happened?"

Shudders coursed through her body, chattering her teeth. She pointed to her closet.

Jacob unpinned the note from Manuel's chest. "Get out while you can. You're next."

A dead body, a threatening note—they meant to kill her. She squeezed her palms between her knees, but they still shook. She shouldn't be thinking of herself. Think about Agent X. How many others will die if—

"That's it." Jacob pulled her suitcase from the closet and set it on the chair.

"What are you doing?"

He pulled her slacks and tops from the hangers and tossed the clothing inside the luggage.

She crossed to him, following him like a puppy. "Jacob, why—"

"You can't stay here." He brushed past her, unfastened her evening gowns from their special hangers and laid the gowns over the suitcase.

"Where are you moving me?" She took the dresses to the bed and folded them.

"Someplace where someone trustworthy can watch you 24/7." He set the last of her clothing on her bed.

"You're playing into their hands, doing exactly what they want you to do."

"That's right." He opened the top dresser drawer where she kept her underwear. "You take care of those things."

"Later." Once he got Manuel out of there and gave her some privacy. She placed her folded clothing in the suitcase.

Jacob opened her bottom dresser drawer, shoved the sweaters and cardigans into her arms. Then he stiffened. Knelt beside the dresser drawer. "I don't know whose side you're working on, but I can't live with your death."

"Don't know whose side—" She threw her sweaters on the

bed, jabbed a finger at her closet. "How can you say that? You think I hung him in there?"

"No. You don't have the strength. But your pal Khalid does." Fury curdled his tone. "Or Dieter."

"My pal?" Her voice rose in one of her warm-up sirens. "Have you forgotten I'm the one who overheard the plot and saw the Romanians?"

"Nope. But that doesn't mean you did overhear them, does it?" Jacob snatched a tissue from the box on her dresser and scooped several objects from her drawer onto the tissue. He rose and held out his hand.

She stared at the used syringe, the small vial labeled with a skull-and-crossbones insignia. Her jaw slacked. "How—how did that get in there?" Then she made herself meet his blistering gaze.

"You tell me."

"I—I don't know. I've never seen those things before. What's in the vial?"

"Probably the poison used in the water bottles." He pocketed the vial. "The poison used on your so-called best friend." He opened the next dresser drawer and rifled through her night clothes.

"You don't really think I'd poison my best friend, do you?" She stalked him from the dresser to the bed as he dumped her belongings on the mattress. "Or anyone else, for that matter."

"The evidence certainly points that way. Maybe your pals weren't so sure whose side you're on now. Maybe they hung him in your closet to remind you it's against the rules to play on both teams." He scooped her shoes from the closet floor and dumped them beside the bed.

"Jacob, I'm innocent." She grabbed at his sleeve. "Someone's framing me."

"Yeah." He shook off her hand. "Everything's a little too coincidental. Maybe you didn't really see the Romanians at that Antwerp café. Maybe you didn't overhear a conversation at all.

Maybe you already knew about the terrorists' plot because you've been in on it from the first."

"How dare you." Riley slapped him. Her fingers connected with flesh and bone, left their imprint on his reddened cheek. She dumped the contents of her suitcase on the floor. "I'm not leaving this boat."

"Oh, yes you are." He grasped her arm with a tourniquet-like grip. "One of the team will take you to the nearest airport and put you on a flight to Vienna."

"You can't make me leave." She tried to peel his fingers from her arm. "I have a contract with the cruise line."

"Tough." Jacob seated her on the bed then tossed her clothing back into the suitcase.

"You are the most exasperating man I've ever met." The splotches on her skin stung like alcohol on a raw wound.

As he started the zipper around the suitcase, the teeth caught the hem of her red silk evening gown.

"Be careful." She leapt from the bed. "Those gowns are expensive. I worked hard to pay for them."

"Yeah. Maybe with a little help from your pals."

She shook her fist at him as he speed-dialed a number on his phone.

"There's been a change of plan. The steward's dead. They left his body in Riley's closet. A vial of poison in her dresser may have been used to poison me. I need a body bag and safe escort for her to the airport."

"I'm not leaving the ship. My performance contract clearly states—"

He chopped his hand in the air, the classic shut-up gesture. Then his shoulders fell. "Right. Yes, sir. Got it."

"Let me guess." She crossed her arms over her chest, unable to resist a half-grin. "I'm still on active duty?"

"Not with me, you aren't." He shoved the phone in his pocket and went to the door. "Lock this behind me, not that it'll do any good."

Riley double-locked the door behind him. Which was worse —finding Manuel's body or Jacob's distrust? She unzipped her suitcase and examined the red gown. Creased but not torn. The tears came, and she let them flow. Tonight's performance promised to be a disaster, hoarse from her scream, her throat congested from crying.

What had she ever seen in that man? And she'd bailed him out with his parents. Why, he was no different from them. He was nothing but a cold-hearted secret agent who cared only about his mission.

As the *River Nymph* prepared to make an unscheduled docking, Jacob waited at the stern for the ambulance's arrival and Interpol agents dressed as EMTs. Outside the staff's area, several passengers chatted quietly. Seated on a chaise near the bow, Molnár flipped another page of his book. A few couples watched the picturesque villages, the hillside vineyards.

Two white swans floated away from the boat's wake, every peaceful image belying the corpse he'd found in Riley's closet, the syringe, the vial of poison.

Jacob gripped the railing, the metal underpinning digging into his fingers. He'd hated doing the bad cop routine on her. Was she innocent? Had she been framed, as she claimed? Or was she their patsy, a dupe, or worse—a willing accomplice?

Making sure he was alone in the stern, he surveilled the deck again then dialed Schwarz and told him about his suspicions. Suspicions he didn't want to have. Suspicions they couldn't afford to ignore.

"I've wondered all along if we hadn't swallowed a fairy tale." Schwarz sighed into the phone. "Trouble is, we need her. If she's actively working for the terrorists and we move her off the boat under house arrest, we could be letting them write the scenario.

Leave her out of the info loop and keep a firm watch on her in Luxembourg."

"Sir, I'm not certain she is working for them."

"We can't afford to take chances. As you pointed out, she was the only one onboard who knew about Manuel's imminent arrest. Maybe they're listening in on your conversations with her."

"Possibly." Jacob tugged his hand through his hair. He'd let his fear for Riles get the best of him. How stupid could he be—letting her know he suspected her of being a double agent? At the very least, if she weren't working unwittingly for the terrorists, he'd wounded her feelings. Too late now to undo the damage.

"But my daily sweeps of our rooms aren't turning up new bugs." One thing was clear, he had no business being an undercover agent. Once again, he'd let his heart get in the way of sound judgment. "Maybe Tudor will realize Riley's cover has been blown and quit using her to ferret out information."

Schwarz chuckled then did a long inhale, probably a drag on his cigarette. "You really do believe in fairy tales, Coulter."

Noel's dead body held in his arms, his final warning, flashed in Jacob's mind. Tudor never left loose ends. Double agents who'd lost their usefulness were killed. "She'll be the next item they tick off their hit list."

18

Day 6: Trier

J acob waited in front of Captain Lundstrom's desk while he finished reading the fax. For a man who'd found out yesterday one of his staff had been murdered, the captain had taken the news with Swedish calm.

Lundstrom laid down the fax. "I trust you got the steward's body off the boat as unobtrusively as possible."

"When the EMTs arrived, the only passenger on the deck was János Molnár. I hung around afterward to give him a chance to ask questions, but he said nothing. Captain, it's imperative I be on today's tour of the American Veterans Cemetery in Luxembourg. Without your intervention, I'm certain Dieter won't allow it. Can you get me excused from serving lunch without raising his suspicion?"

"Do you suspect him?"

Jacob shrugged. "It's possible he's involved in some way. His behavior is odd. Sorry, but I can't go into details."

"I'll see what I can do." The captain gave him a dry look. "Without telling him what you really do for a living."

"Thank you, sir." Jacob left the office and went to the sun deck.

Riley stood by the railing near the gangplank. A breeze toyed with her curls, tossing them in the air like auburn ribbons. The last place he wanted her was at the cemetery. While watching for terrorists, he needed to observe her, see who approached her. If today's events confirmed she was a double agent, he wasn't sure he could survive knowing the truth.

It had been two years since he'd let a woman get this close to him. All night long his mind had roiled with accusations and Riley's protestations of innocence. Somehow he had to focus on his assignment. Afterward, he'd be a doting surrogate father to Noel's son. Life would be simpler and less painful if he closed off his vulnerable points. And Riley Williams was one huge vulnerable point.

RILEY MOVED ten feet down the railing, putting as much distance between herself and Jacob as possible. Shouldn't he be clearing up guests' dishes and setting up for lunch? Already her stomach gnawed at her, wanting more than the toast and yogurt she'd eaten for breakfast, but being in the same room with Jacob had killed her appetite.

Last night had been no easier. He'd hung around the lounge serving drinks, watching her sing her sets and dance with every diehard male passenger. Watched her waltz with Khalid in her one pair of stilettos. Batting her false eyelashes and feigning a confidence she hoped had dazzled the killer and convinced him she couldn't have been the phony steward.

Jacob walked over to her.

"Don't you dare tell me I can't go on this tour, or I'll throw a fit, right here in River City."

"You're not going."

"Oh, yes I am." What made him think he could tell her what

to do? "These veterans gave their lives during World War II."
She thumped her fist on the railing. "Lone Rangers didn't win
the war, teamwork did. Teamwork between the military and
civilians. Female civilians."

"Riles, this is no longer your battle."

"If the Romanians show up today, I'm the only one who can
identify Eagle Eyes."

Jacob glared at her. "Who do you think you are, Mata Hari,
Joan of Arc?"

"Neither." She flipped a strand of hair from her cheek,
joined the passengers waiting at the gangplank. Sora and
Khalid Hosseni were first in line. A few rows behind the
assassins, Mrs. Cochran and the Ackelroyds chatted like old
friends.

"A lovely day for a tour." Molnár slipped in behind her. "Don't
you agree?"

"Yes." Mustering a smile, she angled toward him. "Several of
our passengers may be old enough to have fought in WWII, or
their fathers did. My parents raised us to appreciate those who
sacrifice their lives for their country."

"Or for the greater good."

"Yes, that, too." Maybe she'd misjudged him. Maybe his
interest in promoting her career was genuine.

"May I have the pleasure of escorting you today?"

"Thank you. I'd like that."

"Have you given more thought to those opera auditions? I
would be most pleased to arrange them for you."

"Yes, yes, I have." Heaven knew she needed gigs for the fall.
How else could she pay her rent? But accepting Molnár's offer ...
She tried to read his eyes. Apart from her first dance with him,
he'd been a perfect gentleman. But then, every man onboard
who'd danced with her had made a play for more than the dance
floor. Except the captain.

With three "excuse mes," Jacob bypassed others waiting in
line, cut in beside her, and locked her right arm in his.

He'd better not make a scene in public. For good measure, she elbowed his ribs.

"Pardon me." Molnár stepped to her left. "Miss Williams has graciously agreed to accompany me today."

She couldn't resist a grin.

"Of course, sir." Shooting her eye daggers, Jacob released her and cut in behind them.

"Thank you. He can be a bit possessive."

The line moved forward, and Molnár escorted her down the gangplank. "Then you're no longer—an item—I believe is how you Americans say the phrase?"

Behind her, Jacob cleared his throat.

"Let's just say, we had a lovers' quarrel. But I'm sure we'll resolve our tiff." No way did she want Molnár thinking she was open to his advances, even if they were almost welcome at the moment. "If you could set up some opera auditions during the cruise, that would be great."

"It will be my pleasure." The only thing missing from Molnár's catlike smile were a few canary feathers.

WHAT HAD GOTTEN INTO RILEY? Jacob followed them down the gangplank. If the intel was accurate, she'd be in grave danger today. Unless she was working for the terrorists. Sugar Daddy wasn't the ideal protector. Jacob shoved his hands in his pockets. Like it or not, he couldn't shake his attraction to her. She was brave and compassionate. Which fueled his desire to box Sugar Daddy's ears and throw the predator overboard.

To take his mind off throttling Molnár, Jacob reviewed the Interpol strategy. Men stationed at the perimeters of the cemetery. Phone alerts for sightings of known terrorists. In his opinion, much too thin a plan. Why hadn't Schwarz assigned more men to the op? Did he think the Interpol agents would've been too obvious? Or was he the one who'd betrayed Noel?

Jacob rubbed his sweating palms on his jeans. The lack of backup would make it even harder to watch for terrorists, stop the sale of the vials, and keep Riley safe.

THE BUS PULLED into the parking lot at the Luxembourg Cemetery and Memorial. Riley glanced at Jacob. His body was poised for a swift exit, his gaze radar-alert. Was he expecting the vials to be exchanged here?

Smiling, the guide put the mic to her mouth. "As you can see, we've arrived at the cemetery, a beautiful fifty-acre, wooded site, established December 29, 1944. Many of the 5,076 members of the military buried here lost their lives during the Battle of the Bulge in Belgium and in the taking of the Rhine River.

"Don't miss the stone chapel, its mosaic ceiling of angels and doves, and General Patton's grave. We will be here for ninety minutes. Be back at the bus by eleven, or we will leave without you."

Despite the smile, no doubt Miss Perky meant the threat. Riley waited in her seat while cruise passengers debarked.

At the base of the stairs, Molnár waited for her, his hand extended toward her. Jacob followed her down the steps, his face grim. Today, the Ackelroyds, Mrs. Cochran, and the Hossenis mingled with other passengers from the bus.

"This is a special treat, spending the day with you." Molnár looped her arm through his.

"You're too kind." She let him walk her through the blue wrought-iron gates embossed with gilded laurel wreaths, past the engraved names of the missing, the battle campaign maps. Past the rose gardens, the descending pools of water with sculptured dolphins, the sections of the cemetery shielded by walls of pine trees.

An endless sea of white marble crosses rose from the

manicured lawns. She swallowed over the lump in her throat. *Dear God, please don't let their sacrifice have been in vain.*

Half-hidden by the trees, Brick stood behind the back row of graves. Was he here to watch her, or had she stumbled on the area where they expected the vials to be exchanged? How ironic. Terrorists selling vials of destruction in a cemetery dedicated to those who'd given their lives to insure freedom for future generations.

"Is anything the matter?" Molnár said.

"No, no."

Jacob stood near the entrance to the section, his face hard.

Did Interpol think she had the vials and was about to pass them to one of the bidding terrorists? Leaving Molnár at the head of the row, she strolled past the head stones and stopped at the grave of Private William D. McGee. Tears sprang to her eyes, spilled over her lashes.

Sniffing, she swiped them with the back of her hand. Jacob didn't know her any better than she did this soldier from Indiana, a recipient of the Medal of Honor. There was no mention of how old McGee was when he died March 19, 1945, so near the end of the war. She took a red silk rose from her purse and laid the flower at the base of his cross.

At the grave to her left, a small man in clerical robes made the sign of the cross, then bowed his head. Closing her eyes, she prayed for Private McGee's family. For lives lost, destinies destroyed. The priest walked behind her, his robes brushing her legs. She turned toward Molnár.

Gripping the end of the white cross, he bent over and clutched his calf.

"Are you all right?" She ran to his side.

"Yes." The word came out sharply, his brief smile unconvincing. "Just a leg cramp."

"Do you need to sit?" She looked for a bench, someone to help, but the priest had left the section. Three graves down the row, the Ackelroyds were deep in conversation. Khalid and Sora had positioned themselves at the front and back of the sidewalk.

Strolling with his head down, hands in his pockets, Brick patrolled the last row of crosses. Where was Jacob? He might loathe Molnár, but Jacob wouldn't refuse to help a passenger in need. "Perhaps Mr. Ackelroyd could massage the muscles."

"No, no." Molnár waved her off. "I'm fine."

Rustling pine needles and shadowy movement near the trees behind Brick caught her attention. Eagle Eyes stepped out from the foliage, today without his black leather coat. Her diaphragm seized, grabbed her breath. Once again, she needed Jacob. Now.

With a flick of his head, Eagle Eyes motioned Brick over.

Hitching his thumb in his jeans' belt loop, Brick ambled over to him, and they began chatting.

From their casual stance and relaxed body language, they seemed to be old friends. Cell phone in hand, she did a three-sixty. Snapped a picture of Eagle Eyes talking to Brick then speed-dialed Jacob.

"Do you get good photos with your phone?" Molnár hovered at her side.

"They're not the best." The phone rang twice as she stepped away from him.

"Yes?" Tension riddled Jacob's tone.

"Eagle Eyes is standing in the back row."

"I'm on the way. Stay out of this Riley."

"No. If he leaves, you'll need to know which way he went. I'm safe. Mr. Molnár is with me."

"He's no protection against that guy." Jacob's footsteps pounded in the background, his voice breathless. "Describe Eagle Eyes for me."

"About five-foot-eight. Sturdy build. Dark hair, dark eyes." She headed toward Brick and Eagle Eyes. "Wearing a light-blue shirt and jeans. Too far away to see his shoes." Maybe now Jacob would believe she wasn't working for the bad guys. Interpol would have a picture of one of their agents conversing with a terrorist.

"Where are you going?" Huffing and puffing, Molnár caught up with her.

Hoping Jacob hadn't heard the question, she covered her phone. "Nowhere."

Just then, Brick walked away from Eagle Eyes.

She put the phone to her ear. "Where are you?"

"Got him in sight. Get out of there Riles. Now." The call disconnected.

Brick strolled past the last few crosses and headed away from the entrance to the cemetery.

Keeping near the trees, Eagle Eyes trailed him.

Jacob drew even with her. "Just once, do as I say."

"Be careful." Riley let him get several rows ahead then followed him, Molnár at her heels.

"Something's wrong, I sense it. Please tell me Miss Riley," Molnár whispered.

"I can't. Maybe you should go back to the bus." She picked up her pace. Something was about to happen, she could sense it. This had to be the exchange of the vials.

"No. I will not desert you." Molnár scurried to her side. "Let me help."

Skirting the rows of crosses, Jacob tailed Eagle Eyes as he paused momentarily at each grave. Without warning, the Romanian turned and disappeared among the pine trees.

Jacob pulled a pistol from his windbreaker and darted into the grove.

"Wait here." Riley motioned Molnár back then sprinted into the woods. Sounds of scuffling and thuds came from the copse of trees. Had Jacob recovered enough to take down Eagle Eyes? Maybe he was fighting off Brick. Pine needles crunched under her shoes as she crept toward the noise.

In the middle of the clearing, Jacob lay sprawled on the ground, his gun in the brush near his feet. Eagle Eyes and Brick had vanished. Hawk Nose stood with his back to her, a large rock held over Jacob's head.

"No!" Swinging her purse like a lasso, Riley lunged toward the Romanian and bashed him with the bag. "Stop! Brick, someone —help!"

The rock thudded on the ground. Hawk Nose grabbed her wrists and hurled her like a sack of potatoes.

Currents of air rippled over her face and hands as her airborne body flew toward Jacob and slammed into his chest. Bone-jarring fire tore through her ribs, her spine. She rolled onto the ground, facing Hawk Nose. A weapon. She needed a weapon. But what?

Hawk Nose grabbed the rock, lifted it high over Jacob's skull.

"No!" Riley swiveled her torso and thrust her foot at Hawk Nose's groin.

Shrieking, he dropped the rock and hobbled away through the pine trees, groaning.

Ignoring the shards lancing her muscles and bones, she knelt beside Jacob, dialed for an ambulance, checked his pulse. Alive. Blood matted his hair and forehead. "Jacob, can you hear me?" But his eyes remained closed, his face grey. She stroked his cheek, ice-cold beneath her fingers. How many times had Hawk Nose struck him before she arrived?

Molnár crashed through the brush. "Are you all right?" He reached for Jacob's gun.

"Yes." Riley lunged for the weapon and shoved it in her purse. "But Jacob's been injured. He's unconscious." This couldn't be happening. He'd been through so much.

"Let me help." Molnár crouched beside Jacob and monitored his pulse. "Not good. I'm afraid your friend might not survive. Head wounds can be quite serious. I'll stay with him. You go meet the ambulance." Molnár helped her up from the ground. "Hurry, my dear."

Riley dashed to the edge of the trees then stopped. What if Hawk Nose returned? Molnár would be no match for him, especially if Eagle Eyes came too. "No, I'll wait. You go direct them here, please."

"But you assured your friend I would stay with you, protect you. I can't leave you here alone."

"I think it's best if you guide them here. Please."

A sing-song siren wailed across the trees and her heart zinged. At the moment it was the most beautiful sound she could imagine.

The brush rustled, twigs crackled. Brick tore through the grove, squatted beside Jacob and checked his pulse. "What happened?"

Molnár stood and backed away from them.

"Your friend bashed his head. Where were you when he needed you?"

Brick frowned. "Following a lead," he whispered.

"Yeah, right."

"Look doll—"

"I'm not your doll. Or anyone else's."

Pink raced up Brick's face. He gave Molnár a sheepish look.

How could Jacob have drawn such an arrogant creep for a partner? Gritting her teeth, she kept her voice low. "I want to speak with Jacob's supervisor."

"Did you see something? Tell me, I'll get word to him."

"Uh-huh." No doubt he'd go straight to Eagle Eyes.

In two steps, Molnár was at her side. "May I be of assistance?"

"I—I'm. No."

Beyond the trees, metal clattered on the sidewalk. Within seconds, three paramedics burst through the grove, pushing a gurney over the uneven ground and stopped near Jacob's still body.

She wanted to sag against the tree trunk. Finally. Help was here.

A few feet behind them, a man wearing a grey shirt and black slacks approached. His skin had the pallor of one who spent months indoors. Another man, with slicked-back hair and dressed in khakis, traipsed behind him. Brick stood, his posture not quite at attention. Were they Interpol? Was one of them Jacob's supervisor?

The pale-faced man eyed her then gave Molnár a once-over.

She strode over to Paleface. "Jacob was attacked by ..."

A few yards away Brick and Molnár stared at her like hawks about to pounce on an unsuspecting mouse.

"By ... by some men."

"We'll take it from here, Miss." German inflections colored Paleface's heavily accented English. He shook a cigarette from its packet and shoved it in the corner of his lips.

One of the EMTs removed the blood-pressure cuff from Jacob's arm while his partner inserted an IV into Jacob's right arm. Seconds later the two men loaded his limp body on the gurney.

"I'm going with him."

"But, Miss Riley." Molnár grasped her arm. "What about your performance tonight?"

"I'll figure something out, but I'm not leaving Jacob."

Paleface looked undecided.

"I can identify his attacker," she said to Paleface.

Interest flickered across the man's face. "All right. Come to the hospital."

"She can ride with me," Brick said.

Riley recoiled from him. "No. I'm riding in the ambulance."

"I'm afraid that won't be possible," the slick-haired man in khakis said. "No one is allowed to ride with the patient, Miss ..."

"Williams. Riley Williams." Maybe they weren't Interpol. Maybe they were local plainclothes policemen. She had to reach Jacob's supervisor and warn him about Brick. Without ending up in a Luxembourg interrogation cell while Jacob's life hung in the balance.

What should she do? Riley plucked the pine needles from her clothes. Captain Lundstrom would never release her from singing and dancing tonight. But someone had to stay with Jacob, make sure no one entered the room to finish the job. Trusting Brick at this point was impossible, but he was her only connection to Jacob's supervisor.

Working swiftly, the EMTs clicked the seat belts around Jacob, rolled the gurney out of the trees and past the graves. Paleface motioned Riley to follow him.

Molnár pattered beside her. "If you're sure I can't be of assistance ..."

"Thank you." She tried for an appreciative smile, her lips trembling. "You've been so kind."

Molnár touched his right hand to his heart, gave her a courtly bow then left the clearing.

On the way to the parking lot, Riley walked between Brick and Paleface. The Ackelroyds and the Hossenis were boarding the bus.

As she reached a black sedan, Brick opened the back door and gestured her inside.

Paleface sat beside the driver. "You're riding with us, Brick."

Sporting a smug smile, he climbed in beside Riley. The car swerved behind the ambulance, sirens wailing.

"Are you Jacob's supervisor?" Riley leaned toward Paleface.

"Do you need to talk to him?"

"Yes."

"Go ahead."

"No. In private."

"Miss Williams, if you have something to say, say it. We haven't much time left to apprehend the terrorists."

"What I have to say must be said in private." She crossed her arms, her fists locked inside her elbows.

At the Emergency entrance of the hospital, the car screeched to a halt behind the ambulance. The moment she climbed out, two paramedics whisked Jacob's gurney inside the building. Eyes closed, face ashen, he didn't seem to have regained consciousness.

"Now, Miss Williams." Paleface pulled her aside. "What did you want to tell his supervisor?"

In two steps Brick had moved close enough to overhear anything she said.

"You know Jacob's partner. You can speak freely."

Right. Like she'd do that in front of a traitor. "I want permission to stay in Jacob's hospital room tonight, and transportation to the boat for my performance and then back to the hospital."

"That won't be necessary. Brick will stand guard tonight."

Her toes curled inside her shoes. Not Brick. "How can he do his job if he's up all night?"

"Or you, Miss Williams." Paleface stared her down.

"You need me more than you know."

Cupping his hand around the tip of his lighter and cigarette, he squinted at her, the suspicion in his eyes palpable. He pocketed his lighter. "So, you expect another attack on his life?"

"Yes, I do." By his partner.

Day 7: Trier

RILEY SQUIRMED, searching for a less uncomfortable position on the wooden armchair beside Jacob's hospital bed. Paleface had kept his word and sent a car for her. The performance had gone okay, the dancing worse than ever. No matter how badly she stumbled, Molnár had been a faithful dance partner, his concern for Jacob sweet. But how much more of these nightmarish events could she and Jacob take? This time, they'd meant to kill him.

The door opened, and a nurse entered. A different one from the private-duty nurse Riley had hired to stay in the room with Jacob during her performance on the boat.

A bleary-eyed Brick followed the nurse inside the room.

Why did he bother coming in when the curtains at the large window overlooking the corridor were kept open? Nothing in Jacob's room was hidden from view. The nurse checked his vital signs then tried to rouse him.

Nine-thirty in the morning. Jacob had been unconscious almost twenty-four hours. If he didn't regain consciousness before the *River Nymph* sailed, the boat would depart without him. She would have to honor her contract with the cruise line. And if the exchange of the vials hadn't succeeded at the cemetery, what next? She'd be on her own. Either way, she'd be alone with Khalid.

19

Day 8: Bernkastel

Riley snapped the lid on the last of the plastic containers and stacked them in her straw carry-all. What if Jacob wouldn't agree to her plan? Surely Brick wouldn't horn in this time, unlike at the hospital. Never leaving, eating his meals outside the door, using Jacob's private bathroom.

Once Jacob had regained consciousness late yesterday morning, Brick had remained inside the room constantly, keeping her from telling Paleface or Jacob about Brick's chat with Eagle Eyes. Or showing them her photo of them together.

Covering her mouth, Riley stifled a yawn. If she'd thought the first night's performance during the hospital vigil had been shoddy, it shone in comparison with last night's singing and dancing. Hoarseness had affected almost every note she sang. Then, she'd trod so hard and so often on men's shoes, it was a miracle Captain Lundstrom hadn't thrown her suitcase overboard and personally escorted her off the boat.

Today's plan had to work. Shooting up silent prayers, she hooked her arm through the handles of the straw carry-all. Despite her description of Hawk Nose's attack on them, and how she'd fought him off, Paleface had reacted like a botoxed politician. She'd caught his half-blink. A half-blink that reeked of disbelief, distrust.

A HESITANT KNOCK on Jacob's cabin door tapped out the opening measures of "Turn Your Eyes Upon Jesus." Although Riley hadn't set up a new code song, Jacob shuffled from his bed to the door, moving more like his great-grandfather than himself. The effects of the concussion had better clear up fast, or he'd be no match for the terrorists.

Riley stood in the hallway, a blanket over one arm, plastic containers jutting from the open straw bag in her other hand. Her silky blue slacks and blouse and glitzy sandals didn't look like she was planning a fast escape, nor did her delicately applied makeup hide the dark circles beneath her eyes.

No doubt it was the residual effect of two nights in a hospital wooden chair, her bout of weeping when he'd regained consciousness yesterday morning. The scent of her Chanel No. 5 nearly crumbled his resolve to heed Schwarz's orders not to trust her. Jacob dug his fingers into the doorjamb to keep from sweeping her in his arms and kissing her.

"I fixed a picnic lunch. Care to share it with me?" Her smile flickered, an uneasy question in her eyes.

He hesitated. Thanks to Schwarz's insistence, the captain had ordered Dieter to release him from waiting tables for the day. But his supervisor's warning re-played in his mind. *She could've been assigned to guard you in the hospital to regain Interpol's trust.* Brick's presence had prevented her letting the killer inside the room.

"Okay."

She blew out her air. "Oh good. I—I thought we might eat by the riverside."

"I'll be out in a sec." Jacob shut the door, strapped on his shoulder-holstered Sig Sauer P365, an ankle-strapped knife, then shrugged into a lightweight jacket.

Outside his door, he took the straw bag from her and followed her to the top deck and down the gangplank. With each step, his lungs burned, his breaths harsh gasps of air. Sweat dribbled down his face. What had he been thinking? Agreeing to a picnic when he could barely stagger across his cabin? Once again, he'd fallen for the vulnerable look in her eyes, begging him not to turn her down. *Idiot.*

Casting frequent worried glances at him, she slowed until he walked at her side. Was it worry for his health or what was about to go down? He did another surveil of the area.

"Let's eat over here." Riley chose a spot beneath a linden tree on the grassy riverside bank. A smattering of benches and old town buildings overlooked the water's edge. The occasional car, a few trucks whizzed past the village. Maybe they'd be safer out in the open. He helped her spread the blanket beneath the canopy of leafy branches.

Riley curled her legs beneath her on the blanket and set out the plastic tubs of salad and soup, bread, and pieces of chocolate torte and plastic cutlery. With shaking hands, she poured soup into the bowls, spilling a small puddle on the blanket.

Had she lured him here so the Romanians could finish him off? He bent his left leg to his chest and trailed his hand to his ankle. *Oh Riles, why can't my heart be right about you?*

On the sidewalk in front of the old town buildings, Khalid and Sora Hosseni walked past, a shoulder's width apart, faces tense and on the alert.

Ignoring the green salad Riley put on his plate, the bowl of soup she set beside him, Jacob slipped his hand inside his jacket, his eyes on the killers.

Moments later, the Hossenis turned up a side street and disappeared from view.

Riley forked a bite of the salad, her glances flitting from him to her food.

Barely aware it was wild-mushroom bisque, he spooned the soup.

"I—I know you still don't trust me. I don't know what I can say or do to convince you that I'm on your side. I'd never betray my country."

He tore off a chunk of bread and stuffed it in his mouth, buying time before he answered her. More than anything, he wanted to trust her, but everything seemed to point to Riles as the leak in their conduit.

"You need to see this." She pulled her cell from the straw bag, scrolled through her photos then turned the phone toward him.

Fog wisped through his brain. He squinted at her picture of Brick talking to a man at the edge of the pine trees, just beyond the last row of crosses of a cemetery.

"I took this at the Veteran's Cemetery in Luxembourg, shortly after you left the area. Brick is talking to Eagle Eyes. János was with me, he can verify that's when I took the photo."

"Right." János. Riley's little shadow. Jacob flicked the breadcrumbs from his jacket. "What is it about older men you dig, their silver hair, their money?"

She snatched the phone from his face. "Older men? What's that got to do with Brick and Eagle Eyes? Didn't you notice they're having a conversation, as in—they know each other?"

"Lemme see." Jacob grabbed her wrist and studied the photograph again. Both men stood casually. Brick one hand in his pocket, Eagle Eyes grinning as if they shared a joke.

"Now, do you believe me?" The pleading in Riley's eyes ate at the remaining shreds of his resistance.

There were too many coincidences in this case. And neither he nor Interpol believed in coincidences. "Maybe they know each other, maybe they don't."

"Oh, men. You're all alike. Exasperating." She wrenched her wrist free and tossed the phone on the blanket. "I couldn't show Paleface the picture because Brick was always at his side."

"Who's Paleface?"

"Your boss. I think. He refused to introduce himself in the hospital."

Schwarz must distrust her enough to conceal his identity from her.

"Brick is the one passing information to the terrorists. Or are you so blinded by loyalty clouds you can't see the truth?"

Was she right? Or had Schwarz's insistence she was a terrorist infiltrator cost him his objectivity?

Seconds later, Brick rounded the corner of the side street the Hossenis had taken a few minutes ago, a newspaper tucked under his arm. He sat on a park bench beyond the linden tree and opened the paper.

"Good. Now we know what Eagle Eyes looks like. Too bad you didn't get a good photo of Hawk Nose too. Then we could send you home, where you'd be safe." Away from his doubts about her. Away from the gnawing temptation of his heart.

"For your information, I was too busy banging the bejabbers out of Hawk Nose while he clubbed you over the head. An injury that seems to have permanently damaged your mental capacity." Riley thrust her half-eaten meal in a plastic bag and knotted the top. "Next time they attack you, I'll make sure to snap a photo first." Tears welled in her eyes.

She was either an Academy-award winning actress or—he reached across the blanket and took her hand. "Riles, I want to believe you ..."

She jerked her hand away. "Do you really think I'd help terrorists destroy my country?"

"My heart wants to believe you, but the facts say something else. You're the only one who had certain information about the terrorists before Interpol did. You're often seen in the company of a known terrorist. The poison used on your friend and me was found in your room. I hate to say this, but the plans that fall apart are the ones you know about."

"I didn't know about the cemetery transaction. You

deliberately withheld the information. And I can't refuse to dance with Khalid. You debug our rooms all the time, you've searched my purse. Maybe you're the one they bugged."

If that had been true, his equipment would've indicated it. "How about some of that chocolate cake?"

"Fine." Riley served them each a piece.

With the gusto of a starving man, he tucked into his slab. The plate sat untouched on her lap. Then she nibbled a bite, set the dish aside and stared across the river. Fresh tears pooled in her eyes. Swallowing hard, she swiped at the wetness glistening on her cheeks.

No way could Sora Hosseni pull off such an act. He scraped the last bit of cake and icing from his spoon then dumped his plate in the garbage sack.

A smidgen of chocolate hung in the corner of Riley's lip. Risking a rebuff, he leaned over and dabbed the chocolate onto his finger. The velvet sensation of her skin clung to his. She sat still, the pulse at the base of her neck beating like a scared rabbit.

Succumbing to the urge he'd battled since he'd first seen her picture in the captain's office, he eased her toward him and kissed her. His lips searched hers, tasting chocolate, a hint of wild mushrooms.

To his delight, she slid her arm around his neck and returned his kiss. How good she felt in his arms. As if she belonged there. Drawing her to him, he drank in her floral scent. As he held her, she relaxed in his embrace, her breaths slowed to match his. Then he kissed her deeper and everything he'd ever promised himself about not marrying clattered off the ledge of his mind.

Riley pressed her palm against his shoulder and pushed him back. "No, no, we shouldn't be doing this." She turned aside and threw the empty containers in her straw bag.

"Riles—"

"I'm sorry Jacob. I didn't mean to lead you on." She scrambled up from the blanket. "I can't do this."

"But it was just a kiss."

"No, it was an open doorway. A door to a place I cannot and will not go. I promised Lacy."

Right. The all-consuming, all-important career. Jacob dug his elbows into his knees, his lips still tingling from their kiss. He tried to shut down the clamoring in his heart for more of them. And failed.

Sniffling, Riley crammed the dishes in her bag, her breaths hiccuping in her throat.

No. She was right. He'd promised himself not to get involved, not to hurt a woman the way Noel's death had hurt Christine and their baby son. A son who'd never know his father, never play ball with him. No way did he want the same fate for Riley. And his career as an anti-terrorist agent upped the likelihood she'd be widowed.

Not bothering to hide his amusement, Brick sprawled on the park bench.

An urge to rush the guy and smash the smirk from his face burned across Jacob's chest. He rose and folded the blanket. What had he been thinking, kissing Riley in public, before he knew how she felt about kissing him? "I'm sorry, Riles."

Without waiting for him, she headed up the riverbank to the road. Breaths heaving, he caught up with her and reached for her arm. With panic in her eyes, she edged away from him. He fought the desire to take her in his arms and tell her everything would be okay. But today they'd crossed a barrier. A barrier he never should've destroyed.

Keeping a chasm between them, she headed back to the *River Nymph*, her silence so uncomfortable he wanted to babble his apologies, undo the hurt he'd caused her.

Still seated on the bench, Brick managed a half-serious expression, but the mocking in his eyes remained.

Jacob's fist worked at his side. For now, he'd not mention Riley's pictures of Brick and Eagle Eyes. He'd tackle this one alone.

AT THE GANGPLANK, Riley took her straw bag from Jacob and hurried down the staff staircase to the galley. She scrubbed the containers with fierce strokes. Why did she feel so confused when she was around Jacob?

Riley slapped the dish towel around the containers then put them away. She could still feel the touch of his lips on hers, his arms about her, making her feel so secure. The way her pulse had nearly pounded itself out of her body. Why, why, why had she let him kiss her?

And more importantly, why had she returned his kiss? Riley fingered her lips, not wanting the sensation of Jacob's mouth upon hers to fade. Kissing her leading man in front of an audience was one thing, but toying with Jacob's heart—how could she do that to him? Did his kiss mean he'd decided to trust her, that he no longer considered her one of the terrorists? Or had he been testing her? She headed for her cabin.

At her desk, she put the music books in order for her performance that evening, making sure numbered sticky notes were attached to each song she'd selected that morning.

Never before had she reneged on a promise, and her promise to Lacy was sacred. She'd prayed and prayed over the career, practically making the promise to Lacy a vow to the Lord.

The phone rang. The caller ID read Fréneau. Mustering a brightness she didn't feel, she clicked on the call. "How are you feeling, Frénie?"

"Ah, *chérie*, I know you too well. Something is wrong. Come, tell me. Confession is good for the soul. Unless you got fired and lost me my job."

Which was worse, Frénie probing about her job or telling her the truth? "A man kissed me."

"Is that all?" Frénie's laugh tinkled through the phone. "I thought it might be something serious. Like you were afraid to tell me you got me fired."

Riley squirmed in the chair. Her friend wasn't far off the mark. "No, you still have your position."

"How about I meet you in Strasbourg? Then you won't have to finish the cruise."

"Oh no. You can't—"

"Why not?" Alarm riddled Frénie's voice.

"I—I need to finish the job. The cruise."

"Rileeee. What has happened that you aren't telling me?"

"I ... uh ..." Riley bounced to her feet and paced the room. "I really, really need to stay onboard until we reach Basel."

"Chérie, I am booking my train ticket as soon as we hang up. Something's going on—"

"No. Don't." She had to find a way to convince Frénie to stay in Antwerp. "There's ... there's a man onboard. He and I ... well ... we—"

"Ah, a boyfriend. At last. Tell me about him. I am all eyes."

"It's ears, and he's not my boyfriend." No way was Jacob making it to significant other.

"Chérie, how long are you going to deny you have feelings for a man, feelings that are God-given."

"I'm not denying I have feelings for Jacob. I'm just not going to give in to them."

"Oh, la, la ... what are we going to do with you? Did you ever ask God if devoting yourself to your career was His will for your life?"

"Well ... no."

"Maybe you should. Maybe you are missing out on His best for you. Are you truly happy living out of a suitcase most of the year, schlepping that heavy bag up multiple flights of stairs to those fleabag hotel rooms you stay in?"

"Yes, yes. I love it." Quit probing, Frénie. "I'm very happy."

"Those greasy meals before you sing, ridiculously stupid staging, worrying about your high notes."

"That's all part of an operatic career, part of the sacrifices a singer makes."

"Only if you're an opera singer. In my job we have no high notes to worry about. I enjoy scrumptious meals prepared by a gourmet chef, dancing with wealthy men, wearing beautiful gowns every night, seeing the most exquisite cities in all of Europe. And you see railroad tracks, sit in crowded second-class cars reeking of diesel oil, unwashed bodies, and filthy latrines. All in the hopes of getting another guest contract in some provincial opera house."

"True, but—"

"I want to meet this Jacob."

"No. Absolutely not."

"He isn't a crook like Radu, is he? That Romanian who wanted to marry you."

Riley sighed. "No, Jacob is not a criminal. He's nothing like Radu. Jacob is courageous, kind, thoughtful, sensitive. Radu ... well, he pretended to have those qualities."

"Have you forgotten how close you came to being imprisoned by the security police because Radu was using you to courier information to his rather questionable friends?"

"Don't remind me."

"If you want Vielle Fréneau's advice to the loveless—"

"I don't."

"I tell you anyway because you are my friend. Give this man Jacob a chance. I have a feeling he may be the one for you, *chérie*."

"How would you know? You've never met him. I'll choose my own husband, thank you."

"Oh, so now you will consider marrying?"

"No. Never. I'm sorry, but I need to practice for tonight."

HUDDLING ON HIS DESK CHAIR, Jacob pressed the earbuds closer. What a heel he was, listening in to Riley's conversation with Frénie. But after hearing about Riley's photo of Brick,

Schwarz had been adamant about the phone taps. Maybe he was having Brick's phone conversations monitored, too.

Hmm ... so he was sensitive and thoughtful. Would Riley still think that if she knew he were listening? Jacob sat up straighter. A courier—she hadn't explained it that way to him. Dear God no. His heart sank. This time he'd have to tell Schwarz.

Jacob yanked out the earbuds and tossed them on the mattress. He paced to the left. The right. Jabbed his fist on his palm. How could he have been such a fool? From the moment he made her his prime suspect, his instincts about Riley had been correct. But the last thing he wanted was to be right about her. With everything in him, he wanted her by his side, forever. Not behind bars for life.

20

Day 9: Boppard/Rüdesheim

How long did Jacob intend to give her the iceberg treatment? Riley edged away from him as they waited to tour Siegfried's Mechanical Music Museum, a former knight's fifteenth-century, half-timbered home.

Since yesterday Jacob had been friendly one moment, frosty the next. Dinner together had been downright frigid. He'd lurked at the back of the lounge while she sang and danced with passengers, never leaving the room. Staring at her as if she had topped Interpol's most wanted list.

If only she'd shown him the photos of Brick while they were on the boat instead of suggesting a picnic. Then Jacob wouldn't have kissed her. And her heart wouldn't be in such a quandary. She shoved her fists inside her elbows. If they were going to survive this cruise, she needed to focus on watching for terrorists, not on her mercurial relationship with a man who despised her. Three more days and she'd never have to see him again.

Riley did a slow turn. The people in line were passengers from the boat. Molnár and the Ackelroyds stood at the doorstep.

Halfway back, the Hossenis. She moved closer to Jacob and whispered, "Maybe they're planning to make the exchange today. The Hossenis don't seem the type to appreciate a museum of mechanically generated music."

"I don't know. Khalid hasn't missed one of your performances. And he dances with you every night." Jacob practically spat the words.

Every muscle in her back bristled. Was he calling her singing mechanical? She took a deep breath. Why rise to his baiting? "Dancing with me is a form of religious penitence, like self-flagellation."

"I'd like to flagellate him myself."

"I'll hold him down for you." But her words failed to soften the clench in his cheek. Was he jealous of Khalid's attentions to her? Maybe that's why he was so irritable.

"The cruise is almost over." He looked around the yard. "This better be the day we get a breakthrough."

"We can't lose hope, Jacob."

"In case you haven't noticed, there's been no break since the botched transfer in Luxembourg."

"Botched is good. Not as good as having captured them all, but the sale hasn't gone through."

"You're no glass-half-full girl, are you? You're an over-the-rim woman."

"Singers learn to dust off the dirt and get back into the ring. We can't afford to dwell on the negatives, or we'd self-destruct." She followed their group inside the building, Jacob's sneakers nipping her heels like an overprotective Yorkie.

Their guide, a slender woman dressed in a nineteenth-century jacket, skirt, and feathered picture hat, chatted about the museum's collection, then cranked the handle on a giant cabinet music box. The mammoth, perforated metal disc plinked out "Die Lorelei."

Riley caught herself humming the tune. It could be a great

song on her next recital. If a few opera gigs didn't surface soon, she'd have to book more recitals to keep her bills paid.

"Come along, songbird." Jacob linked his arm in hers.

The entry-hall doors opened, and Brick entered, sidled along a group of women.

"Stay right here." Jacob released her hand. "Do. Not. Move. Understand?"

She nodded. Her nerves shot into full alert as Jacob made his way to Brick.

Seconds later, they retreated to the entry hall.

Why was Jacob leaving her out of the discussion? Did he still not trust her? Surely he didn't expect her to abandon their tour group. She followed them to the organ-grinder waiting in the back corner of the stone-walled room. A monkey in a red jacket and cap pranced along his shoulder, snapping his furry head to the left and right at the gathering crowd. A long wispy beard and bushy eyebrows overpowered the small man's sharp eyes and aquiline nose.

At the smell of dust motes on his shopworn tie and tails, she stifled a sneeze. His rumpled suit looked as if he'd snatched it from an attic trunk.

The Hossenis, the Ackelroyds, and Mrs. Cochran eased into the front of the circle.

Molnár walked over to her. "Are you enjoying the tour?"

"Yes." She'd enjoy it a lot more if Jacob didn't keep abandoning her.

The wizened man wound the handle of a small barrel-organ, vibrating the coins in a dish on top of the instrument. As the cheerful melody bounced off the walls, Riley's ears rang.

Without prompting, the animal grabbed the dish and thrust it toward Molnár. He fiddled inside his pocket then dropped a large coin in the dish. The monkey shrieked, retracted his lips in a rictus, and put the dish on the organ. Then he dug a slip of paper from the organ-grinder's pants pocket, leapt to Molnár's shoulder and shoved the paper in Molnár's breast pocket. Applause tittered around the group.

Riley suppressed a chuckle. Hopefully the animal wouldn't hop on her.

The monkey scampered onto the hurdy-gurdy then extended the dish to the Ackelroyds.

"Shoo, shoo, you filthy beast." Mrs. Ackelroyd reeled backward, her beringed fingers flailing the air. "Get away from me."

"Oh, be still, woman." Her husband plopped a coin in the dish. The monkey fetched a slip of paper and laid it on Mr. Ackelroyd's palm. He pocketed the paper.

Then the monkey's frantic gaze settled on Sora Hosseni. Her eyes narrowed to gun slits. Tremors shook the animal's body. Whimpering, he leapt back onto the hurdy-gurdy.

Maybe Interpol ought to hire the monkey to sniff out the bidders on Agent X.

Hunching over the handle, the gnome-like organ grinder tilted his head toward Riley and gave her a Fagin-like grin. Three blackened teeth protruded from among his yellowed molars.

The monkey hung from the organ grinder's belt, plucked a scrap of paper from the man's pants pocket, and hopped to Riley's shoulder. Its claws pricked her collarbone. She stifled the urge to flick the animal off her shoulder. Whipping his furry tail across her lips, his fingers wiggled inside her blouse and thrust the paper inside the left cup of her bra. Laughter erupted in the room.

"Even the animals are attracted to you." Molnár held up his blank piece of paper. "What is written on yours?"

She removed the slip of paper, flipped it over. Both sides were blank. "A party trick, unless it contains invisible ink."

"And now, if I may have your attention." The docent activated the Hupfeld Phonoliszt Violina, an upright piano with candle sconces and two bowed cabinets above the keyboard.

While the music blared, she opened the cabinets to reveal mechanized violins hung upside down.

In the center of the instrument, a piano roll played a quasi-orchestrated transcription of the tenor aria, "La Donna è mobile," Woman is Fickle. Is that what Jacob thought of her?

The music segued into the next variation on the aria's theme, a dismal picture of what her own life had become. Upside down. Trusted one moment, distrusted the next.

While the docent shut the violin cabinets and pointed out the other instruments, the Ackelroyds, Mrs. Cochran, and the Hossenis lingered near the Phonoliszt.

Riley looked around the room. No sign of Jacob and Brick. She crossed to a table displaying an enameled snuff music box.

With the monkey on his shoulder, the organ grinder pushed his hurdy-gurdy across the room. He strolled past the Phonoliszt, and the monkey jumped to the instrument and pushed a tiny piece of paper under the edge of the wooden panel near the sconce.

This had to be it. The next move on exchanging the vials. She stepped toward the Phonoliszt.

"Charming museum, isn't it?" Molnár came up beside her and cupped her elbow.

"Yes." She tried to ease from his grasp. No way was she letting anyone else retrieve the paper.

"Have you seen this one?" He walked her back to the table with the snuffbox.

She wanted to scream at him to leave her alone. "Yes, I was admiring it earlier." As the last of their tour group disappeared down the hall, she glanced toward the Phonoliszt. The paper was still there. "Excuse me, I need to catch up with the others."

"I have been in contact with the general manager of the Strasbourg Opera. He would like to see your résumé." He slipped his arm through hers. "Do you have a copy I could fax him?"

"Yes, yes I do." Her pulse did a happy dance. Zeroing her

gaze on the paper beneath the sconce, she ran through a mental list of her best audition arias.

Eagle Eyes strolled across the room and paused in front of a mechanical diorama of Turkish figures playing pseudo-Turkish music.

Where was Jacob when she needed him? "Pardon me." Riley eased her arm from Molnár's grasp and dug in her purse for her phone.

"Then I have your permission to set up an audition for you in Strasbourg?"

"Yes, yes, of course." She speed-dialed Jacob. "That's very kind of you …" Five rings and Jacob still hadn't answered.

As she spoke, Eagle Eyes walked toward the Phonoliszt.

Why wasn't Jacob answering his cell? Riley pocketed her phone. Nibbled her lower lip. What if Brick had been sent to lure Jacob away when the exchange of vials went down? The terrorists might have attacked him again. "I'll get you my résumé this afternoon."

"I am happy to have been of service to such a gifted singer."

Seconds later, Eagle Eyes turned down the hall and disappeared from her view.

The next tour group entered and spread out in front of the instruments. Jacob lagged at the end of the line. Eyes alert. Unharmed.

Where had he been? "Excuse me." Riley threaded her way through the new tour group to Jacob's side. "I don't know what you've been up to, but you missed Eagle Eyes. And the organ grinder—"

"Wait here." Jacob brushed past her and hurried down the hall.

Just this once, couldn't he have taken her with him?

Molnár had vanished.

The paper, the paper. She had to retrieve the slip of paper before the docent returned. Riley squeezed through the crowd and headed toward the Phonoliszt.

The docent took her place beside the player piano and began her introduction.

"Excuse me." Riley scooted past the man and woman blocking the Phonoliszt's sconce, reached for the slip of paper.

It was gone.

JACOB SWERVED past two women with toddlers in tow. How had Eagle Eyes gotten past him? Leaving Riley alone in the museum had been a mistake, but Brick's message from Schwarz had been too sensitive to discuss in a crowded place, and Schwarz had banned Riley from all discussion of ops.

She tagged his arm. "Wait for me. I'm supposed to stay with you, remember?"

"Yeah. Sorry about that."

"Where could Eagle Eyes have gone?"

"No idea. Maybe he was meeting someone here. Someone from the boat."

"The Hossenis?"

"Possibly." He steered her past the Ackelroyds, Molnár, and Mrs. Cochran looking at music boxes in the museum gift shop. No sign of the Hossenis. Jacob hurried Riley from the building, down the hill and through the village.

"The organ-grinder's monkey left a piece of paper on the Phonoliszt. Eagle Eyes walked past the instrument. When I went to retrieve the paper, it was gone."

"Great, just great. One foul-up after another. How is it you always manage to be in the center of the action?"

"If you hadn't abandoned me to talk with Brick, maybe you'd have seen Eagle Eyes, too." She looked around the street. "Where's Brick?"

"Taking care of business." He hadn't meant to snarl at her. It wasn't her fault he'd messed up. Again. Jacob seated her at an outdoor table at a café on Drosselgasse, a touristy pedestrian street, then ordered two coffees and dialed Brick.

"Yo."

"Riley spotted one of them at the museum. And possibly a note with information about the exchange."

"Don't you think it's a bit odd—"

"Yes. Nevertheless, we can't ignore this." Jacob surveilled the café, the people in the street.

The waiter brought their coffees. Riley toyed with the wafer on the side of the saucer.

"This may confirm what Schwarz suspects," Brick said.

"Maybe, maybe not. Talk to you later." Jacob disconnected and stuffed his phone in his pocket.

Riley put her elbow on the table and rested her chin in her hand. "Is your conversation cryptic because of where we are or because of me?"

More than anything he wanted to trust her, confide in her, make her part of the team. But his professional training told him to back off. "Interpol business is sensitive. I wish I could share, but ..." The less she knew, the safer they all were.

"I see." She stood, her coffee unfinished. "I'm going back to the boat. I need to prepare my songs for tonight."

Signaling the waiter, Jacob threw enough euros on the table to cover the bill then caught up with her on the street. "Riles, I'm sorry."

"Uh-huh. Not that it's any of your business, but I've accepted Molnár's offer to set up an opera audition for me in Strasbourg. He's been in contact with the general manager on my behalf."

"Strasbourg."

"It's a good house. A great opportunity for me."

"Riles, you can't."

"Oh, yes I can. You don't need me. You're convinced you can break this case alone." She whacked the side of her head. "Oh, that's right. You have a partner. A partner seen talking with one of the Romanians. You're in great hands, Jacob Coulter."

He grasped her arm and turned her toward him. "You can't do the audition. I'm sorry. I know how much it means to you."

"Do you? I guess you still get paid if you don't catch the terrorists. In my profession we get paid only if we sing the performance. And without any performances, I—"

"Riles, please listen. I can't be there to protect you at the audition. They've assigned me somewhere else that day."

"You needn't worry about me. You're the one they've tried to kill."

"Until now." He looked away from the shock riddling her face. If only he'd softened his words, not sounded so brutal. These people had put her through enough trauma.

MAYBE JACOB HAD LEFT her alone in the museum to keep her from finding out the terrorists' plans to kill her. Riley studied his face, but his expression had become inscrutable. "Y—You have proof?"

Glancing over his shoulder, he eased her to the edge of the street, away from pedestrians milling in front of the shops and restaurants. "Yes."

"If I can't go with you on your assignment, where are you planning to stash me?"

"I don't know." He shot another glance over his shoulder.

What wasn't he telling her? "Does that mean no agents assigned for protection?"

"I wish it were up to me to decide." His gaze flitted somewhere on the cobblestones.

"Very well." She crossed her arms, mostly to stop their shaking. "Since you don't know, or won't say, I might as well do the audition. I'll take a taxi, stay off the streets."

"No, Riles."

"It's my life. I have a career to build. A promise to keep. And, as you said, I'm an over-the-brim woman. No half-empty-glass outlook for me."

"Riles ..."

"Thank you for the warning." She threw back her shoulders, thrust her chin at him. "You can't protect me. I can't go with you, so I'll do as I please." Without waiting for his response, she bowled her way past wine-mellowed tourists, each one oblivious to this impending disaster, and headed for the boat. No more was she letting terrorists control her life.

However long she had left to live.

JACOB FISTED the loose change in his pocket until the metal dug into his flesh. He'd really blown it this time. If the terrorists killed her, he'd never forgive himself. And if she survived, she'd probably never forgive him for not trusting her. But he'd taken an oath when he signed on with Interpol.

Keeping Riley about thirty feet ahead of him, he tailed her as she boarded the *River Nymph,* let herself into the staff's private deck area, and disappeared down the staircase. Then he walked up the hill to the jewelry shop near the café.

An elderly man wearing a green apron over his shirt and slacks stepped from behind a small cubicle in the back of the shop. "*Guten Tag*, good day." He popped a jeweler's loupe from his eye and crossed to the display cabinets. "May I help you?"

"I'm looking for a hair clip." Jacob studied the necklaces, rings, and bracelets in the display cabinets. "Something sparkly."

"Of course." The shopkeeper opened a cabinet door and brought out a narrow clip studded with tiny emeralds and rhinestones.

"Yes ..." Jacob turned the piece over, examined its construction. "I'll need several more rows of stones. Do you have any loose ones for sale?"

"No problem." The jeweler unlocked a safe in his cubicle and returned with a tattered leather box. He shook out the contents of a small suede sack on a black velvet tray.

"Can you sell me enough rhinestones to cover the width of my finger?" Jacob held out his forefinger. "And a tube of jeweler's cement? You know, glue."

"Of course." The man rang up the purchase. "Your girl will like this."

"Yes." Jacob's mouth tightened. Hopefully she'd never discover the real purpose of the barrette.

21

Day 10: Speyer

Jacob set the breakfast tray with two mugs of coffee, bowls of oatmeal, and toast on the small table in the staff's area of the stern. Riles stood against the railing, her mouth taut as barbed wire. After their tiff in Rüdesheim, bringing her breakfast was a paltry peace offering. An offering that could end up on his face when she found out why they were meeting.

"I'm really sorry about yesterday."

Sparks of flak spat from her eyes.

He couldn't blame her. Once again, he'd abandoned her when she needed him.

A breeze slapped the boat's flags, and she snugged her sweater around her chest. The early morning light had yet to flood the vineyard-covered hillsides, the crumbling ruins of the castle above the riverbank. He pulled out her chair for her then sat across the table. Chill from the metal seat seeped through his khakis. Which was worse—the cold chair or the frost emanating from her?

Steeling himself for her reaction, he set one of the steaming mugs of coffee in front of her.

She snatched a bowl of oatmeal and *thunked* it on the table. "And we're meeting out here because?"

"Interpol needs your best description of the man you saw leaving the slip of paper at the museum."

Riley clattered her spoon to the saucer. "So now I'm of use to you again. How long will that last?"

"I know this has been rough for you, but they want your description of him. Mine was sketchy. I was too busy watching for suspicious activity."

"Height, maybe five-foot-four. Small boned. Shaggy black hair and a waist-length beard. Caterpillar eyebrows. Poor dental hygiene and three black teeth." She shoved her uneaten bowl of oatmeal toward him. "You need the description of the monkey, too?"

A chuckle caught in his chest. "Have you seen the guy before?"

She scrunched her face, stared past him. "I—I don't think so …"

"And you still think Eagle Eyes took the note?"

"Who else? Our tour group had left the room." She squirmed on her chair. "I was a bit distracted. Molnár was telling me about the audition, and—"

"Yeah, I get it. Tending to your career when we're trying to intercept a ruthless bunch of terrorists."

"That's it." She scraped back her chair and stood, her chest heaving. "I've had about all I can take of you, Jacob Coulter."

He thudded his half-empty mug on the table. The brown liquid sloshed between the slats and dripped on his slacks. "If you want to chase after Molnár, I won't stop you from ruining your life."

"Chasing after—" She turned and stormed down the stairs.

Two more days of working with her. He slapped their almost untouched dishes on the tray. Then maybe he could return to his desk job. And try to forget he'd ever met Riley Williams. The latest intel pointed to a terrorist attack in Strasbourg. Brick's update at the museum had changed their assignments to the EU building, covering the special meetings with every EU minister, secretary, and head of state present. One vial of Agent X could annihilate them all.

RILEY LET herself in her cabin, dug her aria books from her suitcase. Thank goodness she'd chosen a career and not marriage. Not one opera director or general manager she'd worked with topped Jacob's constant flip-flopping. Either treating her like a suspected terrorist or a feebleminded woman. She slammed the aria book and sheet music on the desk.

Forty-eight hours until the *River Nymph* docked in Basel. If they didn't recover the vials of Agent X by then, Jacob and his cronies would have to solve the crisis themselves. She sank onto the chair and flipped through her music until she came to the Queen of the Night's first *tour de force*. He and Interpol had all but called her Public Enemy No. 1, no different from the evil Queen in the opera.

The clutch in her throat ratcheted a notch. Two more days and Jacob would be out of her life. Permanently. Today she'd come close to slapping him for his crack about Molnár. How could Jacob think she was interested in a relationship with that man?

Pacing the room, she started a vocal siren. The vibrations buzzed in her chest, then she slid the pitches upward. Her vocal folds fought back, stiff as dried out rawhide. At this rate, she'd never be able to sing her runs and high notes tomorrow.

How dare Jacob make her feel guilty for pursuing her career? A girl had to pay her rent, didn't she? Focus on the audition. The audition. The audition.

Breathe in. Out. Forget Jacob Coulter. Think contract with the Strasbourg Opera. She sat at the desk and pored over the music, but Jacob's accusations intruded on the countless measures of runs and high *Fs* she needed to re-photograph in her mind. Tomorrow could be the break she needed, the promise of performances and a paycheck for the coming season.

If she could get her mind off Jacob. Romanians and terrorists. Agent *X*.

JACOB FINISHED CHECKING his table settings for dinner. Today the *River Nymph* had cruised past a slew of castles, making lunch service for the guests leisurely. He went to the stern and phoned Brick for intel updates on the encrypted line. The boat's wake frothed and churned, slashing through the silvery streaks of afternoon sun glinting on the river.

"Yo." A yawn crept through Brick's voice.

"What's the scoop?"

"The analysis of the water bottle and vials is in. Same stuff used on Miss Fréneau. Schwarz wants Riley excluded from all further ops."

"What about the note she saw left at the museum?"

"Watch it, partner. Whose side are you on? Like all her other findings, there's never a reliable witness present to back up what she claims she saw. Or heard."

There had to be a way to figure out for certain whose side she was on—his or the terrorists. Jacob disconnected the call, went to his cabin, and changed into his dinner service uniform. One hour until lounge duty, watching men ogle Riles while she sang. But tonight, he wouldn't have to watch her clutched in the arms of Sugar Daddy and Khalid. Local performers were scheduled to board the boat to entertain the guests.

Beneath his dresser light, he examined the hair clip he'd bought for her, patted the extra stones he'd added to it. Dry. With luck, she wouldn't figure out what lay beneath them. Working quickly, he rewrapped the clip in the jeweler's paper and ribbon then dabbed on a bit of aftershave.

Drawing a breath, he knocked today's signal on her door, the first eight measures of "Holy, Holy, Holy." As he put his fist to the door to tap the rhythm again, she opened it, dressed in a creamy gown that hugged her curves. The pearl-like sheen of the fabric accentuated the curls tumbling about her shoulders, her delicate coloring. If she looked any more ravishing, she'd catapult him back into a starstruck schoolboy.

Before he lost his nerve, he pulled out the packet and extended his hand. "This is for you."

"For me?" Riley stared at his gift as if it contained a live grenade.

"I—I wanted to say I'm sorry."

"That's not necessary." She stepped back from him, her face stony.

"Yes, it is." Moisture slicked his palms. What if she didn't accept his gift? "I—I'm really sorry I doubted you." With the gift on his palm, he inched his hand close to the silky fabric at her waist, the warmth of her skin. "Open it ... please."

She rolled her lips into a hard line between her teeth, stared so long at his hand the wrapping paper stuck to his sweaty palm. With a sigh, she took the packet, her fingernails tickling his skin, triggering shockwaves along his arm. She walked to the dresser, hips swaying, the gleaming fabric swishing about her legs.

He shut the door and peered over her shoulder, inhaling the intoxicating scent of her perfume.

With her back to him, she removed the ribbon and paper, then gasped. She held the clip to the light then turned to him. "It's lovely, Jacob." Her gaze slipped toward the floor. "I—I don't know what to say."

"Say you'll wear it tonight. Please."

Catching her lower lip between her teeth, she nibbled off the rose-colored gloss. Her fingers unfurled, leaving the clip unclaimed on her palm.

His heart skipped a beat. Everything depended on her wearing the clip, having her cell phone with her. Especially tomorrow. Otherwise, if the terrorists made good on their decision to take her out, he'd have no way to rescue her.

"It—it would mean a lot to me."

With the intensity of a merciless searchlight, her gaze roved his face. "All right."

The dullness in her voice knifed his chest worse than a slap on the face. After all of his accusations, why should she be eager to accept his gift? Maybe she'd rather have had diamonds from Sugar Daddy.

"You chose my favorite colors, too." She turned to the mirror, swirled the hair above her ear and eased the clip into place. The sadness in her eyes overshadowed the soft light gleaming on the stones.

"It looks stunning on you Riles." His voice went hoarse. He'd never given jewelry to a woman. A pang shot through him. Too bad the gift wasn't a diamond ring. From everything she'd said to him and to Frénie on the phone, Riles would never agree to marry him. And that was for the best, for both of them. "Promise me you'll wear the clip to your audition tomorrow. I can't be there to cheer for you, but I'll be thinking about you. Wear it for good luck."

"No." She held up a hand. "Don't say that."

"Why not?"

"It's bad luck to wish a singer good luck. We say, break a leg."

"That's good luck?"

"Well ... not if it literally happens."

Jacob shook his head. He'd never understand singers. "Give me your phone."

"Why?" She gave him a questioning frown then fished it from her evening bag.

Holding her cell close to his chest, he punched in a new set of numbers, then handed it back to her.

"If I ask what you did to it, would you tell me?"

"Nope."

"I didn't think so." Her voice held all the warmth of dry ice.

He closed her door behind him. *Forgive me, Riles. This is the only way I know to determine whose side you're on.* And maybe protect you.

REPRIEVED. Her one night off from dancing. Lingering in the corner of the lounge, Riley rolled her shoulders, releasing the tension in her neck. The break couldn't have happened at a better time. Now her body would be rested for tomorrow's audition.

During dinner, staff members had enclosed the dance floor with couches and chairs now crowded with chitchatting and well-lubed passengers. Tonight, her front-row fan club, the Hossenis, Ackelroyds, Mrs. Cochran, and Molnár, had taken ringside seats, facing each other like compass points.

Jacob and the other waiters squeezed between the rows, offering drinks and collecting empty glasses on their trays.

The hairs on Riley's arms stood to attention. Opening night electricity charged the atmosphere.

Seconds later, a brass quintet filed onto the dance floor and bowed, accompanied by raucous applause. If she were a betting person, she'd guess it was subliminal relief, not having to dance with her tonight. In ten days, she'd scuffed a lifetime of men's dress shoes. The musicians scooted the chairs and music stands into position, closing ranks.

Garbed in traditional German outfits, two dancers ran onstage. The grey-haired man, dressed in *lederhosen* with white knee socks, bowed once in each direction. Pivoting with him, the petite woman fluttered her false eyelashes and curtsied, holding out the edges of her dirndl skirt. A spotlight overhead gleamed on her flawless skin, her raven, shoulder-length curls.

The instrumentalists blew air through their mouthpieces then with a toe-tapping count from the tubist, launched into a polka. The dancers clomped and whirled and whacked their heels. With each hop and skip, the woman's bosom heaved and jiggled.

Jacob walked over to Riley. "Enjoying your night off?"

"Never happier." Not entirely true, but she'd count her blessings.

At the end of the fourth dance, the male dancer gestured to his partner. She skipped around the front rows, bobbing low curtsies before the guests. Molnár pulled a ten-euro note from his pocket, crooked his finger at her. She strutted over to him, angled one shoulder low. He tucked the bank note in her bosom. Widening her eyes at the crowd, she pursed her lips into an *O* and pressed two fingers to her mouth.

Jacob grunted. "That figures."

"Oh, please. Not tonight." Couldn't they spend one evening together without Jacob's jealousy rising to the surface?

At the next couch, Mrs. Cochran dug in her evening bag and held out a fifty-euro note to the male dancer. The men sitting beside her stuffed ten-euro notes in the dancer's dirndl-clad bosom.

Like a bunch of adolescents, the men stretched over the first row and handed the dancers ten-and-twenty-euro tips. Practically drooling, Mr. Ackelroyd shoved a wad of euros down the woman's dirndl bosom. His stash rolled out and fell to the floor. Fives, all of them. Mrs. Ackelroyd rolled her eyes. She bent over, her hair ornament catching the overhead light, snatched the euros and patted them on the woman's palm.

Wow. Riley blinked. If tomorrow's audition didn't bring in a contract, she could join a local troupe. Tonight's haul looked more lucrative than panhandling her arias on town squares. She thudded her head against the wall. What was she thinking? They were dancers. She'd starve to death.

Khalid motioned to the female dancer and folded a hundred-euro note in the other side of her gathered blouse. A sneer crossed Sora's face.

"A hundred-euro tip." Jacob frowned. "Who did you say stood near the Phonoliszt?

"Lots of people. Eagle Eyes was the last one beside it before the paper vanished."

The dancers bowed, dropping a trail of euros. Laughing, they gathered up the tips and left the lounge. Then yodeling as they entered, a trio of local singers took their places on the dance floor. The quintet segued into German beer-hall songs.

Jacob clutched her hand so hard her knuckles ached. "Did we just witness the bidding for the vials?"

22

Day 11: Strasbourg, France

Riley stepped onto the stage of the Strasbourg Opera, smoothed a wrinkle from her teal silk dress. She breathed in the familiar scent of paint, raw wood, and dust. If today's warm-ups were an omen, her performance promised to be stellar.

No warming up on the train, in the outside corridor that connected the cars, her voice whipped away by the wind. Or in the back hall offstage with fifty other singers wailing through their exercises, all in different keys. Today she'd had the luxury of a private practice room with a mirror and a piano.

Apart from a single bare-bulb lamp onstage, the house was black. No piano. Perhaps they'd left the instrument in the orchestra pit below. Her heart sank. A piano in the pit with no conductor could create ensemble problems. Not good. Not good at all.

Riley squinted at her watch. Ten o'clock—the audition time Molnár had told her on the boat. She paced the wooden boards, did a few shoulder rolls to relax, lip buzzes to keep her vocal folds ready for the stratospheric arias of the Queen of the Night and Zerbinetta's nineteen pages of pyrotechnics.

Moving around the stage, she snapped her fingers, testing the acoustics. Good, a live hall, kinder to a coloratura's voice. She checked her watch again. If the general manager came much later, she'd have to re-warm up her voice. It would've been nice to run through the arias with the accompanist, too.

The custodian crossed the stage. "You are quite early. The general manager will be down to speak with you shortly."

Oh, no, had Molnár gotten the time wrong? Now she'd have to—

A mid-sixtyish man, dressed in a grey jacket and navy slacks, walked onstage. "Miss Williams? Hans Gruber, general manager of the Strasbourg Opera. I'm afraid there has been some mistake. We did not expect you until eleven. Tomorrow."

"Tomorrow?" Her voice shrilled an octave. Molnár must've written down the wrong date. The wrong time. "That can't be."

"Alas, I am afraid so." Gruber spread his hands. "And the pianist cannot come today."

No. No. No. How would she pay her September rent? A vision of her landlady evicting her, luggage on the sidewalk, no place to go, flitted across Riley's mind.

"János can be most persuasive. His offer to—" Gruber flushed. "What I mean is ..."

"What did Mr. Molnár offer you to let me audition?"

Gruber's cheeks reddened. He tweaked his nose and glanced beyond her shoulder. "A substantial financial package to cast you in a starring role."

Her shoulders drooped. Jacob was right. Molnár was nothing but a wannabe Sugar Daddy.

"Come, come, Miss Williams. Many singers launch their career with the nudge of a benefactor."

"Not this one. I'll build my career on my talent, not on a wad of some man's euros." She stuck out her hand. "Thank you for your time. I'm sorry to have troubled you."

"Good-bye." Gruber shook her hand then escorted her offstage. She thanked him again and left by the backstage street entrance. Surely if Molnár expected favors for setting up the audition, he wouldn't have deliberately given her the wrong information.

Shielding her eyes, she stepped into the sunshine.

Across the street, Eagle Eyes stood in a doorway, cigarette in his mouth, scrolling through the phone on his palm.

Her heart did a slow thump on her sternum. What was he doing here—had he followed her to the audition? More importantly, had he seen her come out?

With a prayer the door wasn't locked, she fumbled with the knob then slipped back inside the building. The concierge rose from behind his cubbyhole counter and gaped at her.

"Forgot something." She hurried back onstage before he could question her.

The lights had been shut off. Riley let her eyes adjust to the blackness then made her way stage left to the steps she'd noticed earlier. She crept down them then race-walked up the carpeted aisle toward the foyer doors. Footsteps clipped across the stage. Her gut hitched. Was it the concierge—or Eagle Eyes?

Riley ducked between the last row of seats and waited until the sounds faded. Counting off the seconds, she waited five minutes' worth then slipped into the foyer. She held her breath, let herself out of the building, stood behind a column at the top of the marble steps and scanned the sidewalks for Eagle Eyes. Perhaps he thought she was still inside the opera house. She released her breath and phoned Jacob.

"Yes." His voice was terse.

She told him about Eagle Eyes. "I don't suppose you'd tell me what's going on where you are?"

"Nothing. Lost the Hossenis three blocks before we got here."

"If I can slip away undetected, I'm heading for the Old Town Square and take a canal boat tour, get in my first sightseeing on this trip." She pulled up the Batorama website and booked a tour time online, the last seat available before the *River Nymph* departed. "I'm on the noon boat."

"O ... kay. Take a tram, a taxi. Call me right away if you spot Eagle Eyes tailing you. Or anyone else."

"Aye, aye, captain."

"Riles, this is no joking matter."

"Yeah, I kinda figured that out." She walked past the kiddie street-carnival rides on the square in front of the opera house and headed toward the canal-boat docks on the river. Funny, she'd expected to feel remorse over the cancelled audition. Instead, she felt strangely free.

Every few feet she checked over her shoulder for the Romanians, until she reached the cordoned-off waiting areas at the docks. As she moved to the end of the line, she clicked her online ticket. A cool breeze nipped her cheeks. She hugged her aria books to her chest for warmth. In high-tourist season, she was lucky to get a ticket.

A few yards upstream, a plastic-roofed tour boat bobbed against its moorings as an open-air boat chugged to the loading dock beside her. Two black-uniformed deckhands tied off the vessel and hopped onto the landing. The first man removed the rope blocking the passengers and welcomed her group onboard.

Seventy minutes of peace. No Romanians in sight. For the first time in ten days, she could relax and enjoy centuries-old half-timbered buildings and a regatta of swans oblivious to the world's trauma. One of the men handed her a headset and she sat in a front-row seat. Minutes later the boat *put-putted* from the dock and her headset crackled to life. Tuned in to the taped English tour guide, she settled in her seat. The boat glided upstream, and her sense of time vanished.

As the boat neared the upper end of the canal, the recorded guide's voice announced they were approaching the circular European Parliament building. Small older homes lined the front edge of the massive, glass-and-steel structure. The little houses would be an innocuous hideout for terrorists targeting the EU.

They'd not only have a great view of the building from their backyard, but easier access to the property.

At the EU's gated dock areas, uniformed policemen stood on the platforms. The officers' faces were on high alert, their Uzis poised to fire.

She sat forward in her seat, the muscles in her legs tensed. Was this where Jacob had been stationed today? Scanning the area, she shot up prayers for his protection, for those who worked there.

One of the policemen motioned the boat to turn around. The tour boat did a graceful one-eighty and chugged back down the river.

Near Petite France, the boat entered a lock with concrete walls. Moving almost stealthily, the wooden gates closed around them, hemming them in. Inch by inch, the water level crept upwards, jostling the boat against the sides of the confined space. She glanced at the riverbanks beside the end of the gates. Hawk Nose stood at her left, punching in something on his phone.

Where were Jacob and the police, when she needed them?

On her right, a dark-skinned man dressed in white, from his skullcap to his athletic shoes, fiddled with his cell held directly in line with Hawk Nose's phone.

She peered over the side of the boat. Three small off-white blocks that looked more like bars of soap, hung a few inches above the waterline. Slender cables ran through the blocks. She dug her phone from her purse and dialed Jacob.

"What's up, Riles?"

"Can a bomb be detonated via phones?"

"Yes. Where are you?"

"The boat is stuck in a lock, waiting for the water level to rise."

"I'm on it."

"You'll be too late." She disconnected and clicked open a phone app. Holding her breath and willing her hand to quit trembling, she focused on Hawk Nose and the guy on the opposite bank, the water now lapping the devices on the wall.

"Hello, all you folks out there in Facebook land, this is Riley Williams, videoing on a canal boat tour in a lock at the edge of Petite France in Strasbourg, France. Before you tune me out, the guy with the hawk nose is a Romanian terrorist." Then she swung the phone camera toward the man on the opposite bank. "I suspect this is his partner."

Next, she filmed the whitish blocks on the wall. "According to an Interpol agent, these may be remote-controlled bombs. Picture them detonating. Picture the destruction they will bring to the area, the hundred-plus tourists on this boat or the next one. If you see this video, pass it on. Pass it on to law enforcement. Make it viral. Now."

Working quickly, she shared the video to every Facebook and Twitter account she could think of. *Dear God, don't let these madmen succeed.*

Hawk Nose glanced her way, shook his fist at her.

"Hey, you there. Smile." She stood and pointed the phone's camera at him. "You're on Candid Camera."

One of the deckhands came over to her. "Madame, please be seated."

"Sorry." She took her seat, scrolled through the responses posted to her video. "Good." It was on its way to stardom.

Moments later, singsong sirens echoed between the buildings.

Hawk Nose retreated from the bank, his phone to his ear.

On the other side of the lock, his cohort stared, open-mouthed.

With agonizing slowness, the gates of the lock parted, and the surging current shot the boat forward. Waves of relief flooded her body. Interpol might not have Agent X yet, but one attack had been averted. "Thank you, God. Thank you."

As the boat docked, the deckhands tied it to the posts. She

let the other passengers disembark while she called Jacob and filled him in. "We're safe."

A few yards up the narrow lane, Eagle Eyes stood beside a restaurant menu board, his body half-blocked by the throng of tourists.

"I have Eagle Eyes in sight. Heading after him now." She accepted the deckhand's heft up the steps and onto the ramp.

"It's a trap. Don't follow him."

"Do you want the vials or not?" Tromping up the cobblestoned hill in her high heels, she followed Eagle Eyes as he dodged between the milling crowds and headed toward the Old Town Square. She shoved past dawdling tourists, street musicians, the tempting smells wafting from the restaurants. Her breakfast of coffee and soft-boiled eggs had long since vanished.

"Riles, you've done your part. Get out of there now. I'll have a team sent in."

"And how long will that take?"

"For once, do as I say."

Fifty more feet and she could touch Eagle Eyes' coattails. "As soon as your team gets here."

23

Shabby narrow buildings hemmed in the Old Town Square. Outside the entrance of the cathedral, three elderly women in dirty skirts and blouses waited by the steps, their gnarled hands clutching a worn crutch, begging as people entered the church. A little boy scampered across the pavement, flapping his arms, scattering a flock of pigeons into the air.

Near the center of the square, three mime artists in body paint and period costumes posed on wooden crates, playing to the crowd of photo-snapping tourists in front of them. A perfect place for Eagle Eyes to hide. Riley mingled with the crowd, looking for him. The Ackelroyds and Mrs. Cochran stood farther down the row.

A tin plate or an upturned hat for donations lay near each performer's box. To her right, Marie Antoinette, wearing a white cone-shaped wig and wide panniers beneath her satin gown, pirouetted on her box. She broke off bits of the enormous piece of cake on her palm and flung them at the crowd. Despite their parents' objections, children scrambled for the crumbs.

Next to Marie Antoinette, a flutist in a waistcoat, velvet breeches, and white tights piped a melody from a Mozart flute-and-harp concerto.

With his bowler hat perched at an angle, the black-suited Charlie Chaplin impersonator tottered in a circle around his box, twirling his cane and aping the Chaplinesque gait. He pivoted toward Riley and paused, wiggled his mustache, then his eyebrows at her.

Sidestepping a large metal grate in the pavement, she tucked her opera scores under her arm, took several euro coins from her wallet. If only Lacy were here to see him. Charlie had been one of her favorite actors.

Charlie hopped off his box and strolled along the crowd to her right, tipping his hat at the ladies.

As she laid the coins in his tin, Riley glanced around the square. Hawk Nose and Eagle Eyes stood to the far side of the crowd. Her pulse shot into overdrive. She speed-dialed Jacob, willing him to answer.

"What's up, Riles?"

"Hawk Nose and Eagle Eyes are here. On the square."

"See anyone from the boat, the Hossenis?"

The terseness in his voice put her even more on edge. "Only Molnár walking toward the Ackelroyds, Mrs. Cochran, a few other couples, too."

"I want you to leave. Now."

Riley did a slow three-sixty and her heart sank. The Romanians hadn't budged, but Molnár had vanished, the only person who might've protected her. "Do you have any men here?"

"No one you'd recognize. Riles, get out of there, before they see you. You've either stumbled onto the exchange of the vials, or those men are there to kill you." Sounding breathless, footsteps pounding hard in the background, Jacob's voice rose in near panic. "Stay on the phone ... until I know you've cleared the square ... without anyone following you."

"Okay." Where had Molnár gone? If Herr Gruber had told him she'd declined the audition, Sugar Daddy probably wanted to throttle her himself.

"I'm putting you on hold for a sec while I alert the local police."

Twirling his cane, Charlie ambled down the line, stopped in front of the family beside her. He wiggled his eyebrows at a preteen girl, clasped his hands to his heart, then spread his arms for a bear hug.

Doing another three-sixty, Riley checked the square for the Romanians. Someone brushed against her side and she drew back.

The twinkle in his shrewd eyes assessing, Charlie stood beside her. Giving her a wicked grin, he kissed her cheek then toddled back to his soapbox.

Riley glanced inside her purse. Tissue hung from the corner of the zipper, her euro bills protruded from her wallet. This morning, she'd had four ten-euro notes. Now she had three. How dare he—Jabbing her forefinger at him, she strode toward his box. "That man's a pickpocket!"

Tsking, Charlie shook his head and wagged a finger at her as if she were a naughty child.

"Help—police! He stole ten euros from me."

In a flash, Molnár appeared at her side and took her arm. *Where had he come from?*

"Surely you're mistaken." He tried to edge her away from Charlie's box.

"No, I'm not. That man is a thief. He's using his disguise to rob people."

"Forget about him. He's just a pickpocket." Molnár gave her a bland smile. "Come, tell me about your audition."

On the phone Jacob's voice sounded a thousand miles away.

"Hold on a sec. Mr. Molnár is with me." Riley let him lead her away from Chaplin's soapbox. "I—I cancelled the appointment. You were so kind to set up the audition, but I need to succeed on my own. I hope you understand." She was babbling like a nervous teeny-bopper.

"Hmm ... A pity you changed your mind." Molnár linked his arm through hers.

"No, really. I think it's for the best." She tried to free her arm from his, but he clasped her fingers in his and walked her toward the Romanians.

At some point, Hawk Nose had moved outside a souvenir storefront at the edge of the square. Eagle Eyes stood on the opposite corner of the street.

They'd formed a gauntlet. *Dear God, help.* They were waiting for her. She hugged the cell to her ear. "Jacob, we're headed toward the Romanians—"

Her high heel slipped between the metal bars over the grate, and Molnár stumbled on the pavement. His arm flew out, knocked the phone from her hand. It clattered as it hit the grate and slipped between the metal bars. Freeing her heel, she peered into the black hole below. How would she contact Jacob?

"Leave it." Molnár locked his arm around hers and stepped toward the waiting Romanians. "I'll take care of you, Miss Riley."

"That's very gallant." She lagged behind him, dragging her feet. "But those are the men who attacked Jacob in the cemetery."

"Have no fear. I will protect you."

"Please. Let me go." Molnár would be no match against the Romanians.

The crowd thinned, the last of the pedestrians parting like the Red Sea.

No one to block Hawk Nose from grabbing her now. "You don't understand. Those two men standing at the corners are here to kill me."

"Kill you? I don't think so."

"They're terrorists."

"My dear." Molnár retracted his chin against his neck. "That cannot be."

"I'm working with Interpol."

"Let me help you." He tightened his grip on her arm. "I have a place you can hide until your colleagues arrive. You are alone, yes?"

"Unfortunately."

With every step, he led her closer to the Romanians.

Her heart climbed into her throat. Ten more steps and she'd be trapped in their dragnet.

A dark-haired man in black slacks and shirt elbowed his way through the crowd and blocked her path. A camera with a telephoto lens hung around his neck.

Molnár stiffened. "Do you know him?"

"No."

Aiming the camera at her, the man snapped a shot. "Are you all right, Miss Williams?"

"Yes, she's fine." Molnár drew himself up like a bantam rooster. "But the man in the striped jersey at the street corner to your left is a known terrorist. She says he's here to kill her."

"Got it." The cameraman spoke into his wristwatch.

Why hadn't Molnár mentioned Eagle Eyes? She pointed a finger at the Romanian. "And the man on the other corner, too."

"Trust me, my dear." Molnár patted her hand. "He can only capture one of them."

As the cameraman ambled toward Hawk Nose, the Romanian bolted across the square. With his watch to his mouth, the cameraman jogged after him. Eagle Eyes disappeared down a side lane off the square.

"Come." Molnár hurried her back toward the cathedral, around the left side of the building.

Metal roundabouts crammed with souvenir hats, stuffed animals, and postcards blocked the doorways of several shops. But the area was deserted. Not a tourist in sight.

"You'll be safe here." He led her to a building beside an antiques store and gestured her inside the door.

"Thank you for rescuing me, but I need to return to the boat and prepare for tonight's performance."

"You mentioned two Romanians. Are you certain the other one left?"

With his arm still locked around hers, she glanced around the street. Even now Eagle Eyes could be circling around the block, heading her way.

"Come inside. Please. Before the other man finds you."

If she ran into Eagle Eyes again, he'd kill her. She walked beside Molnár up the dimly lit steps to the fourth floor. Of the two doors in the hall, one faced the front of the building, the other the rear. Judging from the stench of urine behind her, it was a communal toilet.

Molnár unlocked the door facing the street and motioned her inside. "Please."

A foul musty odor, as if an animal had died in the room, hung in the air. Dust motes clung to the sunlight streaming through the six-foot-high windows. Riley hesitated, then took two steps inside the apartment. He locked the door and pocketed the key.

There were no other doors which meant no bathroom. A round table and two chairs stood near the windows overlooking the street. An enormous eighteenth-century ceramic-tile heater dominated one corner of the room. The mattress on the unmade bed was lumpy and badly stained. She clutched the aria books to her chest like a paper shield.

"My friend's needs are simple."

Simple? The place was shabby, filthy. Amusement filled Molnár's eyes, the twitching of his lips. Sweat slicked her palms. What were his intentions? But he'd saved her from the Romanians, pointed out Hawk Nose to the undercover policeman. She tried to breathe deeply but couldn't. Not as long as she was alone in the room with Molnár.

Maybe she'd be safer on the street. "The other Romanian must've given up by now." She turned to go.

"Please." He gestured to the wooden chairs. "Sit." Despite his words, his tone held a command. "I assure you, your troubles will be over soon." His eyes had gone cold.

Her heart clobbered her chest. What had she gotten herself into? She sat on the edge of the chair across from him, feet facing the door, and forced herself to lock eyes with him. Isn't that what they taught in self-defense—stand tall, chin up, shoulders back—show no fear of your adversary?

"You disappoint me, Miss Williams. You had such a brilliant career ahead of you. But you looked—how you say—a horse in the mouth."

"Close enough." She'd pass on any gifts from him. He must be angry she'd cancelled the audition. "I have to achieve my success as a singer without a ... without assistance from a Sug—a benefactor. I'm sorry, I was so eager for a break. And today, I realized the truth."

"The truth? Hmm. That is too bad." Molnár flicked a speck of dried food from the stained tablecloth. "I must confess, my interest in you was genuine." His voice almost purred, his tone oily. "You are a very beautiful woman."

The inside of her mouth turned to cotton. If only she'd listened to Jacob. Now it was too late.

With measured steps, he walked behind her and enclosed her neck in his large hands.

Heat from his palms seeped into her skin. Beneath the pressure of his fingers, her pulse quivered like a cornered animal. She'd never be able to fight him off. "Take your hands off me."

"Such a pity. You'd have found me most generous." Molnár slid his hands to her shoulders. His fingers bit through her flesh, compressing her bones.

She clenched her teeth to keep from crying out.

A knock thumped at the door, and Riley flinched.

"Alas, it's too late now." He gave her shoulders a final squeeze then headed for the door.

Riley leapt from the chair and raced after him. She had to get out of there. Now.

In one swift move, he unlocked the door, and Sora Hosseni

blocked the doorway, a briefcase in her gloved hand, a Louis Vuitton purse over her shoulder.

Clad all in white, from high-heeled boots to leggings and cape, she resembled Emma Peele in *The Avengers*. But Sora Hosseni was no angelic avenger. More likely an angel of death.

"What's she doing here?" Circling her like a predatory feline, Sora skewered Riley from head to toe.

Heart thumping in her throat, Riley held her ground, Sora's heavy perfume washing over her.

"She's your bonus."

Bonus? "I was just leaving." Riley walked past Sora.

"I'm afraid not." Molnár locked the door, repocketed the key.

A chill shot through Riley. Without her phone she had no way to call for help.

"So, little man." Sora pivoted toward Molnár. "Have you got the vials?"

Every muscle in Riley's jaw slacked. Dear God, no. He must be Tudor.

Eyeing Sora's Vuitton bag greedily, he spread his hands. "Alas, no."

"What do you mean, no?" Sora gripped her bag.

"Miss Williams interrupted the transaction. But we'll meet as soon as I have the vials. Expect to hear from me tonight, or tomorrow at the latest."

Riley's feet froze to the floor. "You're a terrorist." *Oh Jacob, it's too late now.*

Lips retracted into an ugly snarl, Sora whirled on Riley, fingers poised to claw her. "I'm going to enjoy this."

Waves of dizziness swept through Riley. She backed toward the table. Her high-school self-defense course would be useless against Sora. "May I ask why a Hungarian would become a terrorist?"

Molnár shrugged. "Since you won't be around to talk, I suppose there's no harm in satisfying your curiosity."

"Sit." Sora pushed her into the chair.

"Working as a facilitator is quite lucrative." Molnár sat across from Riley, drummed his fingers on the table, the rhythm slow as a death knell. "But your foolish scene with the mime artist in the square ruined everything."

"You stupid, meddling little—" Sora whacked Riley's cheek.

Fire knifed through her face, her teeth, her jaw. At least she'd prevented the transfer of Agent X. But she wouldn't live to tell about it. "Then you knew Hawk Nose was one of the terrorists."

"Of course. At the café in Antwerp, you walked past me, returned my smile. The Romanians were there to meet with me, but I saw your reaction to them—you are not a subtle actress—and I had to cancel the appointment."

The phone call Eagle Eyes had received at the café. If only she'd ignored Molnár that day. "They said Tudor was in charge."

"They know me as Tudor. Naturally, that's not my real name. Having lived in Romania, you know many Hungarians are born in Transylvania."

Buying time wouldn't do her any good since no one knew where she was, but she probed anyway. "Brickley Landon is one of your men, too, isn't he?"

"That fool? I set up the meeting at the cemetery so you and Agent Coulter would distrust him. Despite advances in modern warfare, misinformation and divide-and-conquer are still highly effective strategies."

Oh, to slug Molnár, tell him what she thought of him. "Who planted the poison and Manuel's body in my room? How did you manage to be a step ahead of us every time?"

"You bugged the Hossenis' room, so while you danced away the evening with Khalid and me, I bugged your room." Molnár chuckled. "I'm not quite the doddering old man you took me for. I so enjoyed listening to your conversations, your vocalizing—well, I don't think I'll tell you everything."

How dare he violate her privacy. Everything she'd done or said had been heard.

"As for Manuel, Khalid took care of him and hung his body in your closet."

Shudders rippled across her shoulders. Khalid had been in her room.

Sora grated her throat. "Enough of this."

"And now my dear Miss Williams, your A and Q session is over. Sora's dying to get her hands on you."

Riley risked a glance at her killer, the woman's eyes devoid of humanity.

The promises Riley had made to others paraded through her mind. Her promise to Lacy to have that international opera career they'd dreamed about. Her promise to Frénie to cover the cruise job. Her vow not to marry. All her life she'd done what she wanted to do, what others wanted her to do. Not once had she asked God what He wanted for her.

Suddenly all of the goals, the promises, seemed futile. Had she wasted her life? Was this what God had intended for her? Now she'd never know, never get another chance to make the choices God had wanted. *Oh Lord, if only I could do things over. Forgive me for not letting You be in charge of my life, in charge of my promises to others.*

Molnár rose, and with a sickening courtly bow, kissed Riley's hand, his moist lips slicking her skin.

She yanked her hand free from his grasp.

"Good-bye, Miss Williams. I'm truly sorry. A pity you didn't stick to singing. But no man likes to be spurned. Your tenacity has cost you your life." Molnár gave Sora's Vuitton bag another lustful glance. "And now, I leave you in Sora's capable hands. She has a reputation for letting her victims suffer a slow, painful death. Perhaps, if you're lucky, she will make this quick." He rose and walked to the door.

"Wait." Riley dashed after him, but he slipped out. The key grated in the lock. She pounded her fists on the door, bloodying her knuckles. "*Hilfe, hilfe*, help, help."

"You're wasting your time. The building is vacant during the day." Sora set the briefcase on the table, pulled a gun from her purse. As she strode to the door, she screwed on a silencer. "By the way, I never did like your singing." She grabbed Riley by her hair, jabbed the cold metal silencer against her temple. "And you're a dreadful dancer."

Fiery needles seared Riley's scalp. She reached for her hair. "Well ... now my ballroom skills won't be a problem."

"Not for you." Sora dragged her backward from the door then released her.

Riley edged toward the windows, every inch of her scalp on fire.

Her assassin's mouth spread in one of those I've-got-you-right-where-I-want-you smiles.

Oh Frénie, Lacy, I'm sorry I let you down. Riley peered out the window. Four stories above the pavement. No awnings, no balconies, no ledges to break her fall.

Sora crossed toward her, stopped ten feet away. "Your choice. Jump, or I shoot you."

24

"Riley?" Scuffling sounded in the background of her call then a loud clattering rang in his ear. The line went dead. Jacob punched in her number. No answer. Even the GPS device he'd added to her barrette was silent. Could be a satellite communication malfunction. Or maybe interference from tall buildings around her. Pacing his assigned post back and forth, he dialed Interpol's local police liaison, filled the officer in. "How soon can you get men over to the square?"

"Five minutes."

Five minutes too late. Sweat broke out across Jacob's forehead. He described Riley's dress. The officer promised to call him back as soon as someone reached the Old Town Square. "Send me a squad car ASAP." Jacob disconnected then dialed Brick.

"Yo."

"Riley's in trouble. The terrorists are at Old Town Square."

"I'm on my way. Keep talking bro'."

Brick sprinted toward him from his post on the opposite corner of the European Parliament building. Jacob headed away from him, toward the street.

Seconds later, Brick snagged Jacob's sleeve. "Where do you think you're going?"

"To help Riley."

"You'll never get there in time. The Romanians have probably already eliminated her."

Jacob yanked free from Brick's grasp. "Where there are two terrorists, there are likely more. We've seen no one here all morning."

"You'd leave your post to save her when millions of lives are at stake? A suspected collaborator?"

"That tip you received the other day was a big fat red herring." Waving his ID, Jacob whizzed past the security guards at the entrance to the EU compound, Brick's loafers pounding the pavement beside him.

"What about your oath to Interpol, your promise to avenge Noel's death?"

Roof lights flashing, a police car pulled up to the entrance of the EU compound.

"I was wrong. Vengeance belongs to the Lord." Jacob dashed toward the car, Brick dogging his steps. "I can't live with losing someone else dear to me. As for Interpol ... Are you coming with me or not?"

"I'm not. Luring you there is the cleverest move they've made yet."

"You're wrong." Jacob climbed in the back seat of the police car. "Old Town Square. The sale's going down there. Right now."

The driver activated the siren but the singsong shrill failed to part the stream of vehicles. At the rate the car crawled forward, Jacob could've memorized every object in the shop windows. He rubbed his thighs. Flexed his fists. Walking would've been faster.

"Driver." He tapped the man's shoulder. "Try the sidewalk."

Jamming on the horn, the driver steered the vehicle onto the sidewalk. Pedestrians scattered into doorways and against the walls, some shaking fists at them. The car crept past the sidelined pedestrians, Brick's words echoing in Jacob's mind. *She's probably already dead. Already dead.* Jacob clutched his face in his hands. *Dear God, spare Riley. Please.*

"How much farther?"

The driver hiked his shoulders in a Gallic shrug. "Maybe four kilometers."

Two-point-four miles.

———

Is this how her life would end? Riley glanced out the apartment windows. Then fixed her gaze on her assassin. This was a woman who'd threatened to carve her skin into ribbons. "Is your offer for the jump still good?"

"Suit yourself." Sora tightened the silencer on her gun. "Either way, you die."

As Riley edged to the right side of the tall window, her ankle twisted on a hole in the floorboard. She reached up for the latch, the sweat on her fingers slicking the cold metal. "Mind telling me where you plan to release Agent *X*?"

Sora's eyes hooded, a cobra about to strike. "America will never be the same." She motioned Riley to the window with her weapon. "But you won't be around to see it."

"Guess not." Thankfully, she knew where she'd spend eternity. Riley gave the latch a tug. The wooden window frame screeched then shuddered open. Maybe, just maybe she'd survive the jump. Unless Sora riddled her body with bullets.

As if reading her mind, Sora aimed at Riley's chest.

———

Dear God, *please don't let me be too late.* Even though he'd left the EU as soon as her call from the square had been interrupted, anything could've happened since then. The GPS app on his phone beeped her cell's location, but his earpiece tuned to the frequency of her hair clip was still filled with static.

For the device to work, he'd need to get within a hundred yards of her location. A hundred yards with little ambient noise and fewer thick-walled buildings. Jacob hopped from the police car and ran down the walking street toward the Old Town Square, the two French policemen close behind him.

In front of the cathedral, three mimes were playing to a mesmerized crowd. A crowd that included Eagle Eyes, three rows back. Jacob signaled the two French policemen to his side. "That guy in a black leather coat is a Romanian terrorist. He's probably here to collect the vials."

As the two officers eased through the crowd, they formed a pincer move on Eagle Eyes.

A few yards ahead Molnár stood in front of the mime dressed like Charlie Chaplin. Cane in hand, Charlie seemed to be speaking to him. Molnár blanched.

The phone app beeped louder. Turning slowly, Jacob held the cell out and walked toward a metal grate in the center of the square. As he neared the grate, the red location icon pulsated on his phone. He flicked on its flashlight and shone it between the bars. At the bottom of the hole, his flashlight glinted on the shattered screen of Riley's cell phone.

How had her phone ended up in a hole, and where was she? He did a quick three-sixty.

Just then Molnár reeled back from the mime and staggered toward Jacob.

If only the guy would give him probable cause to have him arrested. A task he'd gladly perform while he was on loan to Interpol's police division.

The static he'd been hearing from the mic in Riley's hair clip died. If only she'd say something, give him a sense of which direction she might have gone. Pressing the earpiece deeper, he swerved left. Right. Then walked toward the cathedral.

"Does your offer to jump still stand?" Riley's voice, terse, shrill. *Oh God, no.* The terrorists had her.

Jacob ran toward the left side of the cathedral. *I'm coming, Riles, I'm coming.* Dear God, the last time he'd promised that, Noel had died.

Across from the cathedral, a fourth-floor window in the second building scraped open. Riles climbed up on the sill, her teal dress clinging to her legs, her bare feet wobbling on the wood. Clutching the right side of the window frame, she lifted her face toward the sky, bleak with gathering thunderheads. Her lips parted, moved as if in prayer.

A silent scream ratcheted through him. Waving his arms, he darted toward her. "Hang on Riles. Hang on." His anguished cries echoed off the buildings.

She blinked, looked toward him, her face pale as death. "Jacob?" Then her eyes widened. Feet tottering on the frame, she jabbed her left hand toward him. "Jacob. Watch out."

Footsteps pattered toward him, picked up speed.

Whipping his pistol from his shoulder holster, he whirled toward the sound.

Molnár's eyes held the calculating look of a seasoned commando. Gripping a dagger, he feinted to the left then lunged at Jacob.

With the finesse of a matador, Jacob sidestepped him and pistol-whipped Molnár's skull. Then he rammed the gun against the man's temple. "Drop the knife."

The dagger clattered to the pavement. Jacob kicked the knife aside and shoved Molnár to the ground.

With everything in him he wanted to bash the man's face. Finally, Sugar Daddy had given him an excuse to retaliate. Jacob fisted his hand over the guy's nose. Every muscle in his body urged him to punch, to pulverize Molnár's cartilage and flesh.

Evil radiated from every inch of the man. The vitriol in Molnár's eyes dared Jacob to strike.

Instead, Jacob sucked a breath. Loosened his fist. Dad was right. He'd almost crossed a moral line. Keeping his foot on Molnár's back, he holstered his pistol, cuffed the man's wrists and hauled him to his feet.

One of the police officers ran toward him, his handgun drawn.

"Call for backup." Jacob turned Sugar Daddy over to him. "Terrorists are upstairs." As he dashed up the stairs of the apartment building, memories of chasing Noel's assailants pelted his mind. A chase he'd lost. He rounded the second-floor landing. Then a bloodcurdling scream and a horrible thud sounded from the square below.

Dear God, no, no, no. He'd lost Riley too.

"HEY, Sora. You're too late. Jacob just arrested Molnár." Clutching the window frame with one hand, Riley thumbed her finger at the square below. "A policeman is leading him away."

The gun faltered in Sora's hand.

"Come see for yourself."

"You're lying."

"Nope. Scout's honor." Flashing two fingers Churchill-style, *V* for victory, she jumped down from the ledge, darted behind the closest chair. "Your days of murder are over."

"Not quite." Sora lifted her weapon. Aimed at Riley's heart.

Snatching the chair, Riley aimed its legs toward her assassin.

Sora swaggered toward her, stiletto-heeled boots clicking on the wood floor like the cock of a pistol.

Shifting the chair like a shield, Riley danced to the left. The right. How much longer could she hold out before Sora shot her?

As if tethered to her every feint, Sora's gun arm jerked, synchronized with each move Riley made.

Once again, Riley pivoted. Advanced toward Sora, thrusting

the chair left right, right left, forcing her toward the open windows.

A gust of air whipped her long hair across her face. Sora swiped the curtain of hair from her eyes, her heel trapped in the hole in the floorboard. Curses spewing from her mouth, she fired. The bullet tore through the side rung of Riley's chair.

Mustering her last dregs of energy, Riley lunged toward her assassin, shoved the chair at her gun hand.

A shot struck the ceramic heater.

How many bullets did it hold? Grunting, Riley thrust the chair at Sora again. The remaining rungs crunched into her torso.

The weapon struck the window frame and skittered across the floor. Grunting like an enraged animal, Sora tried to work her heel free of the hole. The stiletto broke, throwing her off balance. Toppling backward, arms flailing, she fell out the window, her shrieks piercing Riley's ears.

The last bit of adrenaline drained from her body and she dropped the chair. Sank to the floor. She hadn't meant to kill her. Disarm her, yes. But kill— Shudders convulsed Riley's body. Gulping great hiccups of air, she hugged her knees to her chest. Safe. She was safe now.

Someone rammed and bashed the door. The wood splintered and a foot thrust through the panel below the lock. More kicks and grunts, and the door burst open. Jacob rushed across the room and scooped her into his arms.

Crooking her arms around his neck, she sagged against the warmth of his chest, unable to control the shivers wracking her limbs. "Al—always gl—glad to see the ca—cavalry."

"Thank God you're okay." He buried his head in her hair, stifling sobs. "Oh Riles ... I thought I was too late."

The scent of his faded aftershave, his sweat, filled her nostrils. They'd both been through so much. But God had answered her prayers and given her a new chance at life. She stroked the length of his jaw. Strong. Incorruptible. Was he supposed to be part of that second chance?

"You're safe now." He lowered her onto Molnár's chair at the table. Called for police backup to remove Sora's body, then unzipped Sora's Vuitton bag and tilted it toward Riley. Banded stacks of five-hundred-euro banknotes filled the satchel. "Must be a hundred-million euros in here." Inside the briefcase, two small vial-shaped forms had been carved into the case's thick foam lining.

"Thank God she failed." Riley rubbed her arms. Today they'd come so close to death and mass destruction. "Molnár took my phone. How did you know where to find me?"

"You're going to hate me. The hair clip."

"What?" She removed the barrette and turned it over.

"I installed a miniature mic and GPS. Unfortunately, the GPS failed, and you have to be within a hundred yards to pick up a conversation."

Her jaw slacked. "You tricked me, spied on me."

"That clip saved your life." He reached for her hand, but she tucked it under the table. "Without that mic, I'd never have found you in time."

"You ... spied on me."

"I'm sorry Riles. Interpol insisted on proof you weren't working for the terrorists."

Beneath the table, she fisted her hands. She'd thought she could trust him. "Well? Are you satisfied I'm a loyal American?"

"Please believe me, I didn't want to do this."

"You haven't. Answered my question."

His glance shot to the left of her. "Yes."

Why didn't he look her in the eye when he said that? "Molnár is Tudor."

"You sure?"

"Yes. He not only admitted it, but said my scene in the square with that little pickpocketing Charlie Chaplin spoiled the transfer of the vials."

"That's great." Jacob squeezed her arms, but she held herself in check. "I always knew there had to be a better reason to slug Sugar Daddy than just his advances on you."

"Can I believe that? You seem to have issues with trust. And jealousy."

He raked his hand through his hair. "You've triggered feelings in me I've never felt for another woman."

"Relationships are built on trust."

"And forgiveness." He knelt beside her, rested his palm on her wrist. "Can you forgive me, Riles?"

She stared at her lap. Who was she to withhold forgiveness when God wiped her own slate clean every time she failed? "Yes, I forgive you."

"Thank you." He lifted her hand to his lips and kissed her fingers.

The sensation of his mouth electrified her skin, kindled flames along every fiber of her nerves. If only he'd take her in his arms and kiss her. Kiss her until she melted into a heap at his feet.

Instead, he stood. "Khalid can flee into hiding, and now we have no idea when or where or to whom Agent *X* will be sold."

"He may not know Sora's dead. Yet."

Footsteps pounded on the stairwell, and Paleface and a team of armed officers burst into the room.

Finally. The cavalry reinforcements had come. With everything in her, she longed to hunker in a corner and have a good cry. Preferably somewhere less seedy.

Jacob handed Paleface the Vuitton bag and filled him in. "We're heading to the boat to search Molnár's room."

"Good. Keep me posted. Have the French police drive you there and wait, in case you need backup. Nice work, Coulter. Both Romanians are in police custody."

"The kudos go to Miss Williams, sir. It was her courage and ingenuity that foiled the terrorists' plans."

"Hmm ..." Paleface stuck a fresh cigarette between his lips.

"Sir, if orders had been obeyed, Riley would be dead, every bidder would've escaped, and the vials would be in the bioterrorists' hands."

"Possibly."

The back of her eyes throbbed. If she weren't careful, she'd have to work on more forgiveness. But at least Jacob had defended her to his boss.

"Come on." Jacob's tone was more of a snarl. He nudged her toward the door. "Let's get out of here."

Outside Molnár's stateroom, Jacob paused and squeezed Riley's hand. "You okay?" Giving him an unconvincing nod, she edged closer to him, her face so wan he wanted to caress her cheeks until they pinked with color. Then plant a few kisses on them. How much more trauma could she take? "No, I mean really."

"Just envisioning what might happen if we don't find the rest of the bad boys or the vials."

"Hey, you're an over-the-rim girl, remember?" He chucked her under the chin.

"Uh-huh."

"C'mon, partner." Jacob grabbed Riley's hand. "We've got work to do, and there isn't much time. You watch for Khalid." He inserted the passkey into Molnár's door and motioned her inside the cabin. "We're looking for anything a normal passenger wouldn't carry."

"After seeing how disguised your listening devices were, that might be hard to spot."

"If in doubt, throw the stuff on the bed." Jacob took Molnár's suitcase from the closet, searched his clothing and papers, patted down the interior for hidden pockets.

Riley rummaged through his dresser drawers, held up a set of converter plugs, several ballpoint pens, three flash drives, a mouse. "What about these?"

"Electronic listening devices. Put them in your purse." Inside the closet he found a small black circle lodged in the crevice of the wall, another one flush with the lintel of the stateroom door. He pocketed his electronic wand and pried out the devices with his Swiss Army knife. "Minicams, state of the art. Either someone else was watching Molnár, or he wanted a record of anyone who entered his room."

"Which may mean someone knows we're in here."

"Possibly." Jacob knelt in front of the safe, held his electronic safe-cracking device near the keypad. "Check the bathroom, will you?"

"Where do you think Khalid is?" Riley called from the bathroom.

"Looking for Sora, the money, and Molnár." The last digit of the code registered, and the lock sprang open. Three passports, a set of earphones, and a small kit with miniature tools and jeweler's glue lay inside. "Bingo."

Riley knelt beside him. "Besides me, who was he listening to?"

"I dunno." Jacob flipped through the passports.

"I don't ever want to see the man again." She shuddered then returned to his bathroom.

"This guy gets around. Tudor Comenici, Romanian passport. Mikael Rackowitz, traveling on a Polish passport. Grigor Tcherpin, Russian passport." He pocketed the documents in his jacket. "Bring me his stuff from the bathroom, please." Wearing Molnár's earphones, he turned on the man's monitoring device.

A crash reverberated in Jacob's ear. "Ow." He tore off the earphones.

"Sorry. I dropped his can of shaving cream."

A sick feeling wormed through him. The sound shouldn't have deafened him. He leaned his forehead against the wall, squeezed his eyes. What a fool he'd been, trusting her, making her his partner. The whole thing had been a setup.

Like some dimwitted sucker he'd fallen for the classic honey trap. Today she'd lost her usefulness to the terrorists, botched Interpol's investigation, the transfer of the vials. No wonder Molnár had ordered Sora to kill Riley.

Tiptoeing toward her, he unholstered his gun and crept to the bathroom door.

25

R iley stared at the pistol in Jacob's hand, her mouth agape. "What are you doing?" Maybe he, and not Brick, was working for the terrorists.

"Put Molnár's things on the bed." He gestured her out of the bathroom with the weapon.

"Not until you put that gun away."

"Do as I say." He aimed the weapon at her heart. "Now." His voice was as icy as Sora's had been, his eyes glittering every bit as coldly as hers.

Had Jacob set her up? After all, he knew the most about being a double agent.

"I said, put those things on Molnár's bed."

"All right, all right." She stumbled toward the bedroom and tossed the items on the spread.

Waving the pistol at her, he motioned her into the bathroom.

Her legs turned to molten rubber. What was he planning to do to her?

"Get in there."

"Why are you doing this? If you're going to kill me, tell me why you're working for the terrorists."

"Me? Working for them? Lady, have you got things wrong.

Now get in there before I use this thing on you." He pushed her inside the doorway and blocked her exit. "You're wired for sound."

"Impossible." She shoved her hands inside her elbows.

"This gizmo doesn't lie." Yanking the electronic wand from his pocket, he brandished the detector at her. "Gimme your shoes."

Balancing on her left foot, then her right, she flung her high heels at him.

With the slowness of an MRI, he ran his detector over every inch of the leather, the soles, the heels.

This couldn't be happening. First she'd been given a choice of jumping out a window or being shot to death and now this. "Jacob Coulter, I swear when this is over—"

"Be quiet." He tossed the shoes into the bedroom then came closer. "Arms out."

No way was she stripping. He could go ahead and shoot her.

Starting at her feet, he ran the detector up the front and back of her legs, over every square inch of her dress, her arms, her hands.

This was worse than an airport security check. They were thorough, but they never treated her as if she were a criminal.

Then he moved the wand over her mouth. Paused it over her left ear. *Buzzbee.* Then the right one. *Buzzbee.* "Take off those earrings."

"They're twenty-four-karat gold. My parents gave them to me." She unscrewed the posts, handed him the earrings. "Don't you dare wreck them." Her bare feet thudded on the carpet as she followed him to the bedroom.

From his small toolkit, he chose a screwdriver, pried the backing off each earring and tweezered a tiny device from inside each gold disk onto his palm.

"What are those?"

"As if you didn't know."

"Jacob Coulter, you're the most infuriating man I've ever known. How should I know? You're the spy."

"So are you."

"I most certainly am not. And if they're all as stupid as you, I'm doubly glad I'm not one."

"Then how do you explain these listening devices?"

"How should I know?" She sat on the opposite side of the bed, as far away from him as she could get. "Maybe that's where Molnár went every night after he danced with me. Maybe he did a little work on them. Like you did on the hair clip."

Beet-red splotches bled across his cheeks. He hated to admit it, but she could be right. Best he could tell, Molnár's room was directly above Riley's cabin. The next-best place to monitor her conversations.

"Or maybe Sora bugged my earrings. I thought she left the lounge because she couldn't stand to see her husband clutching me in his arms." Riley shoved her feet into her shoes. "How come you aren't searching my purse?"

"Because I've checked it for bugging devices every day."

She jerked to her feet, slapped her fists on her hips. "You what?"

Voices murmured in the hall. Jacob put a finger to his mouth.

"What if it's Khalid?" She grabbed her purse.

CASTING GLANCES AT HER, Jacob kept his gun aimed at the door. Whose side was Riley on? The mounting evidence pointed to her complicity with the terrorists.

"Jacob, I swear I'm not working for them. I don't know what I can do or say to convince you, but they'll kill us both."

Either she was a superb actress or the innocence in her tone was real. But which was it? "Put Molnár's toiletries and his clothing in his suitcase."

"You really are into—"

"It's evidence." He moved to the bathroom doorway for a clear shot at whoever entered the room.

Riley packed the suitcase and zipped the bag. "This ought to attract attention."

"Oh, I don't know ... after your arrival on the boat spattered with mud, people probably won't look twice."

"Very funny." She stuck out her tongue at him.

How could he take her seriously as Molnár's accomplice when she acted like an eight-year-old?

"What now?"

"At this point, we're ad-libbing. Guess you don't do that in opera."

"You bet we do, if we forget our words. Are we going to wait here all afternoon? I have a performance tonight."

With his ear to the doorjamb, he listened for the sound of voices. Movement. The hall had gone silent. "Ladies first."

Her jaw slacked. "You're kidding."

"Nope. If you're Khalid's accomplice, you'll be safe enough for the moment, if he spots you. Probably." Jacob motioned her to the door. "I'll be right behind you."

"Oh. I'm the shark bait."

"At the moment, you're the one most likely to walk down that hall and stay alive."

"Wanna bet?" She started for the door.

"Don't forget your luggage."

She rolled the suitcase to the door, her face muscles pinched in disgust. "What did I ever see in you?" Squaring her shoulders, she unlocked the door, peered into the hallway then left the room.

Jacob counted to three then followed her.

At the lower-level deck, she rolled the suitcase through the staff's quarters, left it outside Jacob's cabin then headed toward her room.

"Wait up." In three sprints, he was at her side. "We stick together."

Sparks flashed from her eyes. "I have to clean up for tonight's performance. Alone."

"After I check your room, your possessions."

"Considering your other accusations today, I guess I can handle the humiliation."

Once inside her cabin he checked her room for webcams and listening devices. "I need to examine all of your jewelry."

"Yes, *Mein Führer*." She jerked open her top drawer, dropped her jewelry pouch on his palm. "Search away."

Inside lay two bangle bracelets, a pearl-encrusted cross on a silver chain, and the sparkly earrings she wore during her performances. Somehow he couldn't imagine Sora, a terrorist, wearing a cross. Who was Riley, really?

He wanded the bracelets and necklace. On the diamond-rimmed edges of the earrings, the detector's LED lights and alarm went wild. In the lens viewfinder, a red light pinpointed the location of the mics. Two of them in each earring, embedded among the diamonds.

Using his pocketknife, he pried them out, dislodging several diamonds. No larger than the head of a pin, the mics were state-of-the-art devices used for clandestine government ops. Clearly, Sugar Daddy was no amateur.

She sank on the bed, her mouth agape. "I hope you realize how expensive those earrings were."

"Sorry, Riles." She seemed so shocked. Maybe she wasn't working for the terrorists. If she turned out to be innocent, he had to make up the destruction to her.

"Please leave. I need to get ready for my performance tonight."

"I'll be in my room if you need me."

"Need you? Ha." She escorted him to the door and locked it behind him.

Once inside his cabin, he wanded it for bugging devices then phoned Schwarz and brought him up to date. "Any developments in Strasbourg?"

"No sign of Khalid. The contact person, Charlie Chaplin, has probably gone underground."

Which meant he was no closer to finding Noel's killer than he was three weeks ago.

"What's your assessment of the situation, Coulter?"

"When the boat sails without Sora, Khalid will know something has happened. As long as Khalid's on the boat, Riley isn't safe. I'm not sure I can protect her tonight."

"So, who is she working for?"

"I ... I think, for us." With all his heart, he wanted this to be so. "She's a good actress, but her surprise at my finding the listening devices in her earrings seemed genuine. Right now, she's so furious with me, I doubt she'll let me try to help her."

"Wish we knew what this Charlie Chaplin really looks like." Schwarz cleared phlegm from his throat.

"When Charlie finds out Sora and her money are gone, he may refuse to give the vials to Khalid. We could end up with a turf war on French soil."

"Since Sora was at the Old Town Square in Strasbourg, Khalid may have been there too. He may know about her death." The click of a cigarette lighter sounded over the phone. "Khalid might murder Riley for revenge."

Jacob's gut triple-knotted. *Dear God, please don't let anything happen to her.*

"We need Riley alive as a witness in court. She's also the best bait we have to draw out any terrorists connected with this plot."

Bait? Jacob punched his fist into an imaginary Schwarz. How could the guy call a civilian, a woman, bait? But then, hadn't he done the same thing to her, coming out of Sugar Daddy's room?

"Your orders are to make sure they don't kill her."

"I'll do my best."

"See that you don't fail." Schwarz disconnected the call.

Nothing like a few more notches of pressure. Dinner might be very interesting tonight. Jacob showered, changed into his waiter's black shirt and slacks, then rapped the first measures of the hymn, "I Need Thee Every Hour," on Riley's door.

Far too many seconds later, she opened the door. Her black lace evening gown tastefully accentuated every delicious curve of her body.

"Wow. Do you own a different gown for every night of the cruise?" Idiot. Why hadn't he told her how stunningly beautiful she looked?

"Yes." Her tone was stiffly polite. "For singers, it's a uniform."

At least she was speaking to him. "You look gorgeous."

"Thank you."

An inch of frost seemed to have thawed. "May I come in?"

Riley hesitated, looked away. "I guess so." She stood back and let him ease past her into the cabin.

"My supervisor has ordered me to be your bodyguard."

"Great. So now I'm worth protecting."

"I can't do that while I'm waiting tables. Would you mind wearing the hair clip tonight? I'd hear you scream if you need help."

Her posture went rigid. "Who do you think is going to attack me tonight?"

"Khalid. If he's arrogant enough to return to the boat."

"I tossed the barrette in my purse." She went to the bathroom and applied her lipstick. "You might as well dig it out since you search my bag every day." Icicles dripped from her tone. "I use an evening bag during the performances. Have you been checking that purse too?"

"No." He removed Molnár's listening devices from her day bag, set them on her desk then ran his hand inside the soft leather. "Given how I treated you this afternoon, I'm surprised you didn't throw the clip overboard."

"I considered it."

As he searched an inner pocket, his fingers enclosed over several black-lidded cylinders. Stretching the opening of her purse wide, he held the bag to the light. "Riles, come here."

"Yes?" She strolled over to him, her hips swaying like a siren.

"Look." Hoarseness stole his voice. He shoved the open purse toward her face.

Chanel No. 5 wafted from her throat as she peered inside. "What are those?"

"That. Is Agent X."

26

The shock on her face, her mouth working like a guppy, the pallor—all seemed genuine. How he wanted to believe her, trust her completely.

"How did the vials get in there?" Backing away from him, she sank on her bed then hunched over her knees. "Now you'll never believe I'm not working for the terrorists." Her voice hollowed. "And—and my bugged earrings—I had no idea. Those fiends were using me, and I didn't even know it."

"Didn't you say Charlie Chaplin robbed you?"

"Yes. Ten euros. He must've pickpocketed me to cover up leaving the vials in my purse." Curls fell about her shoulders as she lifted her head. "That's what Molnár meant.

"When I yelled at Charlie, accusing him of being a pickpocket, everyone focused on him. If the police had searched him, he couldn't afford to have the vials on him. But he didn't have time to tell Molnár the vials were in my purse. Right after that, Molnár walked me toward the Romanians. If they had snatched my purse, it wouldn't have put us on Charlie's trail."

"Sounds plausible."

She balled her fists on the mattress. "Those vials make me even more popular, don't they?"

"Yes." Acid fired a pit in Jacob's stomach. "You have any rubber gloves?"

"You're in luck." She took a pair of clear plastic gloves from her cosmetic case. "In case you're wondering, I use them to apply depilatory to my legs."

"Oh." He almost wished she hadn't had any gloves. Having a pair added one more piece of circumstantial evidence against her. With one hand gloved, he carefully inserted a vial inside the other glove, added the second vial then tied off the wrist opening. Then he took off his glove, crammed the wrapped vials inside it and pocketed them.

Riles leaned against her dresser drawers. "What if ... what if we pour out the poison and fill the vials with water? I could offer them to the highest bidder."

"Yeah, right. Schwarz would love the idea." Jacob's voice was morose. "It's too dangerous."

"I'm volunteering to be the bait. As long as you exchange the poison for water."

No one working for the terrorists would suggest pouring the poison down the drain. "I need to call in a Hazmat team to do that. This stuff is deadly. One drop spills and—"

"What are you waiting for? I have to sing in twenty minutes."

"I'm on it." He phoned Schwarz. "We have the vials." Then he told him Riley's idea.

"Great plan."

Jacob gripped the phone so hard he thought the plastic casing would crack. Riles meant nothing to Schwarz. Nothing more than the proverbial means to Interpol's desired outcome. "Unless you get a Hazmat team onboard to exchange the vials for ones with water, she refuses to do this."

"Rather hard to do with your boat underway and a monster storm heading along your route. Or hadn't you noticed."

"I'll arrange with the captain to stop the boat in the middle of the night."

Schwarz said nothing.

"Sir, as long as Agent *X* is on this boat, with only one Interpol agent and Khalid possibly onboard, the situation is highly volatile."

"Brick just called me. Said he saw Khalid board seconds before the boat left the dock."

An invisible sucker-punch hit his gut. Jacob covered the phone, whispered the news to her.

Beneath her makeup, her skin went chalk-white.

"Sir, how soon can you get a Hazmat exchange set up?"

"I'll call as soon as I have definite information. In the meantime, alert the captain."

The phone went dead.

"What's the plan, Kemosabe?" She dug in her purse, pulled out his hair clip and fastened it in her curls.

"Keep you alive."

"I mean Agent *X*. If Khalid knows or suspects Charlie gave me the vials ..."

Jacob's hands went clammy. The assassin would abduct her and use her as a hostage to force him to give up the vials.

"It's going to be okay." She squeezed his wrist, the pressure somehow reassuring. "God has brought us this far."

"Yeah, well, right now I'm having a few trust issues."

"You don't still doubt me, do you?"

"No, no I don't." It was himself he didn't trust. He'd failed to reach her in time today. If God hadn't intervened, Riles would be dead now. "I wish we had an entire team onboard to keep you safe."

"Well, we don't. So if anything happens to me ..." One by one she wove her fingers between his, hers warm against the chill of his skin. "Protect those vials at any cost. You understand me?"

"You don't know what you're saying."

"After facing death today, yes, I do. You've got to promise me to put your duty first."

"I don't know if I can do that."

"You took an oath, didn't you? Our country's at stake. Life is a precious gift. But sometimes life has to be the gift we give others." She hugged her evening bag and the music to her chest and walked to the door. "It's time for my first set. You're supposed to be making arrangements with the captain. Are you armed?"

"Ankle holster. Knife in the pants pocket."

"That's comforting. What are you going to do with the vials?"

"Try to get the captain to put them in his safe."

"And if he won't?"

A swell slammed the boat, rocking it like a cradle cut loose from its stand. He grasped her elbow and steadied her. "I'll worry about that if the situation—"

"Hey." She jabbed him in the ribs. "I thought you said a good agent always has a Plan B."

"Yeah, well, I never said I was a good agent."

"They don't come any better." She stroked his cheek, her touch velvety against his freshly shaven skin. "Or braver."

The tenderness in her eyes nearly undid his determination not to pull her to him, kiss her until they ran out of kisses then somehow spirit her off the boat to somewhere safe. Instead, he traced his fingertips along her arm. "You have to understand Riles, my job has conditioned me to be suspicious of everyone. Will you forgive me for not trusting you?"

Tears spilled over her lashes. "Yes. I forgive you." Swallowing hard, she dabbed at the wetness. "What do I say if Khalid asks for the vials?"

"He won't say pretty please."

"Do I tell him I have them?"

"Do or say whatever you have to, to stay alive, and buy time for me to reach you. I'll be wearing an ear transmitter. Hopefully people think it's a hearing aid."

"Better take it out while I'm singing, or you might be permanently deafened." She gave him that saucy grin. "Then you wouldn't hear me call for help."

RILEY FINISHED her second set and acknowledged the warm applause from the bench. Every seat in the lounge was occupied, perhaps stirred by end-of-cruise nostalgia. Blowing rain lashed the panes with a vengeance. Earlier, the captain had announced the river level had risen three feet. If this kept up, Interpol would never be able to pick up the vials.

Gathering her skirt in her hand, she headed for the ladies' restroom.

As she neared the entrance, Khalid stepped from behind a marble pillar and grabbed her arm.

She stifled a gasp. Dear God, where was Jacob?

With his free hand Khalid squeezed her fingers and drove them back from her palm until she wanted to shriek. "I think you know where Sora is."

"How could I?" Riley gritted her teeth against the pain. Sweat trickled down the inside of her evening gown. Any second now, he'd feel the dampness on the fabric, know she was lying. "Let go of me."

"Miss Williams, are you all right?" Jacob came toward her, his tray of fresh drinks balanced on one palm.

The boat shifted violently to starboard, and she fell against Khalid. His head slammed the marble pillar. Blood trickled on his collar. His grip on her arm loosened, and she staggered free from him.

Jacob's drinks wobbled on his tray as he shifted left and right, his eyes fixed on her.

This would be the first time she'd thanked God for violent weather. "Excuse me, I must go now."

"We shall speak later." Khalid swiped at his scalp, his fingers bloody.

"This is the captain speaking." Lundstrom's voice cut through the crackling PA system. "Due to the unusual violence of this storm, dancing is canceled for the evening. In an effort to prevent injuries, I am requesting all passengers return to their cabins immediately after dinner."

Once outside the lounge, she locked herself in a small unisex lavatory. Only one more set of songs and she could escape to her cabin. Not that she'd be safe there. Not with Khalid on the boat. She did a few deep-breathing exercises. Five seconds before she was due onstage, she returned to the piano and began her third set.

After Riley's third song, Mrs. Ackelroyd rose from her front-row seat. Tonight, she'd poured herself into the lamé dress again, the ubiquitous flower pin in her beehive hairdo. The rings on every finger, bracelets covering every square inch of her forearms, looked as if she'd prepared to abandon ship.

She sashayed on her stilettos across the lounge to Captain Lundstrom then turned, her lips moving as she pointed toward Riley. Then his mouth gaped. Mrs. Ackelroyd pouted, cocked her head to one side then the other. Another pout.

Oh no, what was the woman cooking up?

The captain's hands spread in a placating gesture. Mrs. Ackelroyd pouted again, said something. Seconds later his head dipped in a half nod. With a smug look on her face, she returned to her chair then flashed Riley a sneaky smile.

The notes blurred on the page. Riley's fingers fumbled for the chords. Somehow, she made it through her final set. Applause erupted and she rose from the bench and bowed. Maybe she could get away before—

Mrs. Ackelroyd rushed to the piano. "My dear, I have wonderful news."

"Oh?" Riley gathered her music.

"You'll be dining with us tonight. At the captain's table."

The saliva fled her mouth. If the Ackelroyds were assigned to the captain's table, then Khalid would be there too. "That's very sweet of you, but I don't think staff are allowed—"

"Everything's arranged. The captain's thrilled to have you."

I'll bet. "You're too kind."

"Nonsense, my dear. You've become like a daughter to us."

A shudder crept across her shoulders. With parents like the Ackelroyds, she'd rather be an orphan.

Looping her arm around Riley's, Mrs. Ackelroyd walked her downstairs to the dining room. "You and our nice waiter make such a charming couple."

Riley's feet melted in her shoes.

The seat between the captain and Khalid was vacant. The next two chairs at Khalid's side were empty. Mr. Ackelroyd and a couple whose name Riley couldn't remember, probably because the husband had danced with her only once, had joined the group. Mrs. Cochran sat on the captain's left.

Khalid's gaze seemed to flick between her and Mrs. Ackelroyd, a grim smile playing at his lips.

"Is anything wrong, my dear?"

"I—I think I need to go to my room and lie down."

"Don't be absurd. What you need is a good meal. Get some protein in you." She patted Riley's hand. "Too bad you don't get to dance with all those dreamy men tonight."

Dreamy? Definitely not how she'd describe her dance partners. Riley steeled herself. If she left now, Khalid would be even more suspicious.

Jacob stood near the table, his face ashen.

Hopefully he'd be nearby because dinner would be fraught with conversational death traps.

"Come along, my dear." Mrs. Ackelroyd walked her to the table like a prisoner being led to the gallows.

An internal fist cut off her air. Riley's legs almost refused to cooperate, her ankles wobbled in her heels. Trying for a smile, the corners of her mouth refused to budge. She pulled out the chair next to Mr. Ackelroyd.

"Oh no. That's my place." Mrs. Ackelroyd gave Riley a little push. "You sit on the other side of our dear, dashing Khalid."

Trying for a demure look in his direction, Riley sat beside him, her heart pounding so hard he probably heard the thumps.

She laid her beaded clutch on the tablecloth. Tucked her fingers beneath her thighs to conceal their shaking.

Jacob leaned over Riley's shoulder and poured her a goblet of water. "How long will you be staying?"

"Mrs. Ackelroyd kindly had me invited to dinner." Riley ignored his breaths fuming on her cheek.

"There, Captain, didn't I tell you this would be a smashing dinner party?" Mrs. Ackelroyd beamed at her as if Riley were Her Majesty, The Queen. "A diva at our table."

"Hmm." The captain's assent sounded more like a growl.

"Sir, I really prefer not to eat during a performance ..." *C'mon, Captain, please, please throw me out.*

"But this is a special occasion," Mrs. Ackelroyd said.

"It is?" Riley lifted her water goblet to her mouth.

"Our night at the captain's table." Mrs. Ackelroyd clasped her bejeweled hands and laid her overly rouged cheek against her fingertips. "If only our dear, dear János were here."

Water caught in Riley's throat.

Khalid perked up. "Yes, where is he?"

"Ask Riley." Mrs. Ackelroyd whipped her napkin onto her lap. "She was with him at the Old Town Square today."

"Careful, ma'am." Jacob set a bowl of roasted red-pepper soup on Riley's service plate. "The bowl is extremely hot."

"Thank you." Surviving this dinner would be more dangerous than crossing Niagara Falls on a tightrope without a pole and a safety harness.

"So, Miss Williams." Khalid's hawk-like gaze pinned her, a field mouse trapped in his talons. "Where is Molnár?"

"I—I have no idea."

"But I saw you leave the square with him." Mrs. Ackelroyd slurped her soup. "After you accused that mime artist of pickpocketing. Did he truly rob you?"

"Yes, he stole ten euros from my—me." Riley plopped her hand on the table, rattling the crystal. "Can you imagine that? And such a talented impersonator, too."

His eyes narrowed to gun slits, Khalid stroked his forefinger over his lips.

Right now, a stroll through a mine field might be less risky. Riley forced down a spoonful of the soup.

"But you haven't answered my question, dear." Mrs. Ackelroyd tapped Riley's wrist. "Where did János take you, and why isn't he here?"

"Captain." Mrs. Cochran grasped his arm, sloshing his soup on his white jacket, gaping at him as if he were Attila the Hun. "You've sailed without one of your passengers."

The captain's cheeks matched the color of the soup. "Yes. I know." He dabbed his napkin at the stains on his clothes. "Alas, company policy prohibits us straying from our schedule, madame."

"Two passengers, actually," Mrs. Ackelroyd said. "Unless Sora isn't well. Did she stay in the cabin, Khalid?"

"My wife wasn't there, or in the lounge." Khalid's face darkened. "She isn't answering her phone."

Riley almost breathed a sigh of relief. Since Khalid didn't know about Sora's death, maybe they'd survive tonight, after all.

Giving him a sly smile, Mrs. Ackelroyd tsked. "Oh dear, a lovers' quarrel?"

One sharp intake of breath and Khalid's chest puffed like a peacock. "No, no."

"But my dear boy ..." Mrs. Ackelroyd jutted her bosom in his direction, revealing far too much décolleté, and waved her soup spoon at him. "I've seen that look Sora gives you when you dance with Riley."

Locking eyes with Riley, Jacob cleared Mr. and Mrs. Anonymous's bowls and service plates.

If only he could whisk her away too.

"And now, my lovely girl." Mrs. Ackelroyd turned to Riley. "Where did you go with János?"

"Window shopping." Oops. Wrong analogy.

"But ..." Mrs. Ackelroyd tapped her finger on her chin. "I saw Sora follow you and János."

Riley forced herself to meet Mrs. Ackelroyd's gaze. "Perhaps she was shopping for souvenirs." Swiveling toward Khalid, Riley tried for an innocent glance. "Does your wife collect them?"

"No. She collects trophies."

As in shrunken heads? Riley heaved a drama-queen sigh. "Mr. Molnár and I didn't see any trophy shops."

An I'm-not-buying-this smirk slid across Khalid's lips.

Leaning over her right side, Jacob removed her service plate. "Will you be staying for the main course, Miss Williams?"

She could've grabbed his neck and kissed him for bailing her out. "No, thank you. It's been delightful." As she grabbed her evening purse, she glanced at Khalid.

The assassin's eyes held the hungry look of a lion about to pounce on his prey.

Her diaphragm froze, locking out her breath. If he followed her, she didn't stand a chance of surviving. If she left, they might never uncover any other bidders or bring them to justice.

"Have a nice evening." Jacob pulled back her chair.

"On second thought, I'll stay for the main course." Maybe her last course. Ever. Ignoring Jacob's eyes bugging at her, flipping between are-you-insane and we'll-never-get-out-of-this-alive, she unclasped her purse. "It's time we cut the pretense." She pulled out two small, black-lidded glass vials and set them on the white tablecloth. "I understand some of you are interested in acquiring Agent X. Bidding is now open."

27

W hat had Riley been thinking? She must've used the little vials he'd found the first day in her makeup bag.

The atmosphere around Jacob crackled with electricity. Conversations and laughter from the surrounding tables suddenly seemed a galaxy away. Every muscle fiber in his body twitched, poised for action. He bent close to Riley's ear, felt for his pistol in his ankle sheath. "I thought singers rehearsed stuff before they performed."

"Not low-budget productions." Riley rapped her fist on the table like a gavel. "Now. What am I bid for these vials?"

The captain's face paled, his eyes alert.

"My, my. What do we have here?" Mrs. Cochran looked ready to salivate.

Their eyes wide as half-dollars, Mr. and Mrs. Anonymous squirmed in their chairs.

Nostrils flaring, breaths coming in rapid puffs, Khalid was a volcano about to erupt.

With a mixture of incredulity and grudging respect, Mr. and Mrs. Ackelroyd eyed the vials, then Riley.

Every hair on Jacob's arms stood to attention. Too bad Riles hadn't thought of a simpler way to force Khalid's hand. But she'd uncovered the other bidders too. He slipped his knife from his pocket and tucked the weapon behind his back. Using his pistol would be preferable, but with so many guests in the room, a knife might be safest.

Without warning, Mr. Ackelroyd jumped to his feet and reached for the vials.

Before Jacob could shield Riley from Ackelroyd, she snatched the vials from the table. "Where's my money?"

"You little tart." Spittle flew from Mrs. Ackelroyd's mouth. "Those vials belong to us."

"I think not. You don't look like terrorists to me."

Mrs. Ackelroyd snorted. "You're as lousy a broker as you are a dancer."

Ouch.

"True. But I have the vials."

Fingering her teased mane, Mrs. Ackelroyd hoisted her hair doodad an inch. "I'll have you know we represent the largest terrorist cells in the UK."

Mr. and Mrs. Anonymous shrank in their seats.

So much for the captain's dictum of happy passengers.

Like a gunslinger at a crooked poker game, Lundstrom moved his hands to the tablecloth, his gaze narrowed on the players.

From the other side of the table, Khalid toyed with his dinner knife, observing them through half-lidded eyes, a Bengal tiger biding his time.

Jacob shifted his weight onto the balls of his feet, waiting for their first move.

"Give me those vials." Mr. Ackelroyd whipped a gun from inside his jacket and aimed it at Riley. "Now."

Her shoulders flinched. "Nope. Not until I have your bid. And the money."

"Dear God, help." Mr. Anonymous clutched his wife, cowering in her chair.

"Riles. Give him the vials." Keeping his knife-bearing hand behind him, Jacob stepped toward Ackelroyd. If only she'd listen to him, just this once.

Instead, she flashed the man a catch-me-if-you-can grin and held up one of the bottles, shook it in her fingers like a bell.

Without waiting, Jacob lunged for Ackelroyd, jabbed the knife at the man's gun wrist. The blade connected with bone and flesh. Blood spurted from the wound, splattering Jacob, the carpet.

"Aieeee." Ackelroyd's weapon fell to the carpet.

Jacob shoved him to the ground, pocketed his knife, and cuffed the man.

Without missing a beat, Lundstrom dashed for the weapon and picked it up.

"You'll never get away with this." Ackelroyd squirmed, hunched his knees to his chest, donkey-kicked Jacob in the abdomen.

Fire shot through his gut, knocking the air from his lungs. Groaning, he careened backward and crashed on the table, scattering the dishes.

In a flash, Mrs. Ackelroyd plucked the flower pin from her hair and plunged the four-inch needle-sharp tip toward his heart.

"No!" Riley leapt from her chair and locked the woman's neck in a chokehold.

Jacob grasped her forearm, tried to deflect her aim.

"Drop the pin." Riley tugged her backward and squeezed her larynx.

Gurgling sounds came from the woman's throat. The hairpin fell from her hand and plunked onto the tablecloth.

Struggling to catch his breath, Jacob lumbered to his feet and cuffed her while Lundstrom trained the weapon on Ackelroyd, moaning and writhing on the floor.

With the swiftness of a cat burglar, Khalid snatched the vials from the table and dashed behind the captain.

Jacob barreled toward him, knife in hand. No way was Hosseni escaping.

Before he could reach the killer, Lundstrom bashed the terrorist's head with the butt of the gun. Khalid slumped to the floor, unconscious. Jacob cuffed him, took the weapon from the captain.

The dining room was deathly still. Lundstrom phoned for the security officer and the staff captain then switched on the microphone. "Ladies and Gentlemen, it seems we've had some unscheduled entertainment tonight."

Nervous titters rounded the room.

"Was this one of those murder-mystery cruises?" Mrs. Cochran's voice quavered.

"Explorer Cruises is always looking for innovative ways to make our trips memorable." Lundstrom's nervous chuckle hollowed. "Champagne is on the house. When you've finished dessert, please retire to your rooms until the storm has passed."

At the arrival of the security officer and the staff captain, Lundstrom motioned toward Khalid and the Ackelroyds. "Take these people to my office. Under no circumstances are you to uncuff them or leave them alone."

Riley collapsed in Jacob's arms. "Never again will I describe my opera roles as death-defying."

Curling his arms around her, he snugged her so tightly against his chest the *thump thump thump* of her heartbeats pulsed against his. "Thank God, you're okay. I thought I was going to lose you."

Breath by breath, the tremors in her body eased and her heartbeat synchronized with his.

He buried his head in her freshly shampooed hair. Inhaled the scent of her Chanel No. 5, wafting from behind her ears. "It's over, Riles. The vials are in the captain's safe. If the storm calms enough for the helicopter to land, we'll be ready to exchange them. If not, first thing in the morning, we'll be free of Agent *X* and the prisoners."

She looked up at him, dug her chin into his chest. Tears welled in her eyes. "You did it, Kemosabe. You stopped them."

He stroked the tears from her cheek. "No, we did it."

28

Day 11: Breisach am Rhein

S tifling a yawn, Riley waited for Jacob at the stern. The scent of sodden earth clung to the morning chill. Fallen branches from last night's storm littered the grassy knoll. Shortly after dawn, two crew members had tied off the *River Nymph* at the dock below Breisach am Rhein. A Hazmat van and a SWAT team were already dockside.

She adjusted the collar of her white blouse over her navy sweater, neatened the fabric tucked inside her seersucker slacks she'd changed into last night after Khalid and the Ackelroyds had been escorted to the captain's office.

The night hadn't seemed long, staying with Jacob in the captain's office. Apart from her bedside vigils, it was the most hours she'd spent with him since they'd met. She'd been too keyed up to sleep. Besides, her cabin held too many unpleasant memories, invasions of her privacy, a dead body.

Still dressed in his waiter's uniform, Jacob joined her at the railing, two mugs in his hands. He looked as tired as she felt. "We just searched the Ackelroyd's cabin. Found syringes and a vial of poison under a false top label of insulin.

"Interrogation will probably confirm one of them poisoned Frénie and me and planted the other vial of poison and syringe in your dresser drawer. Captain Lundstrom verified they were passengers on the previous cruise when Frénie became ill." He gave her one of the mugs.

"It's hard to believe people can be so evil." She inhaled the smell of the freshly brewed coffee, letting its steam warm her face, then sipped. "Do you suppose they hoped to get one of their cell members hired to replace her?"

"Very likely. But Lundstrom told us the morning Frénie was hospitalized, she recommended you and that day the captain announced to the passengers a replacement performer had been hired."

The mug clutched in both hands, she sagged against the railing. "Finally, tonight we can focus on our jobs without worrying about terrorists and vials of Agent X."

"Yeah." He sidled closer to her.

On the sidewalk beside the *River Nymph* stood a flower-seller's cart with a red-and-white striped awning. The hunchbacked woman hawked red roses to the passengers disembarking to see the town. Amazing, the gimmicks locals used to engage tourists. Every piece of the flower-seller's outfit, the black dress and white lace collar, black stockings and clunky brogues, belonged in a museum.

Heat from the mug seeped into her palm. The last day of the cruise. The last day to decide about her career, her relationship with Jacob. "In less than twenty-four hours we dock in Basel."

He rubbed a hand over the straw-colored stubble on his jaw. "Guess you're pretty excited about not having to dance every night, getting back to singing opera and those high notes."

"Like every opera singer, I've had to fend for myself in a cutthroat world. On the surface, they're polite colleagues, but scads of young hopefuls lurk in the wings. Your understudy, or choristers, hoping you'll crack on those high notes, or come down with laryngitis."

"You like having those worries?"

"No, but I love to sing. And I promised Lacy ..." But yesterday she'd told the Lord He could be in charge of her life. What did He want her to do? She had to earn a living. "The thought of a nine-to-five job in an office breaks me out in hives."

"Can you live happily ever after if you don't become a household name to opera lovers?"

"Yes. Those minutes in Molnár's apartment made me realize there are more important things in life."

"Like what?"

Like a relationship with you. Like marriage and children. Instead, she said, "While I waited for Sora to kill me, I realized I was pursuing an opera career to keep my vow to my sister. But I'd never asked God what He wanted me to do with my life. Whether or not I pursue that career is now in His hands."

He broke into a grin. "That's awesome."

"How about you? Will you return to your desk job, or stay a field operative?"

"I don't know. That decision may not be up to me."

"Do you like undercover work?"

He shrugged. "I took this job because I wanted to avenge Noel's death, capture his killers, and keep Agent X off the streets. Even as kids, Noel and I dreamed of living out adventures. That's part of what made us pals.

"All I know is that God needs to be in control of my life. If that's in the field, I'll obey. And if I'm to return to the desk job, that's okay by me, too." He sipped his coffee. "But whoever masterminded this crime is still at large and probably plotting his next terrorist coup."

"I know how badly you want to solve this case, but we don't always get everything we want in life. You have the vials. And you spoiled the terrorists' plans to use Agent X."

"No way am I accepting defeat. Compromise." He tossed the remainder of his coffee into the river. "Noel's killers must be brought to justice. And whoever betrayed him to the terrorist cell."

"I agree." With everything in her, she prayed his goals would be fulfilled. She elbowed his arm. "You owe me for the earrings you destroyed. How about a date as payment?"

With a gleam in his eyes, he leaned his back against the railing. "You mean a cruise wasn't enough?"

"And I don't want to have to sing for my supper."

"Or dance ... I suppose ..."

"Dance? You're joking."

"Oh." Jacob made it sound as if the world had self-destructed.

Why would dancing with him be any different? She clobbered feet indiscriminately. "You've seen what I do to my victims on the dance floor."

"Yeah." He slid his arm around her shoulders, buffed his knuckles on her chin. "But you haven't danced with me."

The guy was a hopeless romantic. If dancing was that important to him, maybe this relationship was doomed. Maybe she should end it now, before she hurt him.

The SWAT teams herded the shackled prisoners toward the gangplank, followed by Paleface and the duo from Hazmat. Mr. Ackelroyd's face had taken on a pasty coloring. The side seam of Mrs. Ackelroyd's dress had split, revealing her fleshy thigh. Her beehive hairdo had deflated. Someone had stripped off her rings and bracelets. She shot Riley a murderous look.

Riley grinned at her. "I hear prison accommodations are memorable."

Despite his shackled hands, Khalid strode behind the Ackelroyds with the self-assurance of a sheik, gaze straight ahead, head held high.

As he pulled a dormant cigarette from his mouth, Paleface stopped beside Jacob. "Good work, Coulter."

"Once again, sir, Riley deserves the credit. Her courageous ploy brought these weasels out of their holes."

Paleface sniffed.

"Is he your boss?"

"Yes. Goes by the name of Schwarz."

Every woman who worked under him probably asked for a transfer. She fingered her collar. Then again, maybe he'd betrayed Noel to his terrorist cell. After all, Schwarz had been content to set her up as bait and risk her life.

The penetrating look he gave her made her want to shelter beneath Jacob's arm. Schwarz relit his cigarette and headed down the gangplank.

Should she share her suspicions with Jacob?

Hemmed in by the SWAT team, the prisoners trudged down the gangplank. The flower peddler twirled a rose in her fingers, her eyes beaded on them. She bobbed a quick curtsy and offered the rose to Mrs. Ackelroyd. But the officer flicked it away and prodded his prisoner toward the van.

In mere seconds the Hazmat men stashed the deadly vials in their van and drove off. The knots in Riley's stomach loosened. Thank God the poison was in good hands now. The SWAT team herded Khalid and the Ackelroyds into the rear of the van.

Finally, she could sleep without listening for intruders or wondering if her room were bugged. Schwarz climbed in the front passenger seat, flicked a stream of cigarette ash out the rolled-down window. With lights flashing, the van drove off.

At the top of the hill, Brick stepped from behind a tree, a newspaper folded under his arm, and strolled down the sidewalk.

The old woman rolled the cart halfway up the incline then stopped to wipe her brow with a handkerchief. She picked up the handles and toddled up the sidewalk toward Brick.

The toddle. Riley gripped Jacob's arm. "That flower-seller— it's Charlie Chaplin."

29

"You sure?" Jacob's breaths came faster as he snagged his gun from his ankle holster. "If you're wrong, I'll be arrested for assault and battery."

"Yes. I'd know that Chaplin walk anywhere." Riley started down the gangplank.

Jacob pulled her back. "You stay here."

"Every time you say that I get into more trouble. Isn't it time you worked with a partner? If Charlie thinks you're on to him, he'll run." She looped her arm around his, the scent of her Chanel No. 5 tickling his nose. "How about a stroll, lover boy?"

"You leave this to me. He's probably armed."

"What? That sweet little old lady?" She gave him that maddening grin, slipped her arm around his waist. "Now smile. Pretend we're an item."

"How can you joke at a time like this?" Jacob held his pistol behind his back.

"It's a coping mechanism for stress. I could give Interpol some great tips on this."

Without slowing his step, Charlie glanced over his shoulder.

Keeping his peripheral vision pinned on Charlie, Jacob kissed Riley's forehead. "That better?"

"I certainly hope so."

Charlie peeked at them again. Pushed the cart faster.

"Get down, Riles. Stay on the grass."

For once she did as he said.

Despite the bone-weariness, adrenaline coursed through his muscles. Gripping his pistol in both hands, he spread his legs shoulder-width apart, flexed his knees, leaned forward and aimed at Charlie. Dear God, don't let Riley get hurt. Focus, focus. Take down the bad guy.

Without warning, Charlie dropped the cart handles and reached inside the wagon. He pivoted, aimed a gun at Jacob, and a shot rang out.

Almost without thinking, Jacob returned fire. The pistol recoiled in his hand.

Dark splotches seeped across Charlie's chest. The revolver in his right hand loosened and fell to the ground. He staggered toward them then crumpled on the cement.

In three sprints Brick was at the wagon.

Leaving Brick to take care of the flower cart, Jacob knelt beside Charlie.

Riley ran to Jacob and crouched beside him. "Is he—"

Swallowing over the fist in his throat, he checked Charlie's pulse. "Dead." He'd killed a man. But it had been self-defense. Not revenge. Not vengeance.

"You had to do it." She squeezed his shoulder. "He'd have killed us and harmed others."

But knowing that didn't relieve the emotions roiling inside him. He peeled the wig from Charlie's head, pulled the lace collar from his neck. The scalp was almost shorn of its kinky grey hair, the Adam's apple prominent like a man's. His facial skin had been waxed baby's-bottom smooth.

He called Schwarz, filled him in, then snapped a couple of cell-phone headshots of Charlie and sent them to Interpol headquarters. "Now we wait for computer data to identify him."

"This has to be Charlie. I'd know that walk anywhere. He got careless and slipped into Chaplin's trademark toddle."

The height was right. Clearly, the guy was a master of disguise. "I think he was the dirndl dancer on the boat, the organ grinder."

"Yes, and maybe the priest at the cathedral." Riley snapped her fingers. "Wow. I think he could be the violinist I saw in Antwerp, when I ran into the Romanians." She shivered. "He could've killed us so many times."

"He enjoyed toying with us. I'll bet he basked in his clever deceptions. Charlie probably sold the vials to more than one bidder. Which makes him the mastermind of this entire plot."

Riley brushed debris from the sidewalk off her slacks. "Charlie wouldn't tell them where to find the vials unless the purchasers paid in advance. Maybe the bidders knew Molnár was Tudor. Charlie put the vials in my purse and planned to tell Molnár what he'd done with them, to protect Molnár from them and ensure the vials went to the highest bidder, or perhaps the bidder with the most destructive plan."

Schwarz hopped from the van, his driver at his heels, and headed toward them.

As Jacob stood and helped Riley to her feet, Brick headed up the hill, a knapsack on his back. "Hey." Jacob nudged Riley. "Wonder why he showed up?"

"I saw him by the tree earlier." She gripped Jacob's arm. "He didn't have a knapsack then."

"Get out of here." He waited until she darted across the lawn then unholstered his pistol. Took his stance. "Brick. Drop the knapsack."

Brick spun toward them, a gun in his hand.

"Don't make me shoot." Jacob flexed his knees, steadied his pistol hand. Killing Charlie was one thing but shooting his partner—

A shot rang out and Brick's gun hand jerked. Blood oozed across his shoulder.

"Drop the weapon, Brickley." Schwarz readied for another shot. "Or I'll shoot to kill."

The revolver clattered to the sidewalk and Brick's hands crept upward, red rivulets coursing down his arm.

Jacob cuffed him, snatched the knapsack from his back. Bound stacks of five-hundred-euro notes filled the bag. "Must be two-million euros in here. What's the matter, pal? Interpol pay's too low for you?"

A sullen look mottled Brick's pretty-boy face.

Schwarz ambled over to them, nodded at the knapsack. "Charlie's haul?"

"Looks like it." Jacob handed him the bag. "Odd, Brick knowing where and what to look for. Sir, I'm asking you again. Who was Noel's contact, his case manager?"

Shoving the rucksack in his driver's arms, Schwarz said, "Brickley."

Unable to quit clenching and unclenching his fists, Jacob stared at his partner. "Why, Brick? Why did you betray Noel?"

"You said it yourself, bro. Money's better on the other side."

Riley slid her arm around Jacob's waist, her gaze so tender he wanted to spend eternity in its depths. Instead, he forced his focus on his supervisor.

"Great job, both of you." With a flick of his head, Schwarz motioned his driver to take Brick to the van. "Miss Williams, we couldn't have broken this case without your help." He snatched the smoldering cigarette from his lips, exhaled a stream of smoke. "If you ever consider a career change—"

"No." Jacob draped his arm over her shoulder. "She's sticking to singing."

"Thank you, Herr Schwarz." She laced her fingers in Jacob's hand on her shoulder. "I'll stick to—well—whatever it is I'm supposed to do with my life."

"Suit yourself. Coulter, see me for debriefing the day after the cruise ends. Nine o'clock sharp." Schwarz hiked his eyebrow, took another drag on his cigarette. "We need to discuss your future."

"Yes, sir." Desk job or field work, he'd go with whatever God put in his path.

Snuggling closer to him, Riley nestled against his side. "Thank God, the nightmare is finally over."

"Yeah." Jacob blinked hard, pinched the inner corners of his eyes. *It's done Noel.*

30

Riley disconnected the call from her agent and tossed the phone on her bed. The opera contracts were a godsend, but the gigs complicated things. Tomorrow Frénie would arrive in Basel to join new passengers and the crew for the *River Nymph's* cruise back to Antwerp.

Studying her reflection in the full-length mirror, Riley adjusted the strapless bodice of her white satin gown then swept a few stray curls into the barrette Jacob had given her. No need to wear it, but it was her only memento of him.

As the elevator doors closed around her, she stifled a yawn. Despite only a brief nap today, she'd survived her three sets of songs, playing to an empty front-row couch and an otherwise full house. Guests seemed reluctant to sit where terrorists had sat.

Moments later, the bell dinged. Flashing her curtain-call smile, she entered the lounge. Her last night to crucify men's feet. Thankfully, Captain Lundstrom hadn't deducted men's shoeshines from her pay.

At the head of the dance floor, Johann waited behind his keyboard. Sparkling brighter than a strobe light, his rhinestone jacket nearly blinded her. He nodded at her, a new respect in his eyes.

Two more hours and her agony would be over. Never again would she offer to sub for Frénie or any other dance-related job. But if she hadn't done the cruise, she wouldn't have met Jacob.

With a broad smile on his face, the captain crossed the dance floor, his hand extended toward her.

A groan guttered in her throat. Oh please, God, not more humiliation. Why did Lundstrom have to start and end the cruise the same way? She offered him her hand, and he escorted her onto the dance floor.

"Well done, Miss Williams. I doubt we'd be alive if you hadn't filled in for Miss Frénau."

"Thank you, sir."

"Where do you head next?"

"My agent called during my break. I've been offered contracts at three opera houses for the coming season. Antwerp, Ghent, and Brussels. I'm subletting my apartment in Vienna and renting a place in Brussels for the year."

"Congratulations. I hope to attend one of your performances."

"Let me know, and I'll get you comp tickets. For the front row, if possible." That was the least she could do for him, for not firing her for her lousy dancing.

"My wife and I shall look forward to that." Lundstrom swept her into position, his hand on her back.

A mellow tune, a two-step, flowed from Johann's fingers.

Five minutes of torture. At least it wasn't a cha-cha or a tango. As she laid her hand on the captain's gold-braided shoulder board, she felt a tap on her collarbone.

"May I, sir?" Jacob stood beside her, now dressed in a tuxedo and shiny patent-leather shoes.

Suppressing a smile, the captain released her. "By all means." He stepped to the edge of the dance floor and waited with the other guests.

A gasp escaped her lips. "What are you doing?"

"Dancing with you."

"You'll regret it."

"Wanna bet?"

Wrapping his arm around her, he clasped her sweaty palm against his cool, dry one. He laid his cheek against the side of her head, the heat from his skin seeping into hers. Then she let the subtle pressure of his hands and legs ease her around the dance floor. Slow, dreamy steps. Smooth steps. No stumbles.

As the sinuous melody wafted over her, the stiffness in her arms, her back and legs, dissolved. Even her inhalations synchronized with his. "This—this is fun."

"Told you." He grinned. "So, you're moving to Brussels."

"How did you know?"

"You're wired."

"Oh, the hair clip. I forgot."

"A friend of mine is an opera-lover. Owns a huge apartment. I'm sure she'd rent you a room with kitchen privileges."

"Um, a former girlfriend?"

Jacob chuckled. "She's eighty years old. Her grandson and I work in the same department."

"Sure. Sounds great." If only the music wouldn't stop, but Johann swung into the final bars and the song ended. "Oh."

"You sound disappointed."

"I am. I actually enjoyed dancing, and I didn't stab your instep once. I don't understand."

"That's because you haven't been dancing with the right man." Tucking her arm in his, he led her off the dance floor as Johann swung into a samba. "So, Riles, have you figured it out yet?"

"Figured what out?"

"That we're made for each other."

Not trusting her voice, she nodded.

He walked her behind a marble pillar then thumbed her chin upward. "When you disappeared in Strasbourg, I knew I couldn't face life without you. No matter what, I had to trust someone, even if it hurt."

"Are you sure about this?"

"I'm sure." He trailed a finger across her lips then kissed her.

A current rippled through every inch of her body. She melted into his embrace and returned his kiss. Fighting the urge for more, she forced herself to come up for air.

"One thing I'm certain of." He gave her a cockeyed grin. "The unpredictable, crazy future we'll have together."

Tears pricked her eyes. A life with Jacob at her side. Could her life grow any sweeter?

As he cupped her elbow and led her outside to the stern, the satin folds of her gown swished around her legs.

Surrounded by the chug-chugging of the boat, she sat on the bench, a cool breeze caressing her shoulders. Behind her, the ship's wake glimmered with silver streaks of moonlight. The scent of moist earth almost smelled like Texas. And now she had Jacob in her life. God was so good.

Clearing his throat like a nervous schoolboy, Jacob pulled a small black velvet box from his pants pocket. "I ... I know this can't replace the earrings I damaged."

"You didn't need to do this. I understand why—"

"Yes, I do."

Riley took the box from his palm and snapped open the lid. Soft deck lights glittered on the large solitaire diamond ring, the gold band. "Oh Jacob—" Blinking back tears, she shot him a grin. "I'm going to have a hard time wearing this on my ear."

"I think it would look much better on your ring finger."

Glancing away from the earnestness in his eyes, she cradled her fingers around the box on her palm. This was the moment she'd longed for, prayed for.

With her chin clasped in his fingers, he tilted her face upward. "I don't want to miss out on a moment more of what God has in store for us." Hope and uncertainty flickering in his eyes, he knelt in front of her. "Will you be my wife, Riles?"

"Oh Jacob. Yes, yes, yes."

Breath fluttered in her throat as he removed the ring from its velvet box. She let him take her left hand in his and slip the ring on her finger. Unable to resist the urge, she rocked her hand left and right, the diamond shimmering beneath the deck lights. Never would she have expected an engagement ring could feel so right. Then she slid her arms around his neck and kissed him. The first of many, many kisses to come.

ABOUT THE AUTHOR

Author Sara L. Jameson makes her home in the desert southwest. When Sara isn't working on a novel, she loves dog sitting, reading, cooking, and gardening. In addition to romantic suspense, she also writes historical novels often set in WWII. She loves to write about women facing challenging situations who display heroism and courage and grow in their Christian faith. Her sense of humor has been known to creep into her books.

As a child she dreamed of becoming a singer and a writer. Having done the singing bit, she is thrilled to pursue a career in writing. She enjoys editing and helping writers develop their skills.

NEW RELEASES FROM SCRIVENINGS PRESS

Beneath the Seams

by Peyton H. Roberts

A Social Impact Novel

Fashion designer Shelby Lawrence is launching her mother-daughter dresses nationwide when she receives a photo of the girl who will change her life forever. Runa, the family's newly sponsored child, is a clever student growing up near Dhaka, Bangladesh. Shelby's daughter Paisley is instantly captivated by their faraway friend. As the girls exchange heartwarming messages, Shelby has no idea that a tragedy in Runa's life is about to upend her own.

Dresses are flying off clothing racks when a horrifying scene unfolds in

Dhaka that threatens to destroy Shelby's pristine reputation. Even worse—it sends Runa's life spiraling down a terrifying path. Shelby must decide how far she's willing to go to right a tragic wrong.

Both a gripping exposé of fashion industry secrets and a heartwarming mother-daughter tale, *Beneath the Seams* explores love, conscience, hope, and the common threads connecting humanity.

Rainstorm

by Cindy Bonds

Romantic Suspense

Laurel Ashburn has a scarred past, filled with corruption and pain. After an injury overseas sends her home, she moves back in with her foster mother and to a town that hates her. Being home puts her on a path to find a missing friend. But when she's attacked over and over, who will be willing to help?

Detective Dev Hollister traded in the big city for a slower pace and less crime in rural Arkansas. After rescuing Laurel from an attempted kidnapping, he finds himself intrigued with this headstrong and stubborn woman.

While Dev's job is to protect Laurel, he wants much more than to solve the case. He wants to give her a new life and reason to stay.

Laurel will have to push beyond her dark past to trust Dev with her life. But after losing so much, can Laurel survive one more storm?

Blue Plate Special

by Award-winning Author Susan Page Davis

Book One of the True Blue Mysteries Series

Campbell McBride drives to her father's house in Murray, Kentucky, dreading telling him she's lost her job as an English professor. Her father, private investigator Bill McBride, isn't there or at his office in town. His brash young employee, Nick Emerson, says Bill hasn't come in this morning, but he did call the night before with news that he had a new case.

When her dad doesn't show up by late afternoon, Campbell and Nick decide to follow up on a phone number he'd jotted on a memo sheet. They learn who last spoke to her father, but they also find a dead body. The next day, Campbell files a missing persons report. When Bill's car is found, locked and empty in a secluded spot, she and Nick must get past their differences and work together to find him.

Scrivenings
PRESS
Quench your thirst for story.
www.ScriveningsPress.com

Stay up-to-date on your favorite books and authors with our free e-newsletters.

ScriveningsPress.com